FIVE LE~~SSONS OF A DESI~~GNER

FIVE LESSONS ON WAGNER

ALAIN BADIOU

Translated by Susan Spitzer

With an Afterword by Slavoj Žižek

VERSO

London • New York

First published by Verso 2010
© Verso 2010
Translation Susan Spitzer © 2010
Afterword Slavoj Žižek © 2010
All rights reserved

The moral rights of the author and translator have been asserted

3 5 7 9 10 8 6 4 2

Verso
UK: 6 Meard Street, London W1F 0EG
USA: 20 Jay Street, Suite 1010, Brooklyn, NY 11201
www.versobooks.com

Verso is the imprint of New Left Books

ISBN-13: 978-1-84467-481-7 (pbk)
ISBN-13: 978-1-84467-465-5 (hbk)

British Library Cataloguing in Publication Data
A catalogue record for this book is available from the British Library

Library of Congress Cataloging-in-Publication Data
A catalog record for this book is available from the Library of Congress

Typeset by Hewer Text UK Ltd, Edinburgh
Printed in the USA by Maple Vail

Contents

Translator's Acknowledgements

I would like to thank Alain Badiou, first and foremost, for providing me with the opportunity to translate this work and for his unstinting assistance with the taming of the text, the lectures on which the book is based. We worked on the translation together on several occasions in Los Angeles, and I always came away from these sessions amazed at how cheerfully he would excise sentences that seemed unclear to me, rewriting them without complaint.

I owe a debt of gratitude as well to a number of other people whose help was indispensable. My husband, Patrick Coleman, not only read the entire translation, offering invaluable suggestions, but provided moral support on a daily basis. His colleague in the UCLA Department of French and Francophone Studies, Eric Gans, generously allowed me to draw on his extraordinary knowledge of the French language as he read through the manuscript. I am privileged to have in Ken Reinhard a perspicacious reader and one of the best of friends, whose unfailing support was deeply appreciated. Last but not least, I am grateful to Bruce Whiteman for kindly assisting me with certain music terms.

Preface

As far back as I can remember, Wagner's operas have always been a part of my life. They were my mother's great musical passion, and we had these old black 78s at home on which, amid all the scratches, I used to listen to the forest murmurs from *Siegfried*, or the Ride of the Valkyries, or an orchestral version of the death of Isolde. As early as the summer of 1952, my father, as the Oberbürgmeister of Toulouse, was invited to the 'New Bayreuth' under the direction of Wieland Wagner. We travelled through a defeated, dreary Germany that was still in ruins. The sight of these big cities reduced to piles of rubble insidiously prepared us for the disasters of the *Ring* or the derelictions of *Tannhäuser* that we would be seeing on the stage. I was enthralled by Wieland's quasi-abstract productions, which were aimed at doing away with all the 'Germanic' particularism that for a time had associated Wagner with the horrors of Nazism.

On the Concours Général des Lycées competitive exam I devoted the conclusion of my essay, the topic of which was something like 'What is a genius?', to *Parsifal*. When my father brought to Toulouse's Capitole Theatre a production of *Tristan und Isolde* that was directly inspired by the work that had been done in Bayreuth, I invited my high school friends to attend the opera and sit in the Mayor's box. Already at the age of 17 I was a proponent and champion of this music that was often reviled.

One of the first articles I ever wrote, in the student publication *Vin Nouveau,* was devoted to the monumental production of the Ring Cycle by the same Wieland Wagner, in 1956 this time. I had attended it with my wife-to-be, Françoise, who was immediately recruited to the Wagner cause. And later, much later, in 1979, when invited to Bayreuth by François Regnault, who had worked there, I travelled there to see the so-called French production, by Pierre Boulez and Patrice Chéreau, this time with Judith Balso. As an outspoken partisan of Verdi, she nonetheless devoted a long article, eloquently entitled 'The Conversion of a Verdi Lover', to this astonishing spectacle in *L'Imparnassien,* a journal I had helped found.

There are so many more anecdotes that could illustrate this passion of mine! Truth be told, the maternal heritage, as ever a little hidden from view, a little unavowed, proved to be tenacious and crucial. How many records listened to religiously, how many amazing productions (I'm thinking in particular – just to limit myself to the last few decades – of Peter Stein's *Rheingold,* Heiner Müller's *Tristan und Isolde,* Jan Fabre's *Tannhäuser,* and Warlikowsky's *Parsifal*), how many new singers discovered, how many orchestral interpretations brought forth by imaginative conductors! I'm also thinking of everything that was stirred up in me by the powerful, ambivalent relationship with Wagner found in the series of works that the wonderful artist Anselm Kiefer, meditating in an almost violent way on Germany and its fate, devoted to him. I'm thinking of Syberberg's films, and of so many other things.

And yet, until this book, I had written practically nothing on Wagner, nor is he evoked in my philosophical works, even under the rubric that I myself invented of 'inaesthetics'.

This book possesses something of the diffidence, perhaps, of those fundamental silences that are broken purely by chance.

These five lessons about Wagner would not in fact have existed without the amazing activity of my friend, the composer and critic

François Nicolas. For everything pertaining to that activity, the reader should consult www.entretemps.asso.fr/Nicolas. I would just like to mention three points here.

1. François Nicolas is one of the most original composers at work today. In the important body of work he has produced, I particularly want to direct your attention to the piece entitled 'Duelle', both because it offers a new direction for combining traditional instruments and digitally produced sounds and because, to my great indignation, it was very misunderstood when it was first performed.

2. François Nicolas is a great theoretician of music. He has very clearly shown the relative autonomy of what he calls 'the intellectuality of music' and has provided numerous examples of it. Here, too, I'll restrict myself to one outstanding example: his book *The Schoenberg Event*, in which all the different aspects of the rupture represented by the name 'Schoenberg' in music history are articulated in a strikingly new way.

3. François Nicolas is particularly knowledgeable about the borders of thought, especially those that both separate and join music, mathematics, politics and philosophy. This quasi-encyclopaedic aspect of his thinking, which is a rare thing today, has made of him one of my preferred interlocutors for many years now.

In the first years of the new millennium, François Nicolas, then an instructor at the École Normale Supérieure, where I have been teaching for more than ten years, François Nicolas organized seminars on the relationship between philosophy and music. They were focused in particular on Adorno, who, as a musician himself, has exerted an enduring fascination on the contemporary music scene. He also wrote an analysis of Wagner's *Parsifal* that was so comprehensive and convincing that it overturned everything that had ever been written about this somewhat enigmatic opera.

It was as part of François Nicolas's seminar that I lectured on the relations between Adorno in particular and contemporary philosophy in general, and music in general and Wagner in particular. François Nicolas and I later organized a day-long event devoted to Wagner. As part of his course on *Parsifal* we organized a public conference dealing with that opera. The book I am presenting here is quite simply the reprise of my contributions to the seminar, the Wagner event, and the *Parsifal* conference. Complete recordings of the conferences in which, in addition to François Nicolas and myself, Isabelle Vodoz, Slavoj Žižek and Denis Lévy also participated, are available at www.diffusion.ens.fr/index. php?res=cycles&idcycle=206.

The history of the text is a rather unusual one. My lectures were of course based on very detailed notes, but they were nevertheless not written out. So we began by deciphering them, which resulted in a very imperfect text since it was still heavily marked by an improvised, spoken style. This text served as the basis for the English version, which its translator composed with a virtuosity that can only be called heroic. Indeed, working directly from this French raw material, Susan Spitzer managed to extract from it a fluent, sharply focused English-language text, which must now be regarded as the original written version. It wouldn't be an exaggeration to say that Susan Spitzer is the co-author of this book. The proof is that if a French version exists some day, it will only ever be a translation of this English version!

Finally, I must thank my friend Slavoj Žižek, who is as crazy about Wagner as I am, for his insightful Afterword, as well as for his participation in the *Parsifal* conference. Our dialogue about Wagner is a crucial component of our – in some respects surprising – pairing on the contemporary philosophical scene. And of course, it might seem mysterious that the two philosophers who are instigating the resurrection of the word 'communism' today should also be those who are passionately following the public fate of Richard Wagner and are fighting upstream against the opprobrium cast on him, as much by the majority of pro-Palestinian progressives as by the state of Israel, as much by the dull rationalists of analytic philosophy as by the abstruse hermeneuts spawned by Heidegger.

Let me just note, in conclusion, that Sviatoslav Richter, the great pianist of the Soviet era, who liked to play in the smallest towns in the remote provinces of the USSR and who was also at the piano at Stalin's funeral, always presented himself as a fervent admirer of Wagner, and he could transpose entire Wagner operas, by heart, on his instrument.

Lesson 1

Contemporary Philosophy and the Question of Wagner: The Anti-Wagnerian Position of Philippe Lacoue-Labarthe

My approach to the topic will start off from the question of Wagner as a possible litmus test nowadays – as he has been time and again in the past – for the role of music in philosophy, and, in broader terms, in ideology.

I should mention at the outset an underlying thesis, which I have no intention of proving myself, that posits music as a fundamental operator in contemporary ideology. I'm taking 'music' in its loosest sense here, not as art or intellectuality or thought, but simply as what declares itself as such. In any case, there is really no other formal definition necessary for our purposes.

In this regard, a statement made by Philippe Lacoue-Labarthe in his 1991 book, *Musica Ficta*, subtitled 'Figures of Wagner', can serve as a reference. In that book, Lacoue-Labarthe, an important French philosopher,[1] set forth a host of reflections on the constitutive connections between music in general – and Wagner in particular – and contemporary ideologies, specifically political ideologies. Lacoue-Labarthe put his finger on the critically important role played by music in contemporary ideological formations:

The fact that, as nihilism has taken hold in the wake of Wagner, music, with even more powerful techniques than the ones Wagner

---

1   Philippe Lacoue-Labarthe (1940–2007) wrote extensively on Heidegger, Derrida, Lacan, Celan, German Romanticism, deconstruction and tragedy.

himself invented, has continued to invade our world and has clearly taken precedence over all other art forms, including the visual arts – the fact that 'musicolatry' has taken up where idolatry left off is perhaps a first attempt at an answer.[2]

This text is instructive because it, too, puts forward the thesis that music plays the role of a crucial vector in contemporary ideological configurations; it claims that we are living in an age of 'musicolatry'. This is an interesting term: music has become an idol, it has taken up where idolatry left off, and, when all is said and done, Wagner is the first one to blame for this. It is 'in the wake of Wagner' that David Bowie, rap, and so forth, have arrived on the scene! So what might be called a terrorist function of music has been ascribed to Wagner.

Many signs pointing in this direction could be mentioned, such as, for example, the idea that music is more important than images. Basically, conventional wisdom holds that we live in a world of images and that they have been accorded ideological supremacy. As far as Lacoue-Labarthe is concerned, however, music is actually more fundamental than images in the disciplinary organization of our minds in the world today.

I'm inclined to agree with this idea and I would like to mention, in passing, a few scattered facts in its support that won't be involved in the more fully worked-out theory that I will be presenting.

First, it is certainly true that, since the 1960s, music has become a badge of identity for the younger generation, on a mass scale, and this role is nowhere more apparent, not even in iconography or the cinema, than in music. There does in fact exist an undeniable musicolatry associated with a certain dimension of youth today, and it has emerged in a very specific period of time that can obviously be linked to the techniques of mass reproduction of music developed only in the last fifty years or so.

---

2   Philippe Lacoue-Labarthe, *Musica Ficta (Figures of Wagner)*, trans. Felicia McCarren. Stanford: Stanford University Press, 1994, p.115; translation modified.

Second, music functions as a key organizer in what might be called communication networks, which are used to transmit, exchange and accumulate music. I'm truly amazed by all these gadgets that can hold up to 50,000, 100,000 or 120,000 songs, implying as they do an extraordinary 'musicolatrous' memory. By the same token, music has also become one of the major players in the circulation of capital.

Third, music is an operator in the new forms of sociability, which has clearly been the case from the mass gatherings of the 1960s right up to today's phenomena (raves, for example). More broadly speaking, while music previously played only a marginal role in this regard, its importance has expanded remarkably, to the point where it has now become a key operator in sociability among the younger generation, and even beyond youth.

Fourth, I think music has played a very important role in eliminating the aesthetics of distinction. I call 'aesthetics of distinction' aesthetics holding that there are potentially intelligible, rational boundaries between art and non-art, and potentially transmissible criteria for these distinctions. It is common knowledge that this notion is under attack on all sides today in favour of what I would call an aesthetics of non-distinction, according to which we are pretty much obliged to accept as music anything that comes under the heading of music, even while breaking it down into new journalistic categories. For instance, if you look under 'music', you find 'classical', 'rock', 'blues', and so on. Obviously, 'classical' now designates what would have previously been classified in an entirely different way according to the criterion of artistic distinction. I think it was in music that this staging of the aesthetics of non-distinction was first introduced, in keeping with the democratization of taste and with diversity. It has even become a political theme: take, for example, Jack Lang,[3] who was the first politician

---

3　Jack Lang is a French Socialist politician, best known for having served as Minister of Culture (1981–1986, 1988–1992).

to promote the idea that there are 'musics' (in the plural); that what we are dealing with is egalitarian diversity.

Music has also been a potent force contributing to a certain museographic historicism; that is, a conservative, museographic relationship to the past. Here, first and foremost, can be found the baroque composers, who, having been imbued with a certain valorization of the reactionary, now serve as components of the figure of music in its guise as a complete restoration of its past, as having to approach what it was actually like historically before being revised and reinterpreted.

For all these reasons, I think that, as an introduction to our subject, we can hold on to this idea of music's singular role with regard to the connection between artistic forms in the broadest sense of the term and ideological tendencies or resonances.

But how is Wagner – and in particular Wagner in France – involved in all this? I will be discussing Lacoue-Labarthe's arguments in support of the idea that if music plays an utterly unique aesthetic role in the world today, Wagner is the true forerunner of this phenomenon. The issue of the French debate about Wagner will constitute my second approach to the problem.

Let me mention two very basic reference points in this connection.

First, in the late 1970s, a production of Wagner's Ring Cycle took place in Bayreuth, a production that the Germans in particular regarded as the 'French' one, with Pierre Boulez conducting, Patrice Chéreau directing and François Regnault serving as one of the artistic advisers. This French team struck deep into the heart of the temple, so to speak, because of the forcefulness of their production, which (after the tumultuous incidents of the opening night) met with an entirely positive reception. The so-called Wagner question never came up in connection with it.

What is very striking about this production of Wagner's tetralogy in the late 1970s is the fact that it actually represented a radical transformation, as I see it, in the realm of Wagner productions.

I'm not going to go into the whole history of stagings of Wagner – a very tortuous and complicated history, incidentally, but also a fascinating and really crucial one. Quite simply, to understand it, you have to recall the conditions under which the reopening of Bayreuth took place after the war.

It was hardly an easy task, to say the least. Everyone knew about the ideological compromises between Wagnerism and Nazism, the personal compromises between the Wagner family and the Führer, the way a sizeable number of the top Nazis worshipped Wagner, and so forth. So the question of what would happen after the war was really a very fraught one. It was Wieland Wagner who came up with the solution. In terms of the music, nothing changed: the old guard maintained the musical ritual as such without altering a thing. But the *staging* was radically modified by Wagner's grandson. What did Wieland Wagner's project basically involve? This is a very important issue because all the debates that we will see gravitating around Wagner in the work of Lacoue-Labarthe and other critics also turn on questions of this sort.

I would say that Wieland Wagner endeavoured to rid the production completely of any references to a national mythology and to replace such references with what could be called a pure mytheme, a mytheme that, by virtue of a process of abstraction, would no longer be connected to anything to do with the nation. This process involved purging the stylistics of the production of Wagner in such a way that all the old ideological references would be eliminated so as to arrive at something utterly transnational and timeless, hence 'Greek' in another respect. The extent to which Wagner's work replicated Greek tragedy is a question that would in fact play a major part in the ensuing debates. But here, 'Greek' should be understood in a non-nationalistic sense, which is already a sign that the debate about Greece – the aesthetic debate about Greece as a paradigm – is entirely bound up with the question of whether such a paradigm could or should be a nationalistic paradigm. So the result was what could be called a non-mythological presentation of Wagner, if what is meant by 'mythology' is indeed the founding myth of a nation or a people.

This operation was a success in that Wieland Wagner's production was immediately endorsed (aside from the protests of the conservatives of the Bavarian bourgeoisie) on aesthetic grounds. It was regarded as a genuine theatrical innovation, making the historical reality of the Wagnerian compromise with Nazism fade into the background. Wagner could thus be brought back and staged again, thanks to Wieland Wagner's efforts.

It was precisely against this backdrop, in my opinion, that the French Wagner of the late 1970s, which was still the post-May 1968 period of political activism, of the rediscovered vitality of the idea of revolution, and so on, was situated. I will argue that the Boulez–Chéreau–Regnault production was a demythologized presentation of Wagner. In fact, what was involved now was not a shift from a nationalistic to a non-nationalistic or purged myth but rather an attempt to stage Wagner in a way that would truly theatricalize him, that would reveal the play of disparate forces theatricalizing him and reject any mythification whatsoever of the characters. The result was a theatricalization of Wagner, but note that, in this case, 'theatricalization' means the opposite of the totalizing idea of a mythology.

Similarly, rather than attempting to bring out the continuity of Wagner's music, Boulez's conducting instead strove to highlight its underlying discontinuity. Indeed, when examined closely, Wagner's music can actually be seen to consist of a very complicated play of little cells constantly changing and breaking up; there is thus no essential reason why he should be saddled with an abstract theory of 'endless melody' that would amount to saying that sentimentality is the dominant feature of his music. What we are dealing with here – as is always the case, incidentally, with Boulez – is an analytical kind of conducting, conducting whose aim is to make us hear the complexity of Wagner's compositional techniques behind the flow of the music in the service of mythification.

What really emerged, then, was a new Ring Cycle, in the twofold sense of a new scenographic presentation focused on theatricalizing (rather than mythologizing) and a new presentation of the music that really endeavoured to articulate the principles of continuity and discontinuity in Wagner's œuvre differently. (The aim was not to replace continuity with discontinuity but rather to present the relationship between the two in Wagner's orchestral and vocal technique in a different way.)

In short, an entirely new phenomenon appeared in the late 1970s. 'The French' (with as many scare quotes as you like), or, in other words, an ideological option of the time, appropriated Wagner, not merely as a subject of commentary, as Baudelaire, Mallarmé and Claudel previously had done, but as a means of direct intervention in the production of Wagner and its renewal. This was effectively what the Bayreuth organizers at the time intended: to produce something new and different again, just as Wieland Wagner had done when he took a brilliantly precautionary approach that made the reopening of Bayreuth possible without creating too much of a stir. Not that I want to reduce Wieland Wagner's undertaking, which I myself fervently admired, to something merely precautionary, but it is undeniable that it can also be interpreted that way.

Then, in 1991, Philippe Lacoue-Labarthe's *Musica Ficta*, the essays in which dated from the 1980s, came out. The transformation undergone by the figure of Wagner from the Chéreau–Boulez–Regnault Ring Cycle in the late 1970s to *Musica Ficta* in the 1980s and 1990s strikes me as extremely significant. Note that *Musica Ficta* fits perfectly into the investigation of Adorno's thought that will be undertaken in Lessons 2 and 3 because the last essay in it is in fact devoted to Adorno, based as it is on his commentary on Schoenberg's *Moses und Aron*. What is really striking is Lacoue-Labarthe's opinion that Adorno was not yet sufficiently anti-Wagnerian, that he had not managed to rid himself completely of Wagnerism. So what we are dealing with here is an anti-Wagnerian stance characterized by extreme theoretical violence. We shall see why and how this is the case.

I think it can be argued that by the 1980s there had occurred, along with many other analogous phenomena, a kind of symptomatic reversal where Wagner was concerned. The theatricalized and analytically re-equilibrated Wagnerism of the late 1970s was swept away, so to speak, to make way for a particularly virulent, insidious anti-Wagner campaign aimed at denouncing his work. Let me say a few words here about Lacoue-Labarthe's book.

What is the book's structure and what does it aim to accomplish? Lacoue-Labarthe states that the book describes four different 'scenes' involving Wagner, four conflicts, quarrels with, or dialectical cases of admiration for him: those of Baudelaire, Mallarmé, Heidegger–Nietzsche (considered as somewhat the same in this regard), and Adorno – thus, two Frenchmen and two Germans. These four studies, pointing up four different relationships with Wagner, all arrive at the same conclusion, namely the notion that, despite their apparent conflict with him – a conflict that is perfectly obvious in Mallarmé's case in the form of rivalry; in Heidegger's case in the insufficient necessity of breaking with Wagner; and in Adorno's case in the desire to go beyond him – these thinkers were still in thrall to what is essentially dangerous in Wagnerism. It is an *a fortiori* demonstration, which explains the book's extremely harsh tone. By examining the cases of outspoken anti-Wagnerians or of people who, even if not openly declaring themselves to be anti-Wagnerian, nevertheless competed with Wagner, as did Mallarmé (whose aim was to prove that poetry was better equipped than Wagnerian drama to accomplish the tasks required by the times), Lacoue-Labarthe demonstrates that in precisely these cases the thinkers' anti-Wagnerism was, in actual fact, still altogether inadequate and that they failed to get at the real heart of the Wagnerian enterprise.

What, then, *is* the real heart of Wagnerism, which, despite their repeated attacks on his music, drama and operas, they somehow

missed? In Lacoue-Labarthe's opinion, it is the Wagnerian appa-
ratus as a vehicle for the aestheticization of politics; it is Wagner
as the transformation of music into an ideological operator which,
in art, always involves constituting a people; that is, figuring or
configuring a politics. What is being elaborated here is a vision of
Wagner as a proto-fascist (I'm using the expression in its descrip-
tive sense) inasmuch as he allegedly invented an aspect of opera's
closure by assigning to opera the task of configuring a national
destiny or ethos and in this way ended up staging the ultimately
political function of aesthetics itself.

Wagner supposedly accomplished this by means of a gesture
Lacoue-Labarthe regards as crucial: restoring high art. The basic
lesson he draws from this, which is very similar to the one Adorno
drew, is that it is no longer possible to create art under the banner of
high art, and that, at bottom, the major imperative of contemporary
art lies in sobriety as its key normative value, in the modesty of its
ambitions. (I'll come back later to this very tricky and subtle point,
which Adorno also makes in his own way.) According to Lacoue-
Labarthe, Wagner was the last great artist capable of defending the
idea of high art and precisely in so doing he revealed outright that
the contemporary world can no longer produce anything in terms
of high art except extremely reactionary, dangerous, even secretly
criminal political configurations.

In some of Lacoue-Labarthe's essays, not always ones that
appear in *Musica ficta*, the animus towards Wagner, who is truly
regarded as the primal, unsurpassed paradigm of fascist art, is
explicit. This implies that the Wagner who was demythologized,
theatricalized and restored to his underlying discontinuity (the
Wagner of Boulez, Chéreau and Regnault) should be regarded
as something trumped up, as mere window dressing, or merely
as a disguise plastered over the *essential* Wagner, the one who
remains encrypted in the old categories of mythology, the nation,
the aesthetics of the sublime, and so on. Here we are getting into
a very complicated debate that would require listening to a little

Wagner first in order to be able to pronounce judgement on the matter.

My thesis is as follows: Lacoue-Labarthe's strategy is in a certain way the opposite of the one he announces he is going to use. He intends to start with Wagner taken at face value (not really interrogated) in order to end up proving that Wagner constitutes an inscription, a foundation in the theologico-political realm, and that the essence of this Wagner, patently evident in the effects he produces, will ultimately be revealed to lie in the aestheticization of politics, proto-fascism, and so on. Lacoue-Labarthe's strategy aims to prove that the debates about this Wagner are a sure sign that Wagner's undertaking amounts to a proto-fascist aestheticization of politics. That is why, right at the beginning of his book, he will say, 'Wagner himself is not the object of this book, but rather the effect that he produced',[4] an effect that I myself said at the outset was enormous since, in the final analysis, as Lacoue-Labarthe explicitly states, Wagner founded the first mass art.

If the object of the book is not Wagner himself but only the effects he produced, it is because in a certain way it *is* possible to gain an understanding of Wagner, or to know what lies beneath the name of Wagner, via the effects he produces, which need to be duly pointed out. Yet, in my opinion, Lacoue-Labarthe's book does exactly the opposite: it *prescribes* a certain Wagner on the basis of a theory of politics as aestheticization. Once you've read Lacoue-Labarthe's book, you have a certain idea of Wagner, like it or not – after all, the book is ultimately about Wagner! How can you write a whole book about the effects produced by Wagner without that resulting in a certain figure of Wagner himself? It is absolutely impossible, and this figure of Wagner is delineated here through Lacoue-Labarthe's hypotheses about politics as aestheticization and consequently about the aesthetic role of art in politics. This aspect of things is very interesting inasmuch as we will

---

4   Lacoue-Labarthe, *Musica Ficta*, p. xix.

find this same type of operation in another guise when we turn to Adorno. It is essential to highlight the distinctive features that go into this construction of a certain Wagner, for I believe that that is what we are really dealing with here: a certain figure of Wagner is being constructed, or reconstructed, on the basis of a speculative philosophical determination that in reality has to do with the theologico-political or, if you prefer, with the aestheticization of politics, that is, politics as an artistic religion (which is a possible definition of fascism).

The distinctive features that will gradually go into creating this figure of Wagner must obviously be taken from Wagner himself in one way or another, so we are indeed witnessing what amounts to a *construction* of Wagner. Furthermore, since Wagner is a key name in the realm of ideology, it is always necessary to be aware of what is going on beneath the name of Wagner, that is, to know how the name 'Wagner' has been constructed.

I will now point out four features of this construction that constantly come up in debates about Wagner. And if it can be accepted that such a construction does in fact exist, then it will eventually also have to be accepted that what I'm going to say amounts to a deconstruction, because I will attempt to take apart this figure of Wagner after having shown how it is created.

1. The role of myth

The first, and perhaps most obvious, feature (Mallarmé in particular had a hand in devising this construction) is *the role of myth*, whereby Wagner is regarded as necessarily relying on or formalizing a mythological norm of representation, in other words as basing the representative world of drama and opera in its entirety on foundational, originary myths that play a constitutive role. I would simply remind you here that, while this is undeniable, the Boulez–Chéreau–Regnault production proved that we needn't necessarily interpret it as an *essential* feature of Wagner's work.

I'm surprised to see that Lacoue-Labarthe doesn't mention the latter production, or what he would probably have regarded as its failure. This production would nevertheless have to be subjected to critique in a rigorous, coherent way before it could be claimed that its failure is proof that the mythological is an essential ingredient of Wagner's work. No one will argue that the mythological element isn't present in Wagner, but that alone won't suffice. The real question is that of the essential, organic connection between Wagner's art and the mythological elements that are indisputably to be found in it. There have been in the past, and there are still today, attempts to present Wagner in a way that would free him from all this clunky mythology and that would thereby show how one of the potentialities of Wagner's artistic endeavour is not having to be, strictly speaking, an undertaking beholden to the mythological in the way Lacoue-Labarthe makes it out to be.

The other three features I will discuss are more specific, more relevant, and absolutely critical as well. They concern the role of technology (that is to say, something like the role of the quantitative); the role of totalization; and the role of unification or synthesis.

2. The role of technology

What this means, in Lacoue-Labarthe's view, is that one of Wagner's essential features is his all-out implementation of operatic, orchestral and musical techniques. According to Lacoue-Labarthe, 'musical amplification – and aesthetic accumulation – reached its peak'[5] with Wagner, and this amplification was essentially technological in nature. The theme of technology is introduced via the idea that the amplification of musical techniques in Wagner is entirely in the service of the effect produced and that

---

5   Ibid., p. xx.

once amplification is in the service of its effect we can legitimately speak of technology. Lacoue-Labarthe further writes: 'The truth is that the first mass art had just been born, through music (through technology).' [6] Hence Wagner, by virtue of this facile analogy between music and technology, is supposedly the precursor of music as technical power as defined by the production of effects as an internal norm of artistic arrangement, requiring the most extensive use of musical techniques.

This point could incidentally be developed further, over and above what Lacoue-Labarthe has to say about it. It could be argued that if Wagner needed to have a new theatre built, if he needed the greatest number of musicians, as well as singers whose technical faculties were well above average, and so forth, it was not simply a matter of chance or of the stylistic features of his art but was instead due to the fact that the correlation between the amplification of musical techniques and the effects to be produced is the very essence of his art. Wagner therefore created the first mass art inasmuch as what he created was ultimately a technological creation.

Lacoue-Labarthe reminds us that he is borrowing one of Nietzsche's ideas here. (Nietzsche, as everyone knows, had plenty of excellent ideas, as well as plenty that weren't so great.) This one is taken from a text in which Nietzsche explains that Western music's decline began with Mozart's overture to *Don Giovanni*, in which the full mobilization of the orchestra's capacity to produce an effect of terror and the sacred can already be found. So the overture to *Don Giovanni* was Wagnerian in origin; it was an intra-Mozartian reference to Wagner – which, by the way, isn't wrong, even if we are not obliged to draw the same conclusions from it as Nietzsche did.

This first, entirely obvious point, was expressed early on in a simplistic way: 'Wagner is very noisy', 'All you can hear is the

---

6   Ibid., p. xx.

brass', and so forth, which, in a more sophisticated way, was expressed as: the amplification of musical techniques implemented to the greatest extent with a view towards the technological production of effects and the creation of mass art.

It is striking that Lacoue-Labarthe makes no attempt to examine the real purpose of the techniques used in Wagner's œuvre. Yet this is an interesting question. Although there is undeniably a certain demand for extensive techniques in Wagner, towards what specific effects are these techniques required? If this question is skirted, all we are left with is considering the effects' effect: effects are effects, period. Granted, the point of an effect is to produce an effect, but one can hardly be satisfied with that, given the extreme versatility of Wagner's music. It is an exceptionally dynamic music, contrary to what is sometimes maintained. The question of the effects is actually an extremely complex one, and the demand for the techniques to produce such effects can itself vary a great deal. Wagner's orchestration is treated in its entirety by abrupt cuts, by extremely diverse ramifications; it does not in the least come across as one big monolithic mass. This question is simply not raised, yet it is the one that begs an answer here. Although there is without any doubt an uncommon or innovative demand for technology in Wagner, we still have to make a judgement about the *nature* of the effects and not simply about the mere fact, however undeniable it may be, that effects exist. The latter, in my opinion, is an altogether insufficient reason for lumping Wagner under the heading of technology.

3. The role of totalization

In this case, too, Lacoue-Labarthe restricts himself to Wagner's programmatic dimension, as formulated in his ambition of creating the 'total artwork'. That expression was certainly used by Wagner, who was determined to create the total artwork and as a result, or so Lacoue-Labarthe claims, enacted a gesture of closure: 'The totalizing gesture is a gesture of closure.'[7]

Yet the slogan of the 'total artwork' is no more than that: a slogan. Even though it can effectively be found among Wagner's stated intentions, can artistic endeavours be reduced to the artist's intentions? This is a recurrent debate that I'm often involved in. If we take seriously the fact that art is a process of creating something (I, for one, would say creating a truth), it can obviously not be reduced to the statements of intention that accompany it. I'm not saying that they are irrelevant, that they shouldn't enter into our overall aesthetic judgement of a work of art, but the way that the artist's intentions are systematically emphasized when it comes to the real process of artistic endeavours amounts, in my view, to a contemporary vice that is all the more pernicious insofar as an artist's intentions, while sometimes very rich, may also be very impoverished. Some artists spout nonsense, even about themselves. It cannot be simultaneously maintained that the work of art is not a direct expression of the artist's psychology and that the artist's stated intentions reveal the truth of the work. That is a contradiction in terms.

Granted, Wagner's totalizing ambition cannot be doubted, but we are dealing with a reference to his stated intentions here, and what we would instead need to do is demonstrate in what sense Wagner's work *as such* is a totalization. For the time being I'll leave this question, which can naturally not be settled by the programmatic reference to totalization, aside, particularly since Lacoue-Labarthe himself doubts that Wagner ever achieved such a totalization. For example, as far as the transformation of the stage is concerned, he states that, in actual fact, Wagner did not effect any earthshaking changes and, what's more, such changes did not really figure into his desire for totalization. Lacoue-Labarthe claims, among other things, that Wagner did not bring about any

7   Ibid., p. 12.

genuine transformation of the Italian-style stage, which, by the way, is debatable. In short, contradiction rears its head here too: first he imputes a great totalizing mechanism to Wagner and then he denies that any such totalization was ever operative.

This surely proves that we need to take a closer look, examine what the processes of totalization are, and understand what totalization really means in Wagner's work, which is a much larger undertaking by far. Furthermore, when you read some of Wagner's notes on how the orchestra was conducted and on the state of acting in his own time, he, too, might actually be said to have favoured an ideal of sobriety, since he generally found everything to be very overblown, noisy, terrible, and so on.

In addition, Lacoue-Labarthe says that this issue of totalization should refer us back to the systematic character of Wagner's work. Clearly, the equation of Wagner with Hegel is secretly at work here. In other words, Wagner's systematicity is actually the musical equivalent of Hegel's system, and Wagner allegedly brought to an end a certain type of opera in the history of Western music just as Hegel in a way brought to an end a certain type of metaphysics. Wagner supposedly left to his posterity a task that was every bit as impossible as the one Hegel left to his great successors, a task that consists in continuing to pursue what has already been completed. Thus, we read:

> One might say – not only because it ups the ante where the means of expression are concerned (a move that Nietzsche had already denounced as an art subordinated to seeking an effect), but rather because of its systematic character, in the strictest sense of the term – that Wagner's work left to his posteriority a task every bit as impossible as the one left in philosophy by German idealism (Hegel) to its great successors: to continue to pursue what is completed.[8]

---

8   Ibid., p. 118.

Lacoue-Labarthe's opinion is remarkably ambiguous here. Is this culmination that Wagner's work represents merely a programmatic, illusory one or did it really take place? Is he talking about a real historical fact or does the ambition for totalization, as a fake, deceptive, ideological ambition, actually leave open what it aspires to close? An inability to decide – typical, in my opinion, of a certain kind of Heideggerian thinking – is evident here: the inability to choose between an element that is actually only programmatic and a real historical fact. Did Wagner really bring opera to a close? That is certainly a genuine question, which I am by no means denying, but it is clear that it cannot be posed in these terms. If there really was a Wagnerian closure of opera, it will be necessary to spell out the reasons – in terms of the music, the stage, the drama, and so forth – why it occurred, and not rely exclusively on Wagner's frequently reiterated pronouncements about the total artwork.

4. The role of unification

With this feature, at any rate, we are getting a little closer to the music. Just as Lacoue-Labarthe refers to the total artwork with respect to the question of totalization, he likewise refers, as far as the issue of unification is concerned, to the thematics of 'endless melody', since it is this on which Wagner built his opera. Lacoue-Labarthe interprets 'endless melody' as saturation, which is an interesting point. 'Endless melody', in his view, means 'too much music',[9] that is, music that gets blocked through saturation, the name for which is 'endless melody'.

What 'saturation' means is that Wagner does away with the articulated irreducibility of speech. In other words, the play space between speech and music constitutive of opera's potential theatricality is eliminated, according to Lacoue-Labarthe, by 'endless

---

9   Ibid., p. 118.

melody' in so far as the latter is a unifying saturation, through the music, of all the operatic parameters. So, too much music, as Lacoue-Labarthe no doubt understands Wagner, or at the very least as he criticizes him, means that the music performs a *synthetic* function with regard to the operatic parameters it sets out, and this synthetic function actually nullifies the effectiveness of its words.

We are very close here to Adorno, whose foremost concern was the identity principle. Metaphysically, Adorno considered that the Hegelian dialectic, in exemplary fashion, is a dialectic that does not let difference be, that actually engulfs difference in sameness. As an affirmative – not, indeed, a negative –dialectic, the Hegelian dialectic ends up reducing difference to sameness. In a certain sense, Lacoue-Labarthe says the same thing about Wagner, who, as he sees it, reduces all the possible parametric differences to the 'endless melody'. 'Endless melody' is quite similar to the odyssey of the Spirit in Hegel, that is, to something whose role is constantly to reduce the difference between the discontinuous articulation of speech and the continuous melodic line, or even ultimately to reduce the intra-musical references as well to the flow of the music itself. Wagner, in Lacoue-Labarthe's opinion, created a synthetic music, a music that absorbs its own multiplicities and dissolves them in an undifferentiated *melos*.

There are many interesting passages in Lacoue-Labarthe's work concerning this issue, which is the most important one of all. For example, he charges Wagner with a lack of complexity on account of it. An interesting passage in this regard is the one in which Lacoue-Labarthe examines Adorno's opinion of Schoenberg. He notes that Adorno ultimately considers Schoenberg to be in a position of musical saturation, too. This is why he thinks Adorno is still far too Wagnerian: Adorno fails to see that something utterly different is at work in Schoenberg. Adorno diagnoses the synthetic role played by music in Schoenberg, in *Moses und Aaron*, and Lacoue-Labarthe remarks: 'Once again the style of this saturation is not Wagnerian, if only because the writing is too complex and because it is no longer subordinated to the imperative of a *melos*.'[10] He then goes on to say, 'But all the same, it is saturation.'

Saturation of a non-Wagnerian type would be predicated on a more complex kind of composition, one that would not be subordinated to the imperative of a *melos*, that is, to the imperative of 'endless melody'. This is the crux of the problem. In the first place, is it true that Wagner's composition suffers from a lack of complexity? And, if so, is it true that such a lack of complexity is due to the subordination of all the musical parameters to the 'endless melody'; that is, to a musical line itself endowed with an outwardly oriented power? Once again, I think the key question has not been raised. Lacoue-Labarthe starts off from the programmatic commentary about 'endless melody', but, in actual fact, the consequences he draws from it (lack of complexity, subordination of multiplicity to the unity of the line, and so on) remain unsubstantiated when it comes to Wagner's œuvre itself.

As for the leitmotifs, another tricky point in Wagner, Lacoue-Labarthe claims that the issue hinges on demonstrating that Wagner's music is itself mythological. Here, we come to the nexus of all his objections: the method used by Wagner to unify his own music is conceivable only within mythological parameters. Lacoue-Labarthe tries to relate the question of the mythological not just to the plot, the myths, the gods, the story told by the operas, but to the very texture of the music. The solution Wagner had found to the problem, he says, 'is that the stage action, as well as the mythical units and signifiers, must be constantly overdetermined musically (hence the *Leitmotive*)'.[11] Just as we previously had a theory of 'endless melody', we now have a theory of the leitmotifs as musically overdetermining the mythical elements. So the intrinsically mythological nature of Wagner's nationalistic – and, in the final analysis, political – project is present in the music to

---

10   Ibid., p.121; translation slightly modified.
11   Ibid., pp. 133–4.

the extent that the mythical components are ultimately musically overdetermined. This implies that the leitmotifs are being interpreted here as a musical synthesis of the mythological. Take the Sword motif, for example. According to this theory, every time this particular leitmotif recurs it is actually an instance of a mythical cellular element in the music ultimately infiltrating the unity of the music itself.

There is something that Lacoue-Labarthe overlooks here, namely the possibility that a leitmotif might sometimes play this role only subordinately to *another* role. The fact that the leitmotif clearly has a twofold role in Wagner is a point Boulez strongly emphasized, and rightly so. The leitmotif certainly has a theatrical articulation that can be regarded as mythical, or narrative, but it also functions as a non-descriptive, internal musical development, with no dramatic or narrative connotations whatsoever. As such, it could be better compared with the way Haydn treats little cellular motifs, which are distorted and transformed in his symphonies, producing something that is, strictly speaking, neither a development nor a melody exactly but rather a unique kind of thing.

Thus, Boulez has shown that when you analyze a Wagner score you cannot fail to see that what is called a leitmotif, as a musical gesture connected to the narrative, is not a phenomenon unique to Wagner's music. Very often, on the contrary, an uncertainty in the leitmotifs, a blending of one leitmotif with another, can be observed, because they themselves depend on transformable harmonic or diachronic cells that are like musical modules of sorts. This role of musical modules, that are actually discontinuous at the cellular level and whose transformative principle structures Wagner's musical discourse, is completely overlooked when you claim, as Lacoue-Labarthe does, that the leitmotifs ultimately constitute the mythological dictates in the very fabric of the music.

From this perspective, the damage done by the systematic labelling of the leitmotifs in Wagner can never be regretted enough. For instance, even though you might say 'Oh, that's the Sword motif' when you recognize three notes serving as a transition to another melody, you are nonetheless very well aware that neither Siegfried nor the sword is involved. Sometimes the character is in fact on stage, but at other times he is not.

The issue of the leitmotifs is crucial because it places Wagner at the heart of what is perhaps his own proper innovation, and it is there that a particular brand of ambiguity emerges. Wagnerian ambiguity certainly exists, but it cannot be reduced to the one-dimensional configuration Lacoue-Labarthe ascribes to it. It lies quite systematically in the dual function of what Wagner evokes not only in his musical material but in his scenic or narrative material as well, and even in his poetic material, where there can be found – above and beyond a declarative, explanatory narrative function – an assonanced, repetitive function expressly designed for musical declamation. So in virtually all the components of Wagner's art there can be found a systematic use of a dual function that naturally exceeds any interpretive schema that would attempt to reduce Wagner to the theologico-political.

To conclude this first lesson, then, I think that this construction of a mythological, technological, totalizing figure of Wagner, in which the music effects a synthesis of the mythological imperatives, is being created in keeping with a pre-existing ideal of Lacoue-Labarthe's, a Hölderlinian ideal of sobriety. In other words, it is actually being created under cover of a stance on what contemporary art ought to be, and the Wagner thus constructed serves as its foil. As such, this characterization of Wagner is by and large independent of any real examination of his creative process. That being the case, we might try and describe this Hölderlinian ideal of sobriety from the opposite direction now and inquire as to the nature of this ideal in accordance with which Lacoue-Labarthe imagines the tasks of contemporary art and owing to which he concurs, even while arguing, with Adorno.

First of all, the notion of high art must be dispensed with. Sobriety thus also implies a sort of impoverishment, a humility of artistic ambition, accompanied by a will to detotalization. This does not mean, quite the contrary, that mixing and crossing over from one art form to another are to be prohibited, but that they will always occur instead as fragmentation, detotalization, experimentation. This is the reason why high art will be shifted over to its last explicit representative, in Lacoue-Labarthe's eyes, namely, Wagner.

Another issue in this discussion about contemporary art is the challenging of the overly rigid boundaries between art and non-art. These boundaries are also connected with sobriety and humility in the sense that there is no criterion for distinguishing between art and non-art that is completely self-evidently reliable. In Lacoue-Labarthe's case, for example, this idea appears in the guise of a theory of the contemporary poem as becoming-prose, a theory holding that the essence of contemporary poetry lies in the becoming-prose of the poem. Because the demarcation between poem and prose is precisely what the poem must call into question, the essence of the poem will consist in its making itself impure and becoming prose, rather than in aspiring to be the pure or great poem.

Also prescribed is the renunciation of the immediate form of the sublime as well as of the sublime as a sublime effect or, in a nutshell, the renunciation of effects. Art must humbly accept a certain regimen of absence of effects, the aim of which is to produce the effectless effect, or, when all is said and done, to produce a divorce between the artist subject and the putative public subject. These two must no longer relate to each other in terms of one producing an effect on the other; rather, they are now to be split up, and it is this split that I call the effectless effect, or the divorce effect.

Nor should we forget, of course, the well-known notion that the process must be self-reflexive, since this artistic process must be reflected in its own becoming.

I think it is interesting, then, to note that, in a more general way – with Lacoue-Labarthe's book serving as our reference here

– Wagner is the name for all that is *not* the foregoing, and that it is this that accounts for the fact that he continues to occupy a negative place in the debate about aesthetics. He upholds the project of high art, of totalization, of the idea of the poem as something distinct from prose; he in no way renounces the immediate form of the sublime and the sublime effect; he does not strive for the effectless effect but remains instead within the realm of the aesthetic.

Having arrived at this point, we are now faced with two different questions:

1. Is this prescriptive set of rules for contemporary art justified and, if so, by what?

2. Is it legitimate to make Wagner the foil for this agenda?

It is true – and this problem, which is hardly new, keeps getting worse – that there is a stand that needs to be taken vis-à-vis what might be called the kitsch of waning empires. Without a doubt, every empire nearing its end puts forth its own kitsch, something I would define as a correlation between noise and nihilism, or as noisy nihilism. For instance, we can clearly identify an intentionally kitschy production in the movies today. Over and above the obvious reference to Hollywood, it is a particular form that on closer inspection can be seen to involve a correlation between noise and nihilism or, in other words, an amplification. The technological resources keep being amped up (Wagner is small potatoes indeed next to this!), while, in terms of its innermost core, this amplification is simultaneously shaped from within, as a rule, by an utterly nihilistic vision of the future, together with, quite simply, a wholly external, neo-religious, abstract, dubious logic of salvation. This correlation between noise and nihilism is not in fact unrelated to insecure societies or to waning empires, and Wagner has obviously been retroactively drawn into this trend to some extent. He plays the part of someone who represents the still-artistic presence of this development.

The position he's been assigned is in fact perfectly obvious: He is the one who puts an end to the history of art, closes it, brings it to completion; he is something like the last composer of opera. Lacoue-Labarthe's overview of Wagner's successors is rather odd. He is a little bored, truth be told, by Berg, in whom he locates detotalization, and is delighted by what in his opinion is the significant incompleteness of his *Lulu*. *Pelléas et Mélisande*, as far as he is concerned, is the opera of deconstruction. Strauss, for his part, stands for no more than a vague nostalgia for an opera that is already finished, while Puccini he sees as someone trying to breathe a last gasp into high art but failing – and that's it; after that it's all over.

So the position that has been ascribed to Wagner as someone who brings the history of opera to a close is very clear. What has been completed can no longer be pursued; therefore, Wagner is an integral part of this history just as he is also the first great artist of the kitsch of waning empires, and it is in this sense, moreover, that he is a proto-fascist. Thus, he simultaneously closes and opens up, in that he ushers in the future of mass art. He lays the foundations for the latter even as he brings to a close a tradition that included Mozart, Beethoven, et al.

Adorno already implied as much right from the start of his *In Search of Wagner* when he stated that, all things considered, Wagner is typical of a certain kind of petit bourgeois bombast, of something that actually no longer has what's needed for its purpose and is forced to resort to using an excess of expressive techniques because real historical content is lacking. The same could be said, more or less, about the kitschy art of waning empires: the creative content of the historical epic is lacking, so you fake it by using historical bombast. As a matter of fact, at a time when nothing really matters anymore except the next elections, you can also make *The Lord of the Rings*, or something else of that sort.

But we are still left with the question as to whether this is what Wagner was really all about. Is this typology altogether relevant? It is a complicated question because it assumes that we have an opinion about both aspects of Wagner – the closing and the opening – simultaneously. Wagner's dual role is superimposed on him, and in a certain way he represents the amplified culmination of all of opera's techniques, on the one hand, and the first example of mass art, on the other, so that his actuality is nothing but his historical actuality: at the end of the day, it's something like a big rock concert. The noise, incidentally, was already the same.

Lesson 2

Adorno's Negative Dialectics

What I intend to do now is to look into this problem particular to Wagner's place in philosophy and examine it in terms of a specific question that will be addressed to Adorno: to what extent does his philosophy lay the ground for or construct this place for Wagner? If we take *Negative Dialectics* – the basic text of this lesson – we cannot fail to note that Wagner is completely missing from it, even though it was written by the same Adorno who wrote *In Search of Wagner.*

This approach, which involves trying to determine how a philosophical condition is actually at work in its absence, or, in this case, how music and Wagner can occupy a certain place without Wagner's needing to be mentioned as such, is of great interest to me. Wagner will quite naturally come to occupy this place because in the final analysis it is his own and, more broadly speaking, music's. So we will examine certain aspects of Adorno's philosophy in terms of how they set up the possibility for this function of Wagner as I have just gone over it.

Incidentally, while re-reading Adorno very closely, I was struck by how many contemporary themes he had worked out an approach to early on. I think many of the analyses that became dominant in the 1980s were already present in their primitive form in Adorno. He deserves credit for the fact that, from this standpoint, he really invented something new, and his implicit importance as regards the contemporary French intellectual scene, which is very obvious when you read him today, should be especially emphasized.

This time around, then, I intend to start with *Negative Dialectics*, the important book Adorno completed in 1966. Here too, I will try to highlight what is silently at work in constructing the potential place for this figure of Wagner. I will then end by deconstructing both Wagner and the place reserved for him in such a way as to suggest something different.

In its basic orientation, *Negative Dialectics* is nothing short of a proposal for a new direction for philosophy. It is therefore a work of philosophy in the strongest sense of the term, if it can be agreed that every work of philosophy is a work that reconstitutes or proposes philosophy's place anew. In this case, it consists of proposing a new direction for philosophy, but doing so on the basis of German idealism, that is, Kant and Hegel. We will see why. On the one hand, there is the tradition of Kant and Hegel, *and*, on the other, there is the absolute necessity for formulating a new orientation that is based on this tradition but at the same time abandons it in many respects.

I would now like to present Adorno's project in this extraordinarily dense book (it is quite a feat just to read it!) as I understand it, in five points that boil down what I think is the subject matter of the book.

1. German idealism is the speculative culmination of Enlightenment rationalism. Consequently, if we want to examine Enlightenment rationalism, and Western philosophy more generally, we can in some respects confine ourselves to German idealism, that is, to Hegel and Kant.

2. This German idealism, or in other words this Enlightenment rationalism, has two sides: a negative or critical side (which is very obvious in Kant, of course, but negative in the Hegelian dialectic, too) and a totalizing side as well, with Hegel's absolute or positive dialectic. German idealism is thus a conjunction of critique

and totalization, critique and absoluteness or, when all is said and done, negation and identity. Such is its essential make-up, represented by the Kant–Hegel pair; a pair that, in my opinion, constitutes a fundamental matrix for Adorno.

What interests Adorno, strictly speaking, isn't the Kant vs Hegel opposition, or Hegel's having transcended Kant, or even the need to return to Kant's critique. All of these gestures can be found in Adorno, but what interests him above all is the Kant–Hegel pair, insofar as it is this – not just one or the other of the two terms – that brings Enlightenment rationalism to a conclusion.

3. Once this diagnosis is set up, Adorno's project consists in preserving (while simultaneously going beyond) Kant's critical negativity along with Hegel's dialectical negativity. To Kant's critical gesture, which involves separating or limiting reason's claims, Adorno joins Hegel's dialectical negativity, which is maintained, albeit severed now from its positive absoluteness. Hegelian negativity is thus preserved as purely negative negativity. For this reason, Adorno's doctrines and more broadly speaking those of what would eventually be called the Frankfurt School in the 1960s, which was dubbed *critical theory*, were clearly given the name 'negative dialectics' by Adorno, as a yoking together of critical theory and negative dialectics, of Kant and Hegel now transcended. The following sentence is particularly characteristic of Adorno's project: 'The intelligible, in the spirit of Kantian delimitation no less than in that of the Hegelian method, would be to transcend the limits drawn by both of these, to think in negations alone.'[1] It is thus a matter of transcending this Kant–Hegel conjunction while still preserving it in order to arrive at purely negative thinking. The statement truly sums up Adorno's analysis and project: to bring about negative dialectics on the basis of

---

1   Theodor W. Adorno, *Negative Dialectics*, trans. E. B. Ashton. New York: Continuum, 1973, p. 392.

German idealism as the culmination of the Enlightenment, and to do so under new conditions.

4. *Negative Dialectics* begins, in a way, with a long discussion of Heidegger's ontology because the latter presents itself as another proposal for going beyond Enlightenment rationalism, which Heidegger regarded as no more than a moment in the history of metaphysics. But it actually falls short of doing so, in Adorno's opinion, which is why he won't hesitate to claim (much to Lacoue-Labarthe's chagrin) that Heidegger was a fascist through and through. So Heidegger's ontology, a rival of his own, is ultimately discredited by Adorno because it fails to go beyond Enlightenment rationalism – unlike negative dialectics, which will combine Kant's critique and Hegel's dialectics and transcend them in a new way.

5. The key reference for Adorno's whole undertaking is a break in history. The very possibility for his philosophy is linked to a set of historical facts represented by Nazism and the concentration camps, and this rupture in history is called *Auschwitz*. The method Adorno propounds of an intrinsically negative thinking that would recover Kant's critical heritage and Hegel's dialectical heritage but would sever them from what made Auschwitz possible – from an identitarian assertion in excess of rationality itself – is thus made possible by a historical fact.

This, then, is what I think can be said about the general plan of attack of Adorno's book. Music is hardly apparent in it, and it remains notably absent, moreover, from the body of the whole enormous text, in which can be found merely a few allusions to Schoenberg, Beethoven and Berg. My thesis, however, is that the place for music is being fully set up within it and that if one ultimately wants to understand the importance of Adorno for music theory it can be done much more profitably by studying how the place for music is constructed in a purely speculative text than by looking directly at Adorno's essays on music.

I would now like to sketch out how Adorno goes about setting up this place, the technique he uses to lay the ground for the place for art in general and for music in particular, in *Negative Dialectics*.

This will result in a whole series of questions about both music and Wagner, which will constitute the framework of the next lesson.

1. Let's begin with Adorno's chief concern. In this enormous project, his main adversary is what he thinks is the basic assumption of Enlightenment rationalism: the critical role of the identity principle. *Negative Dialectics* could be said to be one gigantic polemic against the overall effects of the identity principle, along with an analysis of its role in Western rationalism. The identity principle is present in latent form, so to speak, in Kant's critique, in which the theme of the unity of experience, the permanence of the transcendental Subject, and the ultimate unity of the various critiques can be found. Although Kant's critique is a critique of demarcation, of the separation of faculties, and so forth, the action of the identity principle is in the final analysis implicitly at work in it. And it is also explicitly present in Hegel, in the unity of the Absolute, which sublates all things.

So Adorno's target is the role of the identity principle in Western rationalism. Consequently, universalism is suspect in that it consists precisely in the imposition of the One; that is to say, an imposition of identity whereby one thing can apply to everyone, or, to put it another way, it consists in reducing everyone to the same insofar as the same is this universal norm. In this regard, Adorno anticipates by twenty years themes that have become perfectly commonplace in contemporary ideology. There are passages in Adorno that are really quite complex (he is hardly an easy writer) but which have nevertheless become ubiquitous in journals today, as an excerpt like this shows:

> It is precisely the insatiable identity principle that perpetuates antagonism by suppressing contradiction. What tolerates nothing that is not like itself thwarts the reconcilement for which it mistakes itself. The violence of equality-mongering reproduces the contradiction it eliminates.[2]

---

2 Ibid., pp. 142–3.

The linked themes of the need for appreciating differences, the respect for otherness, the criminal nature of identitarian disrespect of differences, and the inevitably violent will to universal sameness are basic themes throughout *Negative Dialectics*. In this regard, what matters first and foremost is really the question of the havoc wrought by the identity principle, culminating naturally in the extermination of the Other in the figure of Nazism, which is at bottom no more than the identity principle – the violence Adorno is concerned with here – pushed to its limit.

All of this is precisely what must be completely contained, circumscribed, and, if possible, eliminated by negative dialectics. Moreover, in one typically concise aphorism, Adorno writes, 'Identity is the primal form of ideology.'[3] To put it another way, to combat ideology, in the vocabulary of the day – 'ideology' being a word from the 1960s, when, as is apparent, it took on a new meaning – is to combat identity.

This takes us to our first question. If combating identity is really what is involved in constructing a place for a new music, does it therefore mean that contemporary art, the music of the future, is that which is capable of subtracting itself from identity? Does it mean that art's proper role, which would be made possible by the end of identity's dominance, would be to demonstrate an ability to subtract itself from identity? Correlatively, does it mean that Wagner represents one of the supreme examples in music of identity's dominance? As we saw in Lesson 1, this is effectively Lacoue-Labarthe's thesis, which holds that unification, a unifying language, or synthesis, is the essential feature of Wagner's musical discourse. If identity is actually the weak link of Western rationalism from which something else – namely negative dialectics – must be constructed, and if music has a unique part to play in this regard, it would mean that music is first and foremost that which is capable of subtracting itself from identity in the world of

_____
3   Ibid., p. 148.

the sensible. This would also constitute a programme for '*musique informelle*': Is music capable of subtracting itself from identity? So that is the first point that can be deduced from the question of Adorno's objective.

2. If identity is the adversary, it follows that difference must be the goal, that difference is ultimately the *telos* of negative dialectics.

The justice rendered by thought to what is other is the crucial element in *Negative Dialectics*: 'Nonidentity is the secret *telos* of identification. It is the part that can be salvaged . . .'[4] (We should note in passing that this is a perfect example of standing Hegel on his head.) What must be salvaged in identification is non-identity, and Adorno goes on to say that 'the mistake in traditional thinking is that identity is taken for the goal. The force that shatters the appearance of identity is the force of thinking . . .'[5]

Adorno's proposition concerning thinking is that it is the force that shatters the appearance of identity and establishes non-identity as *telos*. It should moreover be noted that this non-identity thinking, in Adorno's very style, is both programmatic and ethical. It is not simply, nor even perhaps primarily, a theoretical construct. Besides, as can easily be imagined, the whole book is marked by considerable mistrust vis-à-vis the concept, since the concept always reproduces rationality's identity compulsion. What we have here, then, is a proposition concerning non-identity thinking, or a *telos* of non-identity, of programmatic and ethical difference: 'What would be different has not begun as yet.'[6]

We can gauge the extent to which difference constitutes a programme for Adorno, and once again we encounter that fundamental set of historical circumstances mentioned earlier. Difference is not merely what was repressed by identity; as an expression or an assertion of itself, it has not even begun as yet. We do not really even know what the different *is* yet.

---

4   Ibid., p. 149.
5   Ibid., p. 149.
6   Ibid., p. 145.

As regards ethics, now, we read: 'The subject must make up for what it has done to nonidentity.'[7] From the standpoint of the programmatic aspect of difference, difference must begin, which is only possible in a fundamentally *ethical*, rather than theoretical, context. It is essentially in the context of making reparations, therefore, that difference can begin; we must reconsider the damage that identity has inflicted on difference.

So it can be said that Adorno's system is an ethical historiality; that is, a programme for beginning that can only begin, for this reason, within the realm of *prescription*, not deduction. Assuming, then, that we are still dealing with constructing a place for music, this would lead to the next question: Can music be a programme for difference? Can it be inscribed within a programme for a beginning of difference? If difference has not even begun as yet, can music contribute to, or even play a critical part in, bringing about the beginning of difference? Can art be a locus of making reparations? Does there exist an ethical role for music, and art in general, that, precisely because it would cause difference to begin, would do so in a context of reparations, of fundamental non-violence on the part of identity towards what is different from it? Then, if we stick with the logic of a counter-model, must we maintain that Wagner is the enemy of a programme for difference, that he contributes to making it impossible for difference to begin in music? That is what Lacoue-Labarthe argues in claiming that Wagner saturates and closes the history of music, thereby preventing it from producing its own difference.

To the extent that Wagner represents a culmination of the history of music he is Hegelian, in Lacoue-Labarthe's opinion, for he precludes music from being grounded in the production of difference and thereby perpetuates the violence perpetrated on otherness. Wagner's diatribes against Judaized art can of course be brought up in this context. His unquestionable anti-Semitism

---

7   Ibid., p. 145.

could then be regarded not as a mere personal idiosyncrasy but as a much more fundamental trait implying that the essence of his art, rather than being part of the ethical beginning of difference, would instead lie in an identitarian closure, a closure he certainly brought to the height of its power but which was on that account all the more dangerous.

A somewhat marginal but, in my view, significant point is that Adorno works out all of this again in anti-scientific terms. The deployment of science, he says, has today become a 'mechanical activity'.[8] (Let it be noted in passing that he has a totally Heideggerian view of science and that, on closer inspection, Adorno's proximity to Heidegger is very striking.)

He comes down especially hard on mathematics. According to Adorno, something was borrowed from mathematics (a discipline to which Hegel usually reacts idiosyncratically), namely, the idea that the negation of negation is an affirmation. Ultimately, there is a very odd thesis of Adorno's that I found retrospectively quite interesting. He constantly disparages mathematics, which is unable to produce the genuine self-evident concept of the infinite. Instead, it limits itself to blindly creating a rough approximation of it, while being absolutely unable to grasp it conceptually and consequently remaining on a purely immediate level of the question. Mathematics nevertheless deserves credit, in Adorno's view, for having foregrounded the infinite even if was not able to conceptualize it.

Hegel, too, usually discredits mathematics, which he regards as an external form of thought, and he condemns even speculation about mathematics, moreover, as a fragment of technique. But Adorno thinks the real issue lies elsewhere and can be expressed as follows: Hegel retains something absolutely essential from mathematics, which is that the negation of a negation is an affirmation. Consequently, he preserves mathematics' prohibition of a

---

8   Ibid., p. 388.

negative dialectic since, if the negation of negation is affirmation, it is impossible to have a double negation without ending up with an absolute affirmative:

> To equate the negation of negation with positivity is the quintessence of identification; it is the formal principle in its purest form. What thus wins out in the inmost core of dialectics is the anti-dialectical principle: that traditional logic which, *more arithmetico*, takes minus times minus for a plus. It was borrowed from that very mathematics to which Hegel reacts so idiosyncratically elsewhere.[9]

Thus, Hegel did not ask the right question of mathematics; he did not see that, although the question of the infinite is in fact very important, the logical proposition holding that the negation of negation is an affirmation – and consequently the intrusion into dialectics of a non-dialectical element – constitutes an even more radical borrowing from mathematics that does not respect the laws of negativity.

The principle of double negation as positivity must therefore be abandoned if we are not to be caught up in the mechanical activity of scientific and mathematical logicization. As a result, there arises the question of art and music's real relation to scientificity, to mathematicity and, more fundamentally, to the question of negation. How does the negative element in art, and especially in music, ultimately function? Is there something about music that would compel it to use a double negative, the negation of negation? For instance, isn't the ordinary or classical type of musical finale – of the end of the work, the affirmative context in which the work is resolved – actually the negation of the negative elements that have traversed the agonistic construction of the music's development? Isn't there something Hegelian about musical finales, in that

---

9   Ibid., p. 158.

agonistic, contradictory, or negative elements that have shaped
the work are ultimately expunged through negation? Aren't tonal
resolutions, too – just as Hegel was – prisoners of the logic of the
negation of negation? Shouldn't a music be invented that would
be entirely free from all this, a music that would be the music of
negative dialectics, that would wrest itself away from any process
in the discourse secretly controlled by the question of the negation
of negation?

This could be applied to any number of things: the role of major
vs minor in tonal music, the question of finales, of the resolution
of developments, and so forth. Wasn't it Wagner who took this
aspect of things to the limit by inventing an altogether unique
musical figure whose purpose is to hold back resolution the better
to affirm it? The question of negation in Wagner could then be
approached as Hegelian negation, as negation that is not included
in negative dialectics. The extent to which Wagner's music is a
configuring music is a very important question.

I think there is a very significant, albeit metaphorical, opposition between configuration and constellation in Adorno. At
bottom, Western music has been a configuring music, to all intents
and purposes a music that subjected the multi-branched system
of possible affects to a formal discipline, to a *unifying* formal
discipline in the end. It was this that constituted the configuring
force of music, which configured its own immanent multiplicity.
Adorno suggests abandoning this model and replacing it with a
model of constellation, a kind of dispersive fragmentation in which
the identitarian dominance of form never determines the way the
music is either composed or heard. This is a fundamental issue,
since Wagner could then be considered as the last great model of
music based on configuration, music configuring the system of its
immanent multiplicity and never allowing it to be dispersed into
the figure of constellation.

In more general terms, the philosophy of *Negative Dialectics* can
be said to be that which thinks what is different from thought. If

this idea, that authentic thought is non-identity thought, is strictly applied to philosophy, it means that one must also think that the thinking of authentic philosophy is the thinking of what is non-identical to thought. If we generalize this philosophically, it is not simply the question of the difference of the object that is at issue but that of the access to difference by what from the very beginning is different from thought itself; that is, the thinking of what is different from thought. This is also what is meant by constellation taking the place of configuration, which, according to the definition Adorno deems to be philosophy's traditional one, is thinking that configures thought. Constellation thinking will thus be thinking that lets what is truly different from thought emerge within it.

But how does what is non-identical to thought appear? What is the experience that makes it possible to think what is non-identical to thought? What is the appearance of what is non-identical to thought? The latter obviously doesn't present itself as thought: it necessarily presents itself as affect, as body, even. Consequently, this is the true content of the critical rupture that Auschwitz represented. What was experienced in Auschwitz is something that can in no way be preconfigured by thought. There is no way of relating to what happened there other than by letting it emerge within its own particular context, a context that is altogether heterogeneous with thought and is consequently revealed in what Adorno calls an immediate experience of the essential and the inessential.

Yet, precisely, such an experience is not of the order of thinking, and the only radical proof of the fact that thinking is confronting what is *not* thinking is ultimately provided by its appearance as suffering. For Adorno, this immediate experience of the essential and the unessential finds its measure in what subjects objectively feel as their suffering. What we have here is an extremely intense and in some respects very powerful anticipation of a mode that can be termed victimary; that is to say, the only way difference can be registered is ultimately by virtue of one's being in the position of the victim. It is only in this victimary position, and only within the constellation of experience, that what is different from thought can be registered in a non-configurable way. It is here, moreover, that might also be found the *positive* counterpart, as it were, of *Negative Dialectics*: 'The *telos* of such an organization of society would be to negate the physical suffering of even the least of its members.'[10] The organization in question is the one that would be consonant with the hopes of *Negative Dialectics*.

Furthermore, suffering has to be taken in its most materialistic sense here: it is the body; it is unmediated, unconditional suffering, and negative dialectics would in turn lead, as best it can, to an organization of thought whose *telos* is the negation of the physical suffering of even the least of its members. This is why Auschwitz is the name for a rupture in history on the basis of which a completely different kind of thinking must be mobilized, one that is indeed concerned with what can in no way be organically preconfigured. As a result, the appearance of difference comes about in the objective reality of suffering. So we will have to examine how the question of art, and music in particular, is presented: Is there a connection between music and the appearance of difference as the objective reality of suffering?

This will lead us back to a whole new investigation of the relationship between Schopenhauer and Wagner, for whom the question of compassion, and therefore of suffering, is mythically crucial. How can it be assessed from the standpoint of Adorno's dialectics? What is the ultimate meaning of *Parsifal* from the point of view of *Negative Dialectics*? These kinds of questions arise right away here, and a complicated maze emerges from them, inasmuch as Wagner, it has been argued, ultimately preordains the irreducible experience of suffering to a foretold redemption, meaning that he doesn't really allow suffering to *be* in its otherness but has already reduced it to sameness beforehand. Nevertheless, I think that when you examine the libretto of *Parsifal* this claim is not

10   Ibid., pp. 203–4.

immediately borne out. Rather, it paves the way for a discussion that would investigate how this reduction of suffering to sameness is present in the musical dialectic itself. One quickly becomes aware of how vexed a question this is.

That said, how does Adorno conceive of the present time? What I have discussed up to now has had to do with the relationship between the dialectic and the question of Auschwitz and the victim. A series of parallel statements all characterizing the present time – the time after Auschwitz – can also be found in Adorno.

How can this time be described? In the first place, in terms of the fact that it has become impossible to assert the positivity of existence. Anything that unquestioningly asserts the positivity of existence – anything, for example, that claims to give a meaning to existence – has in Adorno's view become obscene. In *Negative Dialectics* Adorno engages in limited self-criticism regarding the statement he made immediately after the war, to the effect that it had become impossible, obscene, to write poetry after Auschwitz. He now revises what he said somewhat and instead suggests that after Auschwitz one couldn't assert the positivity of anything that was culture, and perhaps even anything that was existence. So, in a generalizing move, he shifts from an aesthetic injunction to an existential one, and, just as the initial aesthetic statement must be generalized to a statement about existence, one must likewise note a radical failure of any idea of culture in the present time. Any thematics of the positivity of something like culture, or of the civilizing role of culture, has in its turn become utterly impossible, and in this regard, he sensibly says, the *criticism* of culture is no better than culture itself; it is part and parcel of it. It has all become utterly incommensurable with difference and it should actually be regarded as the last-minute tactics of identity, which would amount to no more than saying, 'something barbaric happened, so let's be cultured' – the key idea being that the inaugural subjective situation is that of guilt.

Here again we encounter the ethical context of the beginning. According to a statement which, by the way, is very anti-Nietzschean, new thinking can begin only in the context of *guilt*, precisely because life can't be granted any positive value inasmuch as we are merely those who survived Auschwitz. Since the living subject is merely a survivor and as such must forever mourn the dead, it is impossible for justice to be done to the dead of Auschwitz: they died in the total absence of meaning and there is no hope of redeeming their death in any way. Since justice cannot be done, it follows that guilt is unavoidable and, for Adorno, 'existence at large has become a universal guilt context'.[11] It is from this perspective that he sums up the work of Samuel Beckett, who, in his view, holds that today what is, is always more or less like a concentration camp. I personally don't think this is what Beckett is saying, but it doesn't really matter here. Let's just note that he is invoked as a witness to this universal guilt context as being the sole meaning of existence.

These are very dark characterizations, even ones that amount to a deadlock for the present time. The latter is conceived of altogether negatively as a time of dereliction, not so much because we are unhappy as because there is a difference that cannot begin and therefore a justice that cannot be carried out.

Might music, at least, be able to express this dereliction? The idea of music as redemption or relief must be absolutely abandoned, since anything of that sort is impossible in a present conceived of in this way. Nevertheless, could music express this dereliction, this universal guilt, this obscene character of all culture and all cultural critique? This is an additional question that might be put to music, art, and Wagner as well, inasmuch as there is a definite relationship between Wagner's music and dereliction, many illustrations of which can be given. But, once again, where Wagner is concerned, aren't we dealing with a *rigged* relationship with dereliction? Indeed, one can observe in Wagner a relationship that instrumentalizes the state of dereliction to which the music bears

---

11   Ibid., p. 372.

witness precisely in order to stage a forgiveness or salvation that is actually impossible.

If the present time is defined in this way, what imperatives can be deduced from it? Adorno effectively provides us with imperatives for the present time that are all negative, as might be expected.

1. The fundamental injunction is for humankind 'to arrange their thoughts and actions so that Auschwitz will not repeat itself, so that nothing similar will happen'.[12] Incidentally, although this is not our concern for the time being, I would like to point out that the way this imperative is formulated might seem contradictory. It effectively makes use of the notion of resemblance, of 'similarity', hence of a form of identity, whereas Adorno said over and over that Auschwitz was utterly singular and that nothing, therefore, could be identical to it. The injunction should instead be formulated as follows: 'to arrange their thoughts and actions so that a singularity absolutely different from Auschwitz will never – even through a superficial resemblance – bring to mind what Auschwitz was'. At any rate, we must avoid at all costs what constantly happens today: the essence of Auschwitz is declared to be unrepeatable but its repetition is constantly dreaded and affirmed as soon as an atrocity is committed somewhere.

2. The feeling that there will be no relief, that there is no salvation, that justice has not been done must be expressed and made explicit. The slightest beginning of justice consists at the very least in bearing witness to the fact that justice has not been done, or in any case in not pretending that it *has* been. Taking his cue from the Beckett of *Waiting for Godot*, Adorno claims he is expressing the feeling of waiting in vain, which is a fundamental affect, the feeling that the absolute is not going to come. Remarkably, it is at this precise moment that he expressly refers to music, to which he otherwise devotes only a few brief passages in this book. It is a matter of acting negatively, of realizing oneself through waiting

---

12   Ibid., p. 365.

in vain. If waiting in vain is indeed an imperative, then *Negative Dialectics* states that music alone can express it, can bear witness to the fact that justice will not be done.

From our contemporary vantage point, then, in what does the music of waiting in vain consist? Here again, waiting in vain is a crucial Wagnerian theme, constituting the essential texture of the first two thirds of Act III of *Tristan*. If ever anyone might be said to have created a music of waiting in vain, it was Wagner. But once again it might be objected that, when all is said and done, the waiting in *Tristan* is not really in vain since Isolde manages to bless Tristan before he dies, and the tonic chord does after all redeem things at the end. We are nevertheless justified in asking whether the fact that this waiting in vain is ultimately redeemed in Wagner's theatrical dynamics is really the most important thing – or whether, on the contrary, Wagner had such an extraordinary intuition about the intrinsic merit of waiting in vain that he turned it into an unprecedented poetics, an amazing musical system that constantly delays resolutions, thereby creating a state of harmonic uncertainty whose task it is to translate the futility of waiting.

3. The ideal of the open must be opposed to the scientific ideal. Adorno is one of those who went in for the ideal of the open, along with Bergson, Heidegger and Deleuze, among others, all of whom were opposed to the supposedly closed nature of the scientific ideal, to be understood as conveying the idea that the negation of negation is an affirmation, and consequently closes negation. The aim of the ideal of the open, on the contrary, is the idea of a negation such that even negation does not eliminate it: even if negation were to be negated, in other words, it would not be eliminated, and the open would be maintained. The open is the fact of replacing form with formal transformation. The informal, from this perspective, is the possibility of confronting formlessness in a context that would ensure that any form exists only in order to be immediately transformed and that this transformation must itself be erratic, or have no form whatsoever.

Such formal transformation must therefore verge on non-form. It quickly becomes apparent that what is at issue here is a musical question, namely, whether there is any sense in speaking of '*musique informelle*'. Can formal transformation itself be absolutely formless? Is music consequently able to express or represent the open? Isn't it of the essence of music always to be necessarily an immanent proposition of its own closure, or of closure in general? Can music be unequivocally oriented towards the open? Or does it of necessity contain a unique interplay of the open and the closed?

It is this debate that will be ascribed to Wagner's music, and the issue will be whether in the final analysis 'endless melody' is a principle of openness or a principle of closure. Although, as far as Lacoue-Labarthe is concerned, 'endless melody' is what makes possible the closing and saturating of all the parameters of music or opera, it is perhaps no less a principle of openness as well, since it was originally conceived of as a way of putting an end to closed forms. We will therefore examine this contorted dialectic, in whose wake the struggle against the closed itself got caught in the trap of closure.

4. The final imperative is that appearance must be rescued from the totalizing stranglehold of meaning or essence; in other words, the *precariousness* of appearance must be saved from the totalizing stranglehold of meaning. Indeed, all difference does is appear; if it presents itself as corresponding to essence it is because it is not truly different.

Since difference presents itself as what is not already in thought, it initially emerges as something that appears or occurs, like Auschwitz, which is indeed something that occurs, not something that can be preconfigured by thought. Rescuing appearance is therefore the aim of an *ethical* principle above all, rather than an epistemological or aesthetic one: appearance must be absolutely respected, for it is in appearance, in the appearance of body, in the final analysis, that what there is to think first presents itself as being something other than thought.

Adorno writes that 'art is appearance'[13] (it thus has an immediate function) and that there is an 'incomparable metaphysical
relevance' in 'the rescue of appearance, the object of esthetics'.[14]
Aesthetics is being taken in its broadest sense here, both in the
sense of Kant's transcendental aesthetics and more generally in the
sense of the doctrine of appearance, which takes on crucial metaphysical significance given the fact that the rescuing of appearance
encompasses an ethical principle, the principle, strictly speaking,
of difference. So we must ask to what extent music contributes to
the rescuing of appearance. What, in music itself, can partake in
rescuing appearance? In particular, what is the point of this question of appearance in Wagner, that is, of music as the expression of
pure externality?

In any case, we can affirm that, within the possibility for a way of
thinking after the crime, after the catastrophe that was Auschwitz,
the gradual, deliberate and extremely complex construction of a
potential place for art and music does indeed take place in *Negative
Dialectics*. So what is really at stake, when all is said and done, is
the possibility for a music after Auschwitz, for a music that would
somehow be commensurate with the catastrophe, or compatible
with it, a music that would not be debased or unworthy even
though it has to exist against the backdrop of that abyss. And this
music would open a new space for a new assessment of Wagner.

In short, it is a matter of a music that could come after evil, and
this once again raises another question. Adorno, as mentioned,
was the first to expound the thesis that writing poetry after
Auschwitz might be impossible. He later changed the question
inasmuch as, in *Negative Dialectics*, he suggested that it might
not have been the right question, which was rather that of how

---

13 Ibid., p. 404: 'Art is semblance, even at its highest peaks.' Translation
slightly modified so as to maintain coherence between the quotation and
Badiou's commentary.
14 Ibid., p. 393; translation slightly modified.
15 Ibid., pp. 362–3.

one could live, how one could exist, after Auschwitz. The problem became a more comprehensive one, and the question thus became focused on art in general and the relationship it bears to existence. So what is at stake is indeed a music that could come after evil, and the question might also concern whether singing is possible after Auschwitz. But since singing of any sort seems to be incommensurate with Auschwitz, it is also probably a matter of the possibility for a music that would *not* sing, one in which singing would be extinguished. Any music that sang would somehow be inappropriate or incapable of being made appropriate to the post-Auschwitz situation.

This is incidentally one of the meanings that can be given to '*musique informelle*', which is a very broad category when it comes to Adorno. As a first approximation, a very basic definition of it might be: a music that abolishes from within itself the celebratory dimension of song, which is no longer tenable since it is incommensurate with evil in its Auschwitz dimension.

So here is my general thesis concerning Adorno's overall project, in terms of its ultimate relationship with the question of music: *A place is being constructed for a music that might be possible in the historical conditions obtaining after Auschwitz.*

Now, in the second place, what is meant by Auschwitz? What is 'Auschwitz' the name for in this matter? This is another construct found in *Negative Dialectics*, in which 'Auschwitz' does not merely encompass the empirical fact of the massacre and extermination but becomes a philosophical name in its own right, a proper name with its own essential place in thought, in philosophy. It is a paradoxical place, however, since 'Auschwitz' is the name of an imperative for philosophy in the sense that any philosophical thinking must be consonant with the measureless measure represented by Auschwitz, while at the same time 'Auschwitz' names what is forever *external* to philosophy: philosophy's relationship with what is utterly different from it. This is what constitutes the paradoxical dual status of the name 'Auschwitz' in philosophy.

Yet this name is ultimately reconstructed in *Negative Dialectics*, since 'Auschwitz' names what might be called the murderous dimension of identity in philosophy. Needless to say, it is not a matter of identity in the speculative sense that would simply be the essence of Auschwitz, precisely because there *is* no essence of Auschwitz. On the contrary, Auschwitz stands for the absence of essence: the pure murderous figure. The measure of 'Auschwitz' is therefore always expressed by suffering, which in a way cannot be expressed by a concept. So it is a measure that lies within the radical passivity of experience.

It is nevertheless a fact that 'Auschwitz' can emerge as a proper name within philosophy as a correlative of the murderous dimension of identity, as identity pushed to its limits, as the utter subjugation of thought by identity or the identitarian. This is what accounts for the fact that 'Auschwitz' is a proper name precisely for a *negative* dialectics, a dialectics that is in no way subordinated to identity. It also implies, to the extent that there is a place for music in all this, that such a music will have to be one that is radically subtracted from identity's dominance, a music that exists utterly within the realm of difference and transformation, and that nullifies any form of identity. I'll return to this issue later.

It is thus in this name, 'Auschwitz', as the murderous dimension of identity, that all the imperatives of contemporary thought are located, as Adorno sees it. This means that his task will amount to constructing a philosophy of non-identity, a philosophy that accepts that it is dealing with what is altogether different from itself and that endeavours not to make what is different from itself similar, or, in other words, not to make the non-identical identical. Here we have quite a clear imperative as to what a post-Auschwitz philosophy, or in any case a philosophy countering identity's murderous nature, should be: a non-identity philosophy, a negative dialectics, or a philosophy that regards thought as genuine only when it is dealing with what is *not* thought, that is, when it is dealing with something different from itself, especially when confronting the radical dimension in experience of what is not thought, the living subject's suffering.

This project of Adorno's is grounded in German idealism and proceeds by a very unique sort of shuttling back and forth between Kant and Hegel. The elaborate way it is constructed, which is very complex and interesting, won't concern us here, but, in terms of its impact on the question of music, it can be summarized as follows.

What Adorno preserves from Kant is the general notion of critique, the conviction that philosophical thought must be concerned with the question of its own limits. Of course, since it is necessarily the thought of what is different from itself, it must, in a manner of speaking, internalize its own limits critically, because if it is not concerned with its own limits it will remain within the figure of the unlimited and as such will no longer be able to determine what is different from itself. A rather simple but compelling idea can then be noted: once you have a philosophy of non-identity, you have, by the same token, a philosophy that cannot be a philosophy of the unlimited. But a detailed discussion of this would be too complicated to undertake here because we would have to distinguish between the unlimited and the infinite.

To put it in simpler terms, what Adorno preserves from Kant is *the irreducibility of experience*, the fact that it is impossible to dissolve experience in the pure activity of the concept. An utterly irreducible element of passive limitation remains – just as in Kant, passivity, which is the practice of the sensible, is irreducible. Ultimately, there always comes a moment when the sensible produces an impact that cannot be reduced to the pure constructive movement of the concept. In short, there is a non-constructed element in the construction: receptivity. This very fundamental Kantian idea of receptivity – the notion that, since it is impossible to remain within the pure constructive movement of the concept, there is consequently not just a dialectics but a 'pathetics', or a fundamental receptivity – is precisely what Adorno retains. This is because, after Auschwitz, we must open ourselves up to the pure reception of the Other's suffering, to what the Other underwent, and in no way can this be arrived at or constructed by the concept. We have to be willing to accept being open to the Other's suffering with a kind of basic humility, to be open to its impact on us. Philosophically, as Adorno sees it, this idea is already present in abstract form in Kant, in whom we do indeed find the idea of the limits of knowledge, which, on the one hand, is related to the concept, and, on the other, concerns the fact that there exists an absolutely primary sensible receptivity prior to which, in a way, there is nothing. Using a more modern vocabulary, we might call this finitude.

In addition, from Hegel Adorno retains *the work of the negative*; that is, the power of the non-identical or the power of difference as radical exteriority. It will ultimately be a question of connecting (this is Adorno's fundamental idea, in my view) Kant's view of receptivity in experience, of passivity – rather than the Kantian notion of construction, incidentally – with the Hegelian idea of the negative, while eliminating from both of them the supposedly positive outcomes that all these processes might entail. Adorno thus does away with Kant's religious postulates, or the infinitely revelatory role of ideas, along with the dimension of the absolute in Hegel. In this way, he maintains a space severed from its ultimate purpose, which has been eliminated in both cases, a space within which Adorno proposes to connect Kantian limitation with Hegelian negativity. Within this space, thought capable of thinking what is *not* thought, thought open and exposed to what is not thought, can take hold.

I'm oversimplifying things, but it is important to keep all this in mind in order to be aware of the tension specific to Adorno's thinking – not just its results but its tension – which is rooted in this very unique shuttling to and fro between Kant's philosophical inspiration with respect to experience, to passive receptivity, to the limits of experience, on the one hand, and the great Hegelian conception of the negative, on the other.

Assuming we have now arrived at the stage of philosophical testing, in Adorno's sense of the term, what exactly are we dealing with? To which themes will he apply this philosophical inspiration? I think three main themes, the most important ones in terms of both aesthetics and music, can be mentioned.

1. The first theme to be put to the test is a practice of *disunification*, which is directly opposed to the dominance of identity, to the formal unity of experience. Adorno differs importantly from Kant in this regard, for although he does indeed maintain the idea of experience and passive receptivity, there is nonetheless no genuine concept of the unity of experience in his philosophy. On the contrary, there is a constant operation of disunification, which is at the same time an operation of disidentification. It is a question of disuniting what falsely appears to be unified or united and of testing out disunification, including, as we shall see, in terms of music. Adorno privileges a kind of experience that is at pains to establish that which undoes itself, a 'doing' that is at the same time an 'undoing'. The aesthetics that can be dictated by this are readily apparent: a process of formal 'doing' that is simultaneously a disintegration of form, a form that is simultaneously the undoing of form, points to the philosophical theme of disunification, hence of the struggle against identity's dominance.

2. The next theme I want to mention is that of bringing about or testing out what Adorno calls *waiting in vain*, as opposed to any notion of reconciliation or salvation. There is no final reconciliation, no ultimate salvation to be hoped for; we must wait for justice to be done but we cannot entertain the idea of an already accomplished, established, irrevocable justice. We must await justice but we can never regard it as having already come; it is going to come, but it has never yet come; it is supposed to come, but it has never yet come. This might be Adorno's interpretation of Beckett's *Waiting for Godot* and of certain episodes of Berg's *Wozzeck*. Ultimately, this idea, too, amounts to a sort of imperative, since music must produce something akin to waiting, albeit an unresolved waiting

wherein no real outcome of what is awaited ever occurs: Adorno is resolutely opposed to any idea of reconciliation or salvation, to any hypothesis concerning the ultimate harmony of things.

3. Finally, let me mention the system of *negative imperatives*, which consists in establishing that every imperative is actually a negative one. As I already mentioned, the primary imperative for Adorno consists in thinking and acting in such a way that nothing like Auschwitz can ever happen again. This entails that every imperative must really be a negative one. Thus, every imperative derived from *Negative Dialectics* is itself a negative imperative; it is not an imperative positively dictating that such and such must be done but rather one that is always determined by what must never happen again, by something whose repetition must be strictly forbidden. So Adorno is also opposed to any conclusive assertion and thereby to the Hegelian idea of the result. Negative dialectics also implies that something about negation can never be overcome or transcended, that it is not the case that every negation can ultimately be reduced, or is reducible, to an affirmation. Even the negation of the human – inhumanity – will never be redeemed by some higher affirmation: nothing can salvage Auschwitz. Any reconciliation with this radical or absolute negativity is inconceivable; any sort of conclusive proposition must therefore be avoided. The impact this will have on the notion of musical development, in which any conclusion or resolution must be suspended, can already be glimpsed. Once again, we encounter the theme of the absolute necessity of preserving the open, with no final resolution in which negation would ultimately be forgotten or eradicated.

These three themes will thus have an impact on a certain conception of what form, or a work of music, might be, or, in other words, on an aesthetic stance regarding the possibilities for music as it is circumscribed or determined by this philosophical construct.

To the extent that the idea of form – even negative form – or a work of music is provisionally maintained, it must not at any rate be something that unifies or unites. Thus form, if form there is, must be uncoupled from the notion of unity. For Adorno, form cannot be the work of unification in an artwork. Yet it does indeed seem as though such unification is precisely the ordinary definition of form. It follows that Adorno was forced to ascribe nothing but a purely negative meaning to form, or the imperative of form. In effect, form that would in no way be based on the idea of unification or identity in a given undertaking or musical work is form whose imperative would be *not* to be form. What kind of form is not really form, in the sense that any kind of form would be complicit with identity? What would form appearing entirely as its own disintegration be, form whose very essence would be to undo form; that is, to undo the unity assumed to be in the work through the representation of its form?

Second, if waiting in vain is really what is at stake, and if as a consequence there must be no reconciliation or salvation, this would mean that any work having a conclusive resolution must be avoided. There must be no resolution, completion, closure, culmination or finality in a given work of art; the latter must be wholly suspended. Suspended form is form that refuses the resolutive figure of an immanent synthesis, of a synthesis within itself. The latter must remain suspended. Yet, here too, as regards music, the question of the resolution or the possibility of a *telos* of the musical work is a traditional one. There is a history of what resolution consists in, from basic notions of harmony to the question of the nature of an orchestral finale or the significance of the last movement of a symphony, and so on.

Many other examples could be cited; this issue has had a profound impact on the history of music. What is music's capacity for resolving the system of its own tensions? Music creates tensions and proposes to resolve them in every conceivable musical parameter. Thus, a tumultuous history of these questions about resolution, and in particular about what should or should not be considered a resolution, has developed over time. Adorno's position ultimately amounts to abandoning this problematics of resolution in all its guises and instead adopting 'waiting in vain' as a suspended gesture in which '*musique informelle*' – the music of disintegration – can take hold.

Last of all, the heavily negative character of the imperatives would suggest that music should not be structured by any process that would involve sublating its inner negativity. Instead, from within itself, it should negatively confront what is different from itself. (A host of potential negations in music can be noted, including sound, silence, and so forth.) Music should therefore deal with its own otherness. In fact, it has always naturally dealt with its own otherness; it has always consisted of an immanent dialectics, a dialectics of sound and silence, noise and whispering, the audible and the inaudible. So music should of course confront this. According to Adorno, however, the general law of the artwork as a formal work prescribes sublating these inherently negative elements by demonstrating how silence, for example, can ultimately be a parameter of music itself, how silence can be a rhythmic element of sound. Since this Hegelian type of music consists in sublating the immanent negativity it creates, Adorno's view is that music should *not* sublate its negativity but instead let it be and preserve the negative imperative of its being.

We might say, then, that Adorno's position on music, considered at this extremely abstract level, amounts to a thinking of formless form or informal form in the post-Auschwitz situation and consequently in the world today. Three different aspects are involved. First, it is music that terminates the unifying processes of form and consequently tolerates real difference or multiplicity, that is, the genuinely heterogeneous, or, in other words, things that have nothing to do with one another. Second, it is music with no resolution, music that is endless, in a manner of speaking, almost in both senses of the term: it has no ending that is truly essential to it nor does it have an end in the sense of a *telos*; it does not resolve the system of tensions it creates. Third, it must be music that does not sublate its own negative elements and therefore allows within itself the possibility for something different from itself. The consequences of all this are clear, especially as regards specific questions such as silence, non-organized sound, the work's development, its conclusion, its duration, and so forth. All these conventional parameters of the musical work are taken up again and given a negative treatment in the context of negative dialectics.

Lesson 3

Wagner as a Philosophical Question

Now that we have gone over Adorno's construction of a place for music in *Negative Dialectics*, what I intend to deal with is the question of what Wagner has to do with any of it. How does Wagner fit into this sort of philosophical framework?

In his book *In Search of Wagner*, which he wrote quite a while before *Negative Dialectics*, Adorno had already targeted Wagner as his musical foil. Adorno's itinerary was thus marked by a dispute, a fundamental, almost primordial, quarrel with Wagner. From a historical perspective, the fact that this quarrel is a replay of the one engaged in by Nietzsche, the initiator of the first great quarrel with Wagner, cannot fail to pique our interest. In short, taking on Wagner constitutes a genre to which I myself would like to contribute one more variation. In so doing, I will be following in the footsteps of Lacoue-Labarthe, who, like Adorno and Nietzsche before him, considers it absolutely essential for a philosopher to take on Wagner. If I mention philosophers here, it may well be because Wagner is a philosophical musical obsession of theirs. Be that as it may, there is clearly no getting around it: philosophers take on Wagner, and I am going to end up taking him on too. That is the first point I wanted to mention.

It is very interesting to see this sort of thing even in Heidegger, because music can hardly be said to occupy a particularly important place in his work, any more, in my opinion, than does art in general, or shall we say any art other than poetry. I don't think one finds in Heidegger a particularly complex or deep appreciation for non-poetic art. When music does come up in his writing, it is only as a pretext for condemning Wagner. Heidegger, too, was involved in quarrelling with Wagner – an extremely suggestive fact, considering the fondness Heidegger harboured for Nazism during a certain time, and the well-known fact that Nazism, on the contrary, vigorously set about co-opting Wagner, and Nietzsche into the bargain. So it is a very complicated story, because first we've got Nietzsche quarrelling with Wagner, and then we've got the Nazis constructing a certain Nietzsche who would have to be reconciled, or complicit, with Wagner since Wagner was one of the great artistic icons of the Nazi regime! Here, too, an extremely complicated series of debates about Wagner can be noted, as a result of which Nietzsche, Heidegger, Adorno and Lacoue-Labarthe – all following, as the latter reminds us, in the footsteps of Mallarmé and Baudelaire – have come to comprise a history of debates about Wagner. It has proven to be an amazingly rich history, especially if we bear in mind that philosophers' debates about music are a relatively rare phenomenon.

So my thesis is that Wagner created a new situation with respect to the relationship between philosophy and music. It was a new situation because he instituted a special kind of philosophical debate about himself that must inevitably also carry with it a broader debate about music, even if it involves a much more extensive debate about mythology, theatre, and so forth.

In the first place, then, I wanted to highlight this idea of debating about Wagner as a *genre*, particularly as one that became systematically negative from a certain point onward. Nietzsche, Heidegger, Adorno and Lacoue-Labarthe were all involved in mainly negative debates about Wagner, whom they each construed as a foil for one thing or another, and this, I think, constitutes a history that serves as the backdrop to Adorno's construction of a place for music in *Negative Dialectics*. The place constructed for music in *Negative*

Dialectics has as its immediate backdrop this philosophical debating about Wagner and, when all is said and done, the question of 'the case of Wagner'.

Why, then, is Wagner understood or apprehended against this backdrop as the classic example of a negative figure? Why does he ultimately come to occupy this negative place in Adorno? For very specific reasons, which serve as a vehicle for certain theses about, or constructions of, Wagner. I'll go over a few of these now.

1. Nietzsche, Heidegger, Adorno and Lacoue-Labarthe all agree in viewing Wagner as someone who forces musical unity upon a variegated mass, upon differences whose essential character of otherness disappears or dissolves as a result. That is the main charge levelled against him: Wagner created an enthralling, alluring, deceptive, hysterical, shimmering, seductive, sexual (the words keep changing from one writer to the next) musical edifice. As far as Nietzsche is concerned, and this idea is still around, Wagner is the 'old enchanter', the magician of music history, and, in this endlessly seductive guise, he appropriates a motley assortment of elements – narrative, poetic, scenic, theatrical, historical, racial, etc. – a particularly substantial assortment, in other words, that is ultimately all blended together, dissolved and unpresented, in a unity that is forced upon the music owing to the fact that he is an exemplary figure of the superimposition of identity and the diminution of difference.

This idea will be expressed in a variety of ways. Nietzsche, as just mentioned, will claim that Wagner is a great sorcerer or enchanter and therefore the arch-enemy of Dionysian clarity, while Heidegger, for his part, will claim that Wagner is the archetypal metaphysician, since metaphysics, as he defines it, is the supremacy of the One, the capturing of Being by the One. Wagner is an example in music of the One's capturing of Being, of the coming-forth of Being's freedom, in that he creates music that foists its multi-faceted shimmering upon otherness.

2. A second, more political reason to which these writers often refer is that this unity in Wagner's music is ultimately in the service

of a vision – itself unified and identitarian, mythological – of the nation in general and of the German nation in particular. The unification of the music is actually an ideological operation as well. It is the realization in the music of an ideological operation that consists in the triumph – the unified, undifferentiated presentation – of the One in a mythological conception of the foundation of nations, the aesthetic analogon, in the end, of a political foundation of the nation insofar as the latter is ultimately the German nation.

Thus, the unifying regime of the music, the way unity is forced upon it, is allegedly in collusion with a conception of the mythological origins of Germanness such that the musical operation is also and at the same time a political operation by virtue of its mythological resonance. It is precisely the latter feature that allowed the Nazis to co-opt Wagner, though that is putting it mildly; we would otherwise have to speak of Wagner's *pre*-Nazi character, something Lacoue-Labarthe actually does. The term 'proto-fascist' was virtually invented to describe Wagner and it would be possible to speak of 'proto-fascist' music. I won't go into detail about it here, but the reasoning behind it does exist and there is solid support for it.

3. To return now to conceptualization: What is the status of difference in Wagner? It has been claimed, overall, that the melodic line ultimately subordinates all the differences to itself so that the One might reign supreme. But what is the relationship between sameness and difference in Wagner's music?

The argument is repeatedly made that difference in Wagner is actually nothing but the constant postponement of the finale. Despite the fact that Wagner's musical discourse might be regarded as very elaborate, that differentiation constitutes one of its enduring features; despite the fact that he pushed the bounds of chromaticism to the limit in tonal discourse, turning it into tonal uncertainty, and that he could therefore be regarded as having introduced a new way of treating difference in music, the counter-argument nonetheless asserts that this treatment of difference should not be considered genuine since it is not *intrinsic* differentiation but merely the perennial delaying or holding back of the finale. This is a subtle but very important distinction. To say that an innovative, immanent organization of difference can be found in Wagner's music is not the same as to say that there is a sort of 'pathetics' of differentiation in it, which, in the final analysis, comes down to no more than the waiting for a finale that, although constantly deferred, is nevertheless delivered in the end. In other words, if the treatment of difference only amounts to a delayed or held-back finale, or to a use of chromaticism that merely makes you wait before its final diatonic resolution is heard, then the real essence of the treatment of difference in Wagner, over and above his seemingly very differentiated discourse, ultimately comes down to the finale, wherein closure is all the more conclusive precisely because it has been awaited for such a long time.

This is what Nietzsche had already called Wagner's enervating quality. 'Enervating' should be taken literally here: he wears out our nerves precisely because he creates a feeling of absence that, unlike Adorno's waiting in vain, is waiting only because we are left waiting for a resolution that is withheld from us until the curtain finally falls. Nietzsche already claimed that, as far as difference was concerned, this should be regarded as a mystification rather than as a genuine treatment of difference. This is the third reason why Wagner, far from being regarded as a true innovator of principles of difference, is instead accused of being a magician or prestidigitator of identity. After having made a big show of the dove's absence, he finally pulls it out of his hat at the very end, to the delight of an amazed and nervously exhausted audience. If I mention the dove it is naturally because it appears many times in Wagner's tetralogy, and it is a dove, if not a swan, that hovers above the finale of *Parsifal*.

4. The fourth reason why Wagner occupies a negative place is once again something Nietzsche came up with. (It must be said that Nietzsche's passion for Wagner was such that he coined every

negative thing that has ever been said about him. One can easily recognize the vocabulary of the lovers' quarrel in Nietzsche's writings on Wagner, by the way.) It is the role of theatricalization, the way the unification of the music is itself insidiously subordinated in the end to constant theatricalization.

It is here that Nietzsche accuses Wagner of being a ham actor: he is above all a showman, who seeks to get on young people's nerves, in the manner of a hysterical woman. The poor suckers all think they have been entranced by something utterly extraordinary, but in fact there is nothing behind it, nothing but theatre. Of what, then, does this theatricalization in the music consist? Of course, one could reply that theatricalization is naturally present in a music driven by a powerful theatrical impulse. But what those advancing this argument are really getting at is that the music itself is theatricalized *in its very make-up*. This means that, at bottom, the intricate details, the micro-construction of Wagner's music (which, after all, cannot be denied), are ultimately subordinated to gesture, and it is this grand musical gesture that drains the details off like a polluted river, sweeping everything away with it in the end. Thus, everything within the Wagnerian discourse that seems to be pristine, full of detail, subtle, and in a constant state of flux, is subordinated to crass gestures that are actually secretly in cahoots with German militarization.

A very subtle complex of things is in the end reduced to something akin to the military goose-step, to the despicable German aspect of Wagner, in Nietzsche's eyes. It is here that the theatricalization, the casting of the music itself in theatrical form, resides. Incidentally, Nietzsche, it should be stressed, never denied Wagner's genius. When he claimed he preferred Bizet a hundred times over, he was not saying that he thought Bizet was superior to Wagner as a musical genius but rather that this factor of captivating the audience via the grand theatrical gesture, in a music that was in fact infinitely more creative than Bizet's, was what set Wagner's music in the realm of insufferable Germanness, of an ultimate coarseness that destroyed its admirable infrastructure. This is what is meant by the theme of theatricalization.

5. The last reason (and Adorno was of course attuned to this issue) has to do with the spectacularization of suffering. Suffering, a great Wagnerian theme, is ultimately bound up with spectacle, so this argument goes. What is at issue in this spectacularization of the suffering that animates the great scenes in Wagnerian opera is the music's proximity to suffering, which is something that can easily be heard in Wagner. (I should point out that I will deal with this issue more thoroughly later on, but for the moment I'm playing the anti-Wagnerian devil's advocate as eloquently as I can.) Actually, a much more profound effect of heartbreak, of separation, of inner tension can be found in Wagner's music than merely the *sentimentality* of which he is usually accused. There is something about the chromatic dissonances, about Wagner's relation to the orchestra, about his division of the strings, and so on, that, on closer inspection, can be seen to create utterly unique effects of heartbreak. He could therefore be considered a tremendous musician of suffering, not simply because of his plots, even if it may derive from them, but rather on account of the fact that he created a heartbreaking music, a music that in no way comes across as resolutive but instead reveals this very broken-heartedness in its innermost core. In this regard, the chromatic dissonances and other techniques serve to produce a genuine music of suffering, not just a set of gestures or a theatricalization of suffering.

Arguing the same way as before, however, it might be objected that this suffering is in the final analysis bound up with spectacle, that it is merely *displayed* rather than treated as genuine otherness, in Adorno's sense of the term, as an experience of the irreducible. It is on the contrary abundantly exposed and subjected to the overall logic of spectacle. Since suffering in Wagner is not heartbreak per se, it is theatricalized or subordinated to the gesture of spectacle. This is a very important, contemporary question: what is the musical import of the theme of suffering in Wagner? For Adorno, the issue is of the utmost importance. Is suffering truly presented as irreducible heartbreak, or is it ultimately incorporated into the sentimental effects of spectacle? We can see how necessary it is to be precise if this matter is to be settled.

Through a Nietzschean type of logic, the whole issue can be summed up in the conviction that what is being established, in a nutshell, is an ambiguous link with religion. The spectacularization of suffering, the subordination of intricate details to gesture, the finale that is constantly delayed (not unlike the way the Last Judgement or the coming of the Messiah is always delayed), the pervasive mythology of the constitution of the nation, the musical unification of a space lacking any real character of difference, all combine to forge an ambiguous link with religion. Religious material is used over and over again by Wagner, and it might be objected that it is used as *mythical* material, when you come right down to it. In other words, he makes use of a whole range of Christian symbolism in the same way that he marshals pagan symbolism: the Christian materials are brought in as dramatic materials in the same way as Wotan and all the other gods of the Nordic pantheon are.

But the most important point may not necessarily be this use, or attempted use, of Christian material as dramatic and narrative material, or the possible revenge of this symbolism on the intentions of Wagner, who thought he could master Christianity despite the difficulty involved. Rather, the crucial point here is that the ambiguous link with religion is introduced through *indirect* themes, themes that are not merely present in the plot and that, in Nietzsche's view, comprise an ultimate allegiance to religion. They can perhaps be boiled down to two in particular:

- First, there is the theme of *purity*, occurring time and again in Wagner in the oddest varieties, truth be told. Buddhist themes (owing to the undeniable influence of

Schopenhauer) and a few vegetarian tendencies come up here and there, among assorted other varieties.

- Second, related to the theme of purity there is the theme of *redemption and salvation*, which doubtless constitutes a huge question for any particular religion.

It is plain, then, that this connection between purity and redemption, even in the innermost core of Wagner's music, provides an opportunity for detecting an ambiguous link with religion.

From a more trivial, but also more obvious, point of view, the question being raised here is that of the link between sexuality and music. Psychoanalysis can have a field day with it, but in fact it might also be a question that, albeit independent, concerns the religious connotations, which no doubt constitute its most important content when all is said and done.

When I was young, I happened to read a book by a Benedictine music scholar, whose name I think was Dom Clément Jacob.[1] He argued that music is essentially pure, that it is the purest of all the arts in that it does not figure into the invariably somewhat lascivious category of images. It is common knowledge that when you analyze the history of painting, every picture has a tendency to become a nude: it is very hard to argue for the purity of painting from the sixteenth and seventeenth centuries on. Clearly, even paintings such as the many that depict the martyrdom of Saint Sebastian produce an impression that instantly invites psychoanalytic investigation. What is the desire of the gaze, or the gaze as object of desire, as Lacan used to say? In music, though, Dom Clément Jacob discerned a radical purity. But he already had to contend with a thorny problem: the second act of *Tristan*. As far as *that* was concerned, even he was powerless to defend the idea of music's purity any longer.

---

1   Maxime Jacob, or Dom Clément Jacob (1906–1977) was a French composer and organist who also wrote two books, *L'art et la grâce* (1939) and *Souvenirs à deux voix* (1969).

So let's say that there is a singular sexual charge in Wagner, a relationship between music and sexuality that deserves to be clarified. It may be lurking behind themes that seem to be just the opposite: purity and redemption. Just think of those strange characters, the innocent young boys, in lederhosen as a rule, who appear throughout Wagner's work, or even of the young Siegfried, decked out like a backwoods Boy Scout, who has never had sex with a woman and who, when he finally compensates for this lack, gets caught up in a diabolical adventure. We are treated to some rather astounding scenes such as, for example, when he removes Brünnhilde's armour and, at the sight of her bosom, staggers back and exclaims, 'It's a woman!'[2] We are admittedly a little disconcerted, and the music has trouble conveying this.

Nietzsche, of course, noted this issue of the music's erotic charge, but it put him in an awkward position because he normally would have tended to *praise* this aspect of things. Instead, he concluded that the erotic charge in Wagner's music is ultimately subservient to religious themes such as purity, redemption, and so forth. The same dynamic as before is operating here: what could be credited as being an altogether unique creative innovation on Wagner's part – the introduction of a new kind of subjective sensuality into music – is instead treated exactly the same way that his prodigiously intricate inventions in the orchestral sphere were, namely, it becomes a means to criticize him for something. So he is given no credit for it, because this apparent innovation, having been deemed a flaw, is regarded instead as something fraudulent.

Yet it would be hard to deny that Wagner created a new kind of sensuality in music. Even Don Clément Jacob couldn't vouch for the contemplative purity he usually attributed to music when it came to *Tristan*. He had the impression that the two lovers were making love on stage – which is not completely erroneous – in that sort of infinite nocturnal scene, the enveloping darkness of the

---

2   *Siegfried*, Act III, scene 3.

night in which the lovers are hidden. You have to admit that on a pitch-black night like that, the music did indeed have an absolutely erotic effect!

To conclude what I have to say about the ambiguous link between Wagner's music and religion, I don't think that its true aesthetic locus is to be found in the dramatic plots in which Wagner attempted to treat the symbolic Christian material as though it were ordinary mythological material. Instead, the most important question, musically speaking, is whether this new eroticism is inherent in music, and whether, at bottom, Wagner introduced into music what had already penetrated painting long before, as if, contrary to Nietzsche's opinion, Wagner were the first great *pagan* of music, the first to impurify music, to strip it of its natural purity. The question hinges on knowing whether this is something indisputable, that is, whether or not the erotic impurity of sorts that characterizes Wagnerian seductiveness is in the final analysis subordinated to a logic of redemption or purity and whether or not the whole point of this *mise en scène* of the erotic is ultimately only to end up eliminating it ascetically.

It is around all these themes, whose connection with Adorno's whole system (combining as it does the questions of waiting, myth, the negative character of the imperatives) is clear throughout, that the various stages of the 'case of Wagner' were built up and eventually turned him into a 'case', so that, from his own day right up to the present, Wagner has been the focus of fierce debates. I think three phases of these debates can be singled out, in a somewhat schematic way, needless to say.

1. First, there was a debate about Wagner that centred simultaneously on aesthetics and nationality. Was his really a new art, creating new conditions for opera, music, and so on? What was the connection between this new art and the question of nationality (the Germans, the French, etc.)?

The question concerns art's principal functions and how they are connected to nationality. Even Mallarmé's debate with – and mainly against – Wagner was defined by these terms. That debate, after all, involved pitting French exceptionalism, ultimately rooted in the French language, against Germanic mythology and the aesthetics of music. The debate about both aesthetics and nationality thus constituted this first phase, which began with Baudelaire, or right from the time Wagner was trying to win recognition from the French. It was basically a Franco-German debate. In fact, when Wagner had *Tannhäuser* performed in Paris, he did so in order to win recognition at the Paris Opera, which he regarded as the premier opera company in Europe. Since things went badly, he ever after held a terrible grudge against France. That is why it was an explicitly nationalistic debate, which could be labelled 'Wagner and the new art' and 'Wagner and Germany'.

2. Next, I think that, in the period between the two world wars and briefly thereafter, there was a political and ideological debate, originally initiated by Nietzsche then later revised in the context of Wagnerism's compromises with Nazism, when the issue of Wagner's anti-Semitism started to be brought up again, along with the reasons why Hitler was such a fervent admirer of Wagner, the politics of Bayreuth under National Socialism, and so on. A critical inquiry into the political and ideological nature of Wagnerism thus developed, and in it, too, widely divergent positions were voiced. It is telling that this period witnessed, among other things, both Heidegger's polemic against Wagner, whose great contextual complexity I mentioned earlier, and the publication of Adorno's first essays. This time the debate can be labelled: 'Wagner and fascism', 'Wagner and anti-Semitism', or 'Wagner and Nazism'.

3. Finally, continuing up to the present day, a debate about music and philosophy has been going on. Note that the various debates overlap: in this latest one, for instance, the question of 'Wagner and fascism' is naturally still considered to be relevant. In this new debate about music and philosophy, the one we are dealing with here, what does Wagner signify in terms of the attempt to forge a new link between the two? What is Wagner's role with respect

to the possibility, or impossibility, of creating a new link between music and philosophy? Is it a negative, or mainly negative, role, as many people claim?

I would therefore situate what I am trying to say here as a contribution to this third phase, which combines the other two and consists in suggesting reasons why we may find in Wagner today some support for a relationship between music and philosophy that would differ from the one in which Wagner has always played a negative role. However, it would obviously not amount to a return to the fatuous Wagnerism – so blatant were its religious connotations – that was rampant, in France as everywhere else, in the late nineteenth to early twentieth century. The thesis I have in mind is a much more limited one, namely, that a close examination of Wagner's undertaking will enable us to elucidate both why there has been such obvious tension between music and philosophy for so long and how the parameters of this tension might be analyzed.

This will all be examined in the next lesson, which will deal with numerous examples from Wagner's work.

For the time being, though – to conclude and return to our point of departure – I'll examine Wagner in terms of his relationship to Adorno, in connection with the now widely held idea that form can occur only as formal transformation, that it does not consist in imposing the One onto given materials but consists instead in the very process of formal transformation. What needs to be shown, including in terms of music, is how form resolves or dissolves itself in the process of its own mutation, on the basis of which '*musique informelle*' can be prescribed.

This raises a very general question about Wagner, which has to do with his capacity for transformation. There is a different colour scheme in each of his operas, which can be identified in just a few measures, for reasons that are hard to explain. Yet this very striking variation in colour won't suffice to settle the crux of the following issue: Can Wagner's music be characterized in formal terms in a fairly unambiguous way? Are there Wagnerian 'gimmicks', so to speak, that are absolutely typical of him? Of course there are, but there may also be something more: on a deeper level, is the essence of Wagner's music reducible to such 'gimmicks', or does it involve transformative protocols that are far less apparent?

This transformative capacity is not exactly the equivalent of what is heard outright; rather, it consists in the way in which what is heard is determined by what is *not* heard. In other words, it is tantamount to the formal role of silence in Wagner's music, as opposed to the way Wagner is often simply reduced to the obvious power of his music. Granted, the power of the sounds themselves *is* obvious, aphrodisiac at times, or militaristic, or saccharine, at others; there is a little of everything. But, for us today, is this really what Wagner's music is about? Isn't there actually an inaudible operation, something far more subtle and subterranean, at work in it? Examining this phenomenon would amount to what I think could be called a somewhat 'microscopic' approach to Wagner's itinerary. It would have to be illustrated, no doubt by using thinner cross-sections of his music.

Specifically, there is a problem concerning transition that is quite interesting. Nietzsche claimed that Wagner arranged things in such a way that there would be *only* transitions in his music and that it is precisely in this way that he pulls the wool over everyone's eyes, always keeping things moving and overexciting us with transitions. But we need to take a closer look at this. What is the nature of transition in Wagner? How is it really structured? How do we get from one speech to another, and what is the relationship between this new procedure and the traditional system of breaks in opera? This would lead us, finally, to the question: What is the distinctly Wagnerian organization of opera's movement itself, of the inextricably musical and dramatic, or undecidable, interplay between the music and the drama?

As we know, this was the major problem in traditional opera, with which Wagner wanted to break. Composers before Wagner would simply resort to discontinuity to connect the music and the

drama. They always included a moment for telling the basic facts
of the story otherwise than by singing. That is why there was the
recitative, or even parts of the opera without any music whatsoever. Consequently, the connection between the drama and the
music was *decided* rather than being undecidable. It was projected
into an explicit formal device resulting in a break. Considered
archaic after Wagner, the break was nonetheless an extremely
rational way of dealing with the connection between the drama and
the music. Wagner, for his part, proposed something else, namely
that the interplay between drama and music should become undecidable, that no decision between the two be made via discontinuity. This implies that discontinuity was not actually eliminated but
was instead displaced. It has sometimes been said that discontinuity was replaced by continuity, which is not exactly true either. It
would be more accurate to say that discontinuity changed place,
because it was now treated on the basis of continuity and not the
other way around, even though it still remained present.

   This is the issue I would like to conclude with, because I think
that it is probably the most important problem for us today, not
only in terms of music but also, in my opinion, in terms of philosophy. The question of the relationship between the local and the
global, between continuity and discontinuity, or of the nature
of transitions, is a major question in every branch of philosophy
and specifically (I'll just mention this in passing) in politics. If,
in effect, discontinuity is no longer expressed politically in the
traditional figure of revolution, how then *is* it expressed? Should
we conclude that there is no longer any discontinuity whatsoever (an idea that is ultimately analogous to the idea of the end
of history)? Or should we instead think that discontinuity is
concealed behind the overwhelming appearance of continuity?
The latter question is in my view a typically Wagnerian one.
Indeed, Wagner has generally been interpreted as someone who
submerged discontinuity in continuity (yet another of Lacoue-
Labarthe's leitmotifs), whereas I think that Wagner displaced

discontinuity in such a profound manner that it came to act as a new figure of undecidability between narrative drama and music, and that in so doing he invented a new model of the relationship between continuity and discontinuity.

Lesson 4

Reopening 'The Case of Wagner'

1. Overture

As we have seen, the name *Wagner*, the signifier *Wagner*, has been an issue in the music-and-philosophy problem for a long time now. I have argued that it plays an utterly singular role, and I think that, as far as we who have witnessed the end of the twentieth century are concerned, this is due to what could be called the conjunction of two cycles: a genealogical one and an ideologico-political one.

The genealogical cycle, which is actually an intra-philosophical or intra-aesthetic one, sets out the history of how the case of Wagner was built up or developed, or, in other words, how it was *constructed*, since it is a construction that does not derive directly from Wagner's work itself. There is no doubt that Wagner very much wanted a case to be made of him; he did his best to ensure that this would be so, and Nietzsche wrote some fine pages on the unmistakably histrionic aspect of Wagner's personality. But, in fact, both the construction and the dramatization of the case of Wagner went on well beyond that and eventually became a kind of enterprise in their own right, extending from Baudelaire to Lacoue-Labarthe, François Regnault, Slavoj Žižek and myself, by way of Mallarmé, Nietzsche, Thomas Mann, Adorno and Heidegger.

It is a hefty case – unparalleled, in fact – where a musical matter is concerned. And it has turned Wagner into a sort of crucial hermeneutic focal point in terms of the relationship between philosophy and its artistic condition, its musical condition in particular, from the middle of the nineteenth century right up to today, or from what could be called the period of modernity to the period of so-called postmodernity. It is an extremely interesting fact that − in France, at least − Baudelaire, the poet traditionally considered to be the first to have invented the essential figures of modernity, should also have also been the one who so brilliantly initiated the construction of the case of Wagner.

This first, genealogical cycle was followed by an ideologico-political cycle. Its roots are also in the nineteenth century, but in my view it extends from the 1930s up to today, when it is still altogether relevant, its centre of gravity being the correlation between Wagner and the origins of Nazism. The empirical basis of this cycle, which is at once distinct from and yet connected to the first cycle, is indubitably inscribed between Wagner's anti-Semitic statements, on the one hand, and the co-opting of Wagner by the top Nazis, on the other.

So I think that the case of Wagner in its contemporary guise is located at the intersection of these two cycles: on the one hand, the philosophical genealogy of the construction of the case of Wagner, and, on the other, the Wagner question examined, apprehended, and articulated anew in light of the central importance today of the question of the destruction of the European Jews, of anti-Semitism, of Nazism. Wagner, like many others, was implicated in all this, but his position is an intrinsically genealogical one, which has led to the expression often used about him, by Žižek in particular, to the effect that there is something *proto-fascist* about Wagner. The case of Wagner is thus both an aesthetico-philosophical case and an ideologico-political one.

In this regard, I think there are two intellectual references for our purposes, both of which have proved to be entirely decisive in terms of the way the case was handled after the Second World War.

First (in lessons 2 and 3) there is Adorno, from his youthful book on Wagner right up to his far-reaching examination of whether art was possible after Auschwitz. Clearly, Adorno is positioned in a highly significant way at the juncture between the two cycles, which is why his role is so important, after all. He took a stand not only on the necessity for leaving Wagner behind philosophically but also on the question of what art might be after Nazism and the destruction of the European Jews.

The second reference is Syberberg and all his films. These films comprise an utterly extraordinary set of analyses, especially as regards the various cycles that constitute the case of Wagner. Let me just remind you what they are. In 1972 Syberberg made *Ludwig: Requiem for a Virgin King,* a film about King Ludwig II of Bavaria that is saturated through and through with Wagner and is at the same time a film about the relationship between Wagner and Germany. Syberberg's 1975 film *The Confessions of Winifred Wagner* consisted of an enormous interview the film-maker conducted with Winifred Wagner, the person responsible, so to speak, for turning Bayreuth over to Hitler, which made her a major witness to the whole affair. Then, in 1977, Syberberg made *Hitler, A Film from Germany,* a seven-hour-long film about the question of Hitler, Nazism and, once again, Wagner. Finally, in 1982, he made *Parsifal,* a film version of Wagner's *Parsifal.* These films are all very important because what is articulated and featured in them is the issue of the relationship between Wagner and the question of Germany.

Germany may well have been the word that enabled the two cycles I just mentioned to intersect, since Wagner can also be considered one of the great artistic interpreters of the question of Germany. The linkage between the genealogical and ideologico-political cycles, as regards the prevailing current of thought about Wagner, is generally made by pinpointing the abstract principle of what might be called a *conservative revolutionism* in Wagner's artistic philosophy or in its underlying metaphysical foundation. The

usual line of argument of the anti-Wagnerian currents dominant
in this case since Nietzsche's day has been that Wagner's aesthetic
philosophy – essentially his artistic doctrine – lies in the way the
principle of conservative revolutionism, or what Marx had called
feudal socialism, is enacted.

There are many arguments in support of the theory that Wagner
is the great artist of feudal socialism and I am by no means presenting it as a trivial one. Proto-fascism, to use a more modern term, is
a post-Nazi recuperation of feudal – actually Wagnerian – socialism; that is, the conservative revolutionism that, when viewed
from today's perspective, allegedly played a genealogical or foundational role in the properly fascist dimension that feudal socialism took on in National Socialism. Accordingly, the theory runs as
follows: Wagner brought about a break – which is undeniable with
respect to a certain number of points – as far as both music and
the stage were concerned. It is impossible to ignore the fact that
opera after Wagner was no longer the same opera as before, either
musically or scenically. However, this break was essentially a
backward-looking one. The argument constantly advanced is that
having an artistic and ideological project of a feudal socialist or
conservative revolutionary type is essentially backward-looking
because it is pegged to the theme of a new mythology. The function of art, for Wagner, was supposedly to create a new mythology. More to the point, according to a description Nietzsche came
up with that has been parroted ever since, a new but overblown
kind of sensuality was introduced to keep the audience pinned
to their seats, or to unite them, in accordance with the following
question: What must be done to bring the people's spirit and the
Idea together? That was the agenda.

To bring about such unity, you would have to keep the audience
mesmerized so as to foist the ultimately proto-fascist solution to the
question upon them, because this solution supposedly amounted to
introducing a new mythology (this is Lacoue-Labarthe's and many
other critics' major theme) located on the other side of the divide

between the old gods and the new God of Christianity. Wagner's overblown sensuality and the whole network of artistic techniques he invented would be deployed to foster in the audience a hypnotic state that would make it possible to subject them to mythological configurations aimed at transcending the divide between the old gods and the new Christian God. This new mythology would thus be a paganism of the death of the gods – a paganism of the Greek gods, though in their twilight state, or their Germanic equivalents (the system is actually one and the same) – hence, a paganism of the death of the gods and/or a sublated Christianity.

This is the question about the real meaning of *Parsifal,* which is still being debated today because, quite frankly, it is not all that clear. Lesson 5 will be devoted entirely to this issue. At any rate, the opera ends with the idea of the redemption of the Redeemer. A second redemption is required, whereby Christianity is actually sublated by being reaffirmed. There is consequently something Nietzschean about this idea that a reaffirmed Christianity is ultimately acceptable, not as a religion per se but precisely as a new mythology, as a mythology integrated into the mythology of its own affirmation. The homeland of this new mythology would then be Germany. There would be a new mythology, beyond both paganism and Christianity, with Germany as its site. This idea was not entirely new, since already for Hegel the site of the Absolute Idea was Germany, or Prussian bureaucracy. Wagner's Germany, as we shall see, is more ambiguous. When it comes to Wagner, the question 'What is Germany?' becomes really complicated.

We would thus have a teleology of art arrived at through musical and dramatic innovations. As you know, Wagner aspired to realize the synthesis of art through the total artwork. So we are afforded a teleology of art whose aim is to impose a mythology that would ultimately overcome the opposition between Greece and Christianity, and this teleology is linked to a political radicalism, a revolutionary radicalism transferred onto the affirmation of the Nation. It is therefore the classic example of what Benjamin called an *aestheticization of politics*, which is the theme that will run all through this critique of Wagner: there is an aestheticization of politics in his work or, in other words, the intersection of a mythological teleology of art and a radicalism that ultimately assigns the theory of revolutionary rupture to the constitution of the nation.

So, as this accusation would have it (I'm playing the prosecutor for the moment here), the techniques Wagner used are of necessity impure, pernicious – one might almost say disgusting. You hear this over and over again when it comes to Wagner. Because Wagner's is a music of overblown seductiveness, it effectively makes use of partly new techniques that are essentially impure or pernicious from the standpoint of the music's development. This point, about which Nietzsche displayed great acuity, is very important for two related reasons, in my opinion. Wagner's techniques are impure, first of all, because they are *dialectical* (they possess the impurity together with the arrogance of dialectical techniques, which always claim to be overcoming all the differences and contradictions that have been created in the music) and they are impure, second of all, because they are actually of the order of *artificial constraints*. Although there is something innovative about the constraints, they nevertheless prove in the end to be artificial ones that are subordinate to something other than the music itself.

2. The accusations against Wagner redux

We can now proceed to a systematic presentation of what I would call the six major accusations that have been levelled against Wagner, from the point of view of theatre, or of aesthetic criticism, this time.

1. The first accusation targets Wagner's reducing of the melodic line to a principle of continuity (cf. the theory of 'endless melody') whose paradigm is actually the artificial unity of lived experience. The real paradigm thus consists in configuring the flow

of the music on the model of the subjective flow. It is a sort of discursive emotion imposing identities, and this imposition of identities as identities of lived experience is precisely what lends Wagner's music and Wagnerian continuity its dimension of extramusical fascination: the music's effect is not really immanent but is instead always filtered through a subjective paradigm of emotion that remains extrinsic to it. This is our first issue, then: the radical critique of what is hidden, as it were, beneath the 'endless melody' model.

2. The second of the charges of which Wagner stands accused concerns a certain recuperation of suffering and compassion – crucial themes in Wagnerian drama – whereby the former is actually dissolved in the rhetoric of the latter. To put it another way, rather than being truly and genuinely confronted, the Other's suffering is dissolved in a rhetoric of compassion. The upshot of this is that we get idiotic young men in lederhosen who, as they stand around dumbfounded watching someone writhe on the ground in excruciating pain, are suddenly struck by a revelation, the revelation of a new god. This really amounts to a kind of poor man's Schopenhauer; that is, something like an articulation of suffering that, instead of being the point at which all rhetoric comes to a halt, as Adorno would have it, on the contrary *fuels* the rhetoric. Thus, the unbearable, rather than being apprehended in the present, is in fact subjected to becoming, and it is the *music* that produces this, meaning that it is not solely a dramaturgical issue.

Compassion is the redemptive or artificial name for this submission of the pure present of suffering to a becoming that constitutes its dissolution in rhetoric. As a consequence, the suffering character in Wagner is always presented as being the *result* of a musical predetermination, whereas it is obvious that the whole thematics of the pure present of suffering implies that suffering is not a result but an *experience* first and foremost. One must first be open and receptive to such an experience. Wagner allegedly sidesteps all this, however, and consigns suffering to the rhetoric of becoming.

3. The third accusation levelled against Wagner is that his basic strategy is dialectical in the bad sense of the term, assuming that a good one even exists: differences are nothing but the means for getting to the affirmative finale. It does indeed seem as though we are immersed in differences, dissonances, discontinuities, but the bottom line is that it is really all about reconciliation. That is what the affirmative finale epitomizes, and dissonance is explored not from the standpoint of its future development but rather from that of its ultimate elimination, even if the latter is delayed, slowed up, or particularly convoluted. There is a fundamental kind of craftiness about Wagner, which is in line with the French composer Barraqué's remark to the effect that no creative inroads whatsoever were made in Wagner's music as far as modifying musical language was concerned; there is merely a protracted, crafty practice of subjecting every difference to the finale, or what ultimately amounts to the production in the music of an equivalent of absolute knowledge as a resulting figure, as a terminal figure of discursivity.

4. The fourth accusation targets the following: in addition to the dialectical strategy, and underlying the overblown sensuality by which it is conveyed, there actually exists the device of a rational framework in Wagner's music. In other words, if you want to subject suffering to the sublimation of becoming, you will obviously have to force things and come up with a device to make it all work. So in Wagner's musical potpourri there is actually a rational framework that ultimately subjects the music to the narrative.

This is a crucial point that was already made by Nietzsche and again by Thomas Mann and that is entirely brought to bear by Lacoue-Labarthe. The idea is that if you want to use a dialectical strategy in music in conditions that are not exactly those of inherited or traditional forms such as the movements of a symphony, for example, but rather in a discourse giving the appearance of continuity – presenting itself as 'endless melody', that is, without any of the devices of formal discontinuity – you must first proceed in such a way that the music assigns all the differences to a resolution. Since this resolution is not exactly classical resolution, however, but another sort of thing altogether, you secretly subject the musical discourse to the narrative, meaning that theatricality ends up controlling the musical process as such. Form, where Wagner is concerned, is the artificial imposition of narrative signs upon the music. Form constantly imposes narrative signs that act as a rational framework underlying the apparent continuity of the music. This is the function of the leitmotifs, which are regarded in this polemic as the imposition of signs upon the music so that it will be in the service of the result.

5. The fifth accusation amounts to the claim that the proof of all the foregoing charges lies in the fact that Wagner was unable to create any genuine *waiting*. Adorno's critique is a very specific but, to my mind, highly significant one: the proof that we are in the present actuality of things is that waiting might be waiting *in vain*, waiting that is in fact not dependent on what comes after all the waiting. Here is where Adorno's contrasting of Wagner and *Waiting for Godot* comes in: Beckett, he holds, is the dramatist of modern waiting, whereas Wagner is the dramatist of waiting that is still metaphysical, of waiting for the final result. Wagner's shortcoming lies in his inability to create a kind of waiting that might be something other than the eventual fulfilment or even the reward afforded by the fruits of its end result.

6. The sixth – and perhaps the most important – charge is that, for all these reasons, Wagner's music turns out to be incapable of creating an experience of time, that is to say, incapable of being a creation or even a thinking about time, because it acts as a device to artificially superimpose signs upon a duration that is itself subordinated to its own result. As a consequence, time is blocked. Wagner was therefore unable to create a new conception of time as such. For everyone who thinks that music is ultimately one of the modes for a thinking of time, Wagner represents an essential failure because of his inability to accomplish as much. In particular, his notorious *longueurs*, the fact that he always seems to

go on for too long, is merely the structural sign of this inability to create a new experience of time. Wagner's music is *necessarily* too long, because it is actually just a bogus conception of time. Try as one might to shorten it or make cuts in it, it will remain the same length, as everyone has experienced: cut a Wagner opera in half and it will still seem just as long.

You can interpret this phenomenon in a variety of ways. You can claim, for example, that it is precisely because there is such a remarkable temporal creation in Wagner's music that it is extraordinarily resistant to being cut, and that this creation is present even on a *local* level, even within a single measure. That is in fact how I would interpret it. But the hostile interpretation asserts that it's no wonder the music always seems too long: it is because there is no true or authentic creation of time in Wagner. So we get the unbearable feeling that a temporality that is not really genuine, a temporality we cannot enter into, is being inflicted upon us. This stems from the fact that the duration, or length, of Wagner's music is reducible to repetitive patterns that are not really linked to the authenticity of an experience of time but rather to the production of a certain number of effects. Temporality is subjected to the production of effects, resulting in a music of the effect, which, as such, cannot genuinely, immanently produce a new experience of time.

3. The question of 'high art'

These, then, are the six main charges of which Wagner stands accused, charges that essentially turn him into a symbol of the failure of high art, of the end of high art, in the sense that the aim of high art in music is to create a new figure of greatness through the creation of a new experience of time. High art is not something realized in a static figure of greatness but is instead an innovative conception of greatness itself. This was clearly Wagner's own point of view, but he supposedly failed in his endeavour.

Nietzsche thought that the project of high art should be replaced with that of 'great politics'. The older Nietzsche was utterly obsessed with the project of 'great politics'. Nietzsche's and Wagner's final conflict, as I see it, really had to do with the fact that Nietzsche had arrived at the conclusion that what was needed at the end of the nineteenth century wasn't high art but 'great politics' and that Wagner's so-called high art was in no way a 'great politics' or a substitute for it. So Wagner had to be cleared away and forgotten in order for a 'great politics' to come into being. Later came the idea that the quest for innovation in music should do away with the mythical project of high art altogether and no longer be based on it. This new vision of things can thus be called a 'subtractivism': what must be 'subtracted' is the old, idealistic conception of greatness. Such subtractivism has dominated not only music but a good deal of twentieth-century art as well:

- Poetry must become indistinguishable from prose. It must give up striving to embody or impose the metric grandeur of language and return instead to a more modest norm of language.

- The imperative of form in painting must give way to the fleeting precariousness of installations that disintegrate without ever creating a paradigm of stable greatness or eternity of any sort.

- Dance must become the display of the real, ephemeral, or tortured body.

- The novel as a general synthesis of history is impossible;

- As for music, it must be atonal, athematic, informal, etc.

Defined in this negative way, Wagner became a necessary figure insofar as he essentially stood for the culmination of high art. From this
standpoint, Wagner might almost be said to occupy in the history of
the arts the position that Hegel holds in the history of metaphysics; he
is the Hegel of art in the sense that he brought to an end, through his
systematic failure, the project of high art as a project apposite to the
absoluteness of its subject matter. This comes down to saying – and
in my opinion it is why Wagner has remained a 'case' – that what was
once again argued in regard to Wagner amounted to the equivalent of
the critique of metaphysics in its expressly artistic guise. These arguments can be boiled down to two main theses. High art is impossible
and should be subjected to critique or deconstructed because: first, it
is the aestheticization of totality, it presupposes totality, its basic aim is
the seductiveness of totality; and second, in order to achieve the latter,
it is forced to adapt to its aim dialectical techniques, techniques that are
at the same time artificial constraints.

So Wagner – like Hegel, incidentally – has survived (they are
both doing pretty well, after all!) as the boundary stone indicating
the end of something, the monumental boundary stone on which
is engraved 'Here ends the project of high art' or 'Here lies the last
great metaphysics.' Wagner stands as the big mausoleum in the
graveyard of impossible grandeur. In this sense, that is the reason
he has been maintained as a 'case'.

What I intend to do, then, is to create a counter-current with respect
to all of this. I will attempt to argue that, although all the aforementioned accusations may indeed be coherent, significant, and forceful,
the time has now come to write an additional chapter that would go
against the grain of the various accusations targeting Wagner. As
is always the case when you propose to write an additional chapter,
it is because you position yourself elsewhere – elsewhere vis-à-vis
the majority opinion holding Wagner to be the Hegel of music, and
therefore elsewhere vis-à-vis the question of high art.

I would say that the position I'm staking out is that we are on
the cusp of a revival of high art and it is here that Wagner should

be invoked. My hypothesis is that high art has once again become part of our future – I have no idea how this is so, but I am absolutely sure of it. Greatness is no longer merely part of our past; it is part of our future as well. Needless to say, it is not the same kind of greatness as before. So what is it then?

It is surely high art, but high art *uncoupled from totality*, that is, high art not as the aestheticization of totality but rather only to the extent that it is uncoupled from totality. Thus, it is clearly greatness of a new type. This could be expressed as heroism without heroizing, for example, or greatness subtracted from the paradigm of war, or something similar. There are a variety of ways of putting it. This new type of greatness might be constitutive of our present circumstances, in which case we might be poised between two different Wagners now.

The first Wagner is the one I have been discussing up to now. I don't mean to imply that such a Wagner doesn't exist (which would be absurd since the case for him has been duly constituted and argued), but that he is entirely connected to the hypothesis that high art is finished. He occupies the position of high art as something over and done with. But if high art is also a creative project for the future and not merely the end of something, if its revival is on the horizon – even if artistic life today is to some extent subject to unavoidable trial and error compared with what high art uncoupled from totality might be – then Wagner can be brought back again using different means, and we would then have a second Wagner. We need to regard Wagner as someone who said something about high art that can be understood in a different way today from how he himself understood it, or in a different way from how those who constructed 'the case of Wagner' understood it. That would be my hypothesis.

This being the case, Wagner cannot be approached exclusively in terms of totality, since what we are dealing with is greatness uncoupled from totality. We will therefore have to venture into Wagnerian fragmentation. This does not necessarily imply that totality will have to be ignored but rather that its trail can be picked up in fragmentation or in localization: at the point where continuity and dissonance, the local and the global, confront each other both musically and dramatically. If Wagner is made to appear in his own unique mode of fragmentation – in his becoming, in his artistic process, even on a microscopic level, so to speak – here where this clash between continuity and dissonance, between the local and the global, plays out, then I believe he can be defended against the six charges we outlined above. We can switch from being the prosecution to being the defence, since the matter itself will obviously have changed; it will no longer be exactly the same trial as before.

4. Wagner's asceticism

What I would like to try to do now is represent the defence in this new trial of Wagner. But let me begin with something I think it is important to say about what I'd call Wagner's ascetic resolve. Wagner has so often been sneered at as the great sorcerer, the sensualist, the lover of the erotic, or the 'old magician', as Nietzsche called him, typically using one of his remarkably ambiguous expressions. (Wagner was probably the only great passion of Nietzsche's life, and when he had to sacrifice him for 'great politics' he went about it with some very ambiguous phrases, like 'old magician', which is a horrible but also wonderful expression.)

But to return to Wagner's ascetic resolve: Prior to Wagner, what were opera's sensual pleasures (since we are dealing with eroticism, after all)? Everyone agrees that they were abundant. Among opera's great sensual pleasures, which are very obvious to us today, are the ensembles, or, in other words, opera's – as opposed to the theatre's – ability to make people speak and sing together, hence all the trios, quartets and choruses. In the history of opera before Wagner, some remarkable things can be found when it comes to the overt sensuality expressed by certain ensembles, such as the one in *Così fan tutte*, which is utterly erotic, unparalleled as far as this phenomenon is concerned. Or the quartet in Verdi's *Rigoletto*, of which even Victor Hugo was envious, despite the fact that he claimed he didn't like his own poetry to be set to music. This sort of thing went on after Wagner as well: to give but one example, the women's trio at the end of *Der Rosenkavalier*. Yet giving it up all up was one of Wagner's fundamental acts. That kind of sensuality would henceforth be over: there were to be no more trios, quartets or quintets, only very modest and rather perfunctory choruses, or occasionally fairly sentimental ones.

This renunciation of sensuality, which was something relentlessly pursued by Debussy in Wagner's wake, can be chalked up to one essential reason, I believe: the sensuality of the operatic ensemble derives from a musical function that serves to unify multiplicity. The sensuality is its concrete manifestation, realized in the quasi-murmuring play of multiplicity. It is something like the multiple murmuring within unity. Indeed, this is really what the subjection of difference to finitude amounts to. It is moreover always a distinct form, with a clear-cut beginning and end. It is a fragment of the One in which the multiple murmurs, and it is this that Wagner will give up.

This phenomenon must be taken very seriously. Despite the fact that Wagner gave up sensuality in his music, he has actually often been accused of subjecting difference to finitude or closure. It is really ironic that the composer so accused should be the very one who was the first to announce that he was going to give it up! It was nevertheless objected that his renunciation wasn't genuine because he was purely and simply incapable of such a thing; he could do no more than make people go on talking endlessly. As a matter of fact, he was just as capable as anyone, if not more so, and it is this issue that I would like to begin with.

There are two major examples in Wagner's work in which the residue, so to speak, of what he gave up has survived, and these examples prove that he could have produced hundreds more like them. First, in *Götterdämmerung*, there is the formidable tragic trio (whose composition is quite Verdiesque) in which Brünnhilde, Gunther and Hagen vow to kill Siegfried, and then there is the quintet in Act III, scene 4 of *Die Meistersinger*. Without telling the whole story of Wagner's operas here, although it is often easy enough to do so, let me explain where this quintet comes in. From the philosophical point of view that concerns us, there has been a terrible riot in Act II of *Die Meistersinger*, a scene of unremitting conflict in which the various characters' intrigues gradually lead to a kind of carnivalesque free-for-all throughout the whole town of Nuremberg. Everyone comes running out into the street, shouting and yelling all over the place, and the various intrigues all become hopelessly entangled until nobody knows what is what.

Then, at the beginning of Act III, the main character, Hans Sachs, the master singer par excellence, comes up with two things as a sort of lesson about, or assessment of, the riot. First, he gives up his artistic authority and passes it on to young Walther, the representative of the new art. So we have a figure of renunciation/ transmission, whereby the old master abdicates his artistic author-ity and passes it on. (Of course, since he is the one passing it on, he can also hold on to it.) Then he gives up his position of authority in love: despite his love for Eva, he gives *her* up to Walther too. In short, he bequeaths both the music and the woman to Walther. But he nevertheless keeps something for himself, as we shall see later.

The quintet occurs in Act III, after Sachs's decision to give these things up. Why is there a quintet at this point? I think it is precisely because we are dealing here not with the consequences of a heroic, affirmative decision but with those of a *renunciation*: Sachs has really decided to give up these two things, and, as a result, a new sort of peace comes about, featuring the young couple, Eva and Walther, and, as an amorous counterpoint to them, the newly reconciled couple, David and Magdalena, with Sachs, standing for renunciation, in the middle. It is not a matter of the subject's soli-tude, then, but rather of his relationship to the community. I would like to stress that this is the only quintet in Wagner's entire œuvre, and it is linked to the instability typical of a tentative state of peace that has been dictated by renunciation rather than affirmation.

We will now turn to the character of Hans Sachs and examine the first accusation levelled against Wagner at the same time.

5. *Wagner against identities*

The first charge brought against Wagner takes him to task for having granted a paradigmatic role to lived emotion in the composition of the melodic line. This thesis amounts to saying – since it is a dramatic, not just a musical, conception – that subjective identity in Wagner is something like the invariant of the melodic line and that this can be the case because the paradigm of the line is emotion, the lived emotional experience of subjectivity.

I would like to put this thesis to a real test by using Sachs's monologue at the beginning of Act III of *Die Meistersinger*. We just saw how, at the end of this act, in scene 4, Sachs stood alone, both vulnerably and ironically, so to speak, between the two couples. Now I would like to backtrack and show how the moment Sachs makes his decision occurs, in terms of the music. Here we have a real test of the nature of the relationship between the melodic line and subjectivity. The decision Sachs will make, as I have already said, involves a twofold renunciation: the renunciation of his established position of artistic authority and the renunciation of his position of mastery in love. I also mentioned that the background to this in Act II was a chaotic commotion: the schemes and intrigues of the various characters, the confusion in appearance, the total disarray of the set.

In his monologue, Sachs goes over the various factors determining his decision. This strikes me as very important because it runs counter to the idea that the paradigm of the melodic line is nothing more than subjective emotion. In actual fact, the monologue runs through the conditions on which Sachs's decision is based and enables him to move forward, from the anguish of conflict and suffering to a tentative peace of sorts. Thus, the melodic line, rather than being a line of identity, is one of transformation, whereby an emotional torment that has been very powerfully expressed at the beginning turns into a tentative state of peace. This is the subject of Sachs's decision without the decision itself being explicitly mentioned. The decision is made *as the transformation is occurring*.

In essence, I would like to argue that what Sachs goes through here is something that is in no way the unfolding of an identity; rather, it is the plasticity of a metamorphosis. On the whole, it is more Deleuzian in this respect than anything else, since what serves as the subject is not the unfolding of the consequences of identity, as has often been claimed, especially on account of the leitmotifs. There is an extraordinary sort of plasticity about the transformation, which is what accounts for the fact that the affective tone is utterly fluid and that the music produces this fluidity, rather than imposing any identity whatsoever.

Sachs's monologue is a typical example of what might be called the *decision monologue* scene in Wagner, that is, a monologue in which something is resolved without the explicit nature of the decision being apparent. Indeed, the decision is arrived at entirely by means of the character's inner transformation or by what might be called the immanent inflection of the themes.

In this regard, I would like to point out that Wagner's themes, by virtue of the way they are interwoven and follow each other in rapid succession, play two simultaneous roles, and it is this dual role that really accounts for the singular innovation of the theme in Wagner.

- The themes do in fact serve to structure the narrative at times. I'm thinking, for example, of the evocation of Midsummer Night in Act II of *Die Meistersinger*, when the Spring theme effectively comes in.

- Themes also play a much more crucial role, however, in that they actually serve as a vehicle for subjective development. What will enable a subject to be different by the end of a monologue like this, for example, is structured much more crucially by the *transformative* role played by the themes than by their mere indicative role. Boulez, incidentally, always strongly emphasized this point: the essence of the Wagnerian theme lies in its potential to be transformed. It is this transformation that really conveys the subjective metamorphosis, thereby making the decision appear immanently, not in terms of 'I was such and such a way before, but now I am different' but rather in terms of a change from one state to the other in the discourse itself.

What I am saying is that if you want to know what the deep connection between music and drama in Wagner ultimately is – the essential question regarding the new opera as he conceived it – the most important thing to remember is the fact that, in Wagner, *dramatic possibilities are created through the music*. The music does not simply reinforce or support a pre-established dramatic situation, even if the text in fact is always already there; it creates dramatic possibility as such. In other words, the subjective process of the decision or the figure of the emotion as a dramatic possibility is built right into in the music.

I think we have a very clear example of this phenomenon here: at the end, when Sachs says how things will be able to be handled now under the changed circumstances, his new potential for action shows that we are truly in the presence of a different Sachs. But the way he has changed, this new dramatic possibility that will influence the course of the action thereafter, is actually something created by the *music*, not by the text or the drama, really, since the text does not have a lot to say about this metamorphosis, even though it has taken place. Thus, it is the music that effectuates the drama, and this is an essential truth about Wagner's work. The music is not something coming from without to illustrate the subject's evolution; on the contrary, it is truly the unpredictable inner impetus of the transformation.

I must stress this notion of unpredictability. It is not the creation or illustration of a necessity that is involved; it is really the creation of a *possibility*. It is first and foremost the unpredictable creation of a dramatic possibility that, in terms of the music, could easily go in a completely different direction. For example, it is absolutely clear that the possibility for the quintet is contained in what I have just described, because the subjective possibility that Sachs might be the central figure in the quintet simply does not exist prior to there being the melodic line of the monologue. So we are not dealing with just a dramatic possibility but rather with the musically constructed possibility for new dramatic situations: the new Sachs will be the Sachs of a tentative new peace and, it might moreover be said, of a new alliance. The possibility for a new alliance between art and the people is ultimately the true content of this whole process.

6. Music and suffering

This provides us with a very interesting approach to the second issue, namely, the theory that Wagner instrumentalized suffering through a rhetoric of compassion and never restored it as an experience in the present.

I maintain exactly the opposite. Suffering does indeed exist in the present in Wagner's work – not always, naturally, but very often – and perhaps even especially. In the history of opera I can really see only one true heir to Wagner: Berg. There is certainly something very Wagnerian about Berg, not as far as the technical aspect of things is concerned, but as regards his conception of the connection between music and drama.

How did Wagner manage to create suffering in the present? By creating the present of subjective splitting as such in the music. Previously in opera, subjective identity was often a matter either of conventional character types or a calculus of combinations thereof: characters took on their identities within a variety of combinations of different subjective typifications. Even in Mozart, character typing is certainly a lot more deliberate than it is in Wagner, but it fluctuates according to the way the plot and the characters are combined. It is moreover for this reason that the ensembles are so important. In Mozart, the finale of each act is crucial because it is there that occur the instances of subjective identity brought about by combinations of character types.

Subjective identity functions differently in Wagner because, rather than taking on his identity from any such combination of character types, or even really from the plot, the subject essentially takes on his identity from his own split, from his own inner division. This constitutes a radical shake-up of the notion of subjective identity as a *combinatoire*, a notion that in my opinion still prevailed, to all intents and purposes, in opera just prior to Wagner. I would say that the suffering subject, for Wagner, is nothing other than a split that cannot be made dialectical, that cannot be healed. It is a split in the subject that really establishes an inner heterogeneity without any hope of genuine resolution.

Just because there are episodes of reconciliation in Wagner's operas does not mean that this split is not expressed as such in the present. It is not expressed in the plot sequence in which it occurs; rather, it is expressed as a present of absolute suffering. At bottom, Wagner's great suffering characters are really creative new testaments to their own suffering *in the present*, even if the story might later undergo some new twist or other. Regardless of whether it is Tannhäuser, Tristan, Siegmund, Amfortas or Kundry, these characters all display a radical split that can be neither dialecticized nor healed, and this split is conveyed by what I would call a music of heartbreak. Wagner is truly the inventor of a music of heartbreak, which is expressed in the composition of the music itself by virtue of the fact that, by using the potential heterogeneity of the themes, he reveals and communicates an exceptionally intense split that is really a split in the subject in its guise as irresolvable suffering.

The example we will use to illustrate this – the classic one as far as this issue is concerned – is *Tannhäuser*. This opera is traversed by, or composed of, three splits that are woven together but that are nevertheless one and the same.

First of all, Tannhäuser himself is a character deeply divided about love. Torn between two conceptions of love, he cannot give up either one, although they are outwardly and socially incompatible. The basic make-up of these two conceptions of love is strictly conventional, as can easily be seen: carnal, pagan love, symbolized by his relation to the Venusberg and Venus, on the one hand, and the courtly, quasi-religious love of the world of medieval knights, on the other. We are poised between Antiquity and the Middle Ages, between the pagan and Christian conceptions of love. Tannhäuser is torn, however, because he has experienced both types of love to the extreme.

Moreover, as regards both these types of love, there is the fact that Tannhäuser is a great poet, a great musician whose singing has won over not only Elisabeth, a character devoted to the Virgin Mary of Christian chastity, but also Venus, a character representing pagan sensuality. Just between us, it is as though Wagner were saying, 'As a great musician, I'm entitled to all the women, to all the different types of love!' If we consider Tannhäuser the great singer as representing Wagner the man, it implies an interesting claim about what being a great musician ultimately means in terms of entitlement. But if we consider him from the vantage point of how his character is constructed, the division is really presented as an utterly unbearable split. So this is the first great split in the subject.

Second, it is a matter of a historical split, as I said, a split between the strictly ordered world of chivalry and the anarchic world of individual wandering: how, in effect, can desire be reconciled with the knightly order?

Third, it is a fundamental, symbolic split between the gods. This posed a very significant problem for Wagner, who was torn between the pagan gods – via Venus and the Venusberg – and the God of the Christian religion. Ultimately, it is the question of femininity, divided between Venus and Mary as emblematic of two different kinds of love as well as of two totally different cultural or symbolic contexts. However, this split occurs *within* Tannhäuser; he is at bottom nothing other than this split, the consequence of which is his utter inability to remain in any one place.

The theme of the character who cannot stay put is a very interesting one in Wagner. It can already be found in *The Flying Dutchman*. But one cannot fail to note that even Wotan, the great god of the Ring Cycle, ends up as 'The Wanderer'. He cannot stay in one place, either. At the end, we see him with his big hat on his head, wandering all over the world, watching what is going on; a spectator, actually, of the complex unfolding of his ultimate downfall. Such is the typical Wagnerian character. Here, too, we need to take account of how complicated this all is: Wagner is also the great poet of the character who cannot remain in one place, who is bound to wander. Wagner was himself without question a wandering character. As you know, he was banished from a number of German states for many years on account of his having been a revolutionary.

Slavoj Žižek touches on this topic in *Opera's Second Death*.[1] I find his Lacanian hermeneutical reflections on Wagner very interesting. Regarding Wagner's anti-Semitism, Žižek poses the remarkable question: 'Who is the Jew in Wagner's work? Who is

---

1   Slavoj Žižek and Mladen Dolar, *Opera's Second Death*. New York and London: Routledge, 2001, p. 148, fn. 10. A further elaboration on this point can be found in Žižek, 'Brünnhilde's Act', *Opera Quarterly*, Vol. 23, no. 2 (Spring–Summer 2007), pp. 199–216.

the *Wandering* Jew, when all is said and done?'; not merely 'Who is the Jew?' in the way the question is usually asked owing to the often stupid, completely disastrous pronouncements Wagner made about the Jews' role in society. The Wandering Jew is a character with whom Wagner actually identified profoundly. In the end, it is Tannhäuser, the Flying Dutchman or Wotan himself. Wagner, who was in a certain way the eulogist of the Holy Roman Empire, of the dear little town of Nuremberg, who wanted nothing more than to settle down somewhere, and who built his own musical temple in Bayreuth, was in actual fact saddled with an underlying identity that amounted to a kind of compulsion to wander, an inability to remain in place. He projected this onto a whole slew of tortured wanderer characters whose inner split renders them incapable of staying put.

This compulsion to wander gave rise to some extremely striking, wrenching scenes in *Tannhäuser*. For example, while the hero is ensconced in the Venusberg, with sensuality galore, sexual pleasure all day long, there is a scene in which he *begs* Venus to let him leave, since he feels that only the gods are capable of experiencing constant pleasure. This scene, in Act I, is incidentally magnificent, utterly passionate and heart-rending. But in Act II, when Venus does finally let him leave, albeit not without a warning, everything quickly turns sour. No sooner has he been summoned by the knights to a song contest in which ideal love, love for the Virgin Mary, chastity and so on, is to be celebrated, than he asks what all this nonsense is about. The knights don't have a clue about love, only *he* really knows what love is, he boasts, then launches into his big song extolling erotic love. They all want to kill him then, and he is saved only because Elisabeth, who loves him profoundly – precisely because he is able to say such a thing, as opposed to the perfect courtly knights, who are all a bit effete – rescues him. And then off he goes wandering again.

Basically, what we are afforded here is the dramatization of the inability to remain in any one place, hence of a being-between-two-worlds that constitutes subjectivity as a split and is constantly expressed as a tearing apart or essential suffering. But, like anyone exhausted by being torn between two things, Tannhäuser will try to find a solution that would transcend the split and reconcile him. He's advised to go to see the Pope – that sounds familiar today – so off he goes on a pilgrimage to Rome to seek absolution from the Pope.

This business about the Pope is very odd, by the way. Wagner had no relationship with Catholicism and one wonders why the papacy is involved here. As it turns out, this Pope is useless: he condemns Tannhäuser to hell for eternity, with no hope of redemption. This is one dogmatic Pope, in short, and he plunges Tannhäuser into total despair since the only solution that was recommended to him for healing his inner split has not worked. So he returns from this pilgrimage to Rome totally undone, relegated to his inner split by the Pope's verdict and tempted, naturally, to go back to the Venusberg, whereas, in the beginning, he had desperately begged Venus to let him leave, having been unable, as we saw, to remain there either.

At this point in the opera we are confronted with an absolute present of suffering with no possible remission. The passage traditionally known as the 'Rome narration' is Tannhäuser's account of his trip to Rome, in which he tells everything to Wolfram, the friendly knight who has always been secretly, chastely in love with Elisabeth. He has of course seen Tannhäuser gain the upper hand over him, but he is kind to him all the same and willing to listen to the account of his sufferings. This 'narration' is an extraordinary present, public expression of the utter devastation caused by irresolvable subjective splitting. It is a matter of taste, but I don't think you can find many other examples as powerful as this one of the total devastation of someone who has experienced to the utmost degree an absolutely irresolvable split and is consequently condemned to be nowhere.

I remember a production of *Tannhäuser* in the 1970s[2] in which the stage set portrayed a devastated Germany. '*Germania nostra*' was shattered, with a Wolfram who actually looked a bit like Brecht there as a representative from East Germany to bear witness to Tannhäuser's sufferings. What I would just like to point out, as I did a moment ago in connection with Sachs's monologue, is that there is something distinctively Wagnerian about the way the split subject is musically constituted here. As regards the treatment of the text itself, the story always comes undone little by little: even though it may be completely narrative at the beginning, it gradually comes undone, as if it were being incrementally subjectivized under the pressure of the music.

The split subject is presented by means of an interweaving that I think can be seen on closer inspection to be typical of Wagner's method, namely, an interweaving of four terms, or techniques.

- First, there is usually a recitative bordering on ordinary speech, which is actually not dependent on any one specific melodic scheme and which will return at other moments.

- Next, there are really wrenching lyrical passages, crescendo-like thrusts of the voice that stretch the music around a few words rather than a few sentences. We are afforded a dynamics of isolated words rather than of the text.

- And then there's the orchestration. As far as this is concerned, I can only offer a description, as opposed to a technical analysis, of the relationship between two elements in the orchestration per se, irrespective of the thematics. There is something like a subterranean layering

---

2   The production in question had Zubin Mehta conducting the Bayerisches Staatsorchester. René Kollo sang the role of Tannhäuser.

phenomenon that is often conveyed by the low brass instruments or the low strings, together with broken ascending chords of sorts – an oceanic dimension, if you will, based on the deep, low music. Then, in contrast to this, there are the high-pitched tremolos or the oboes. The relationship between these two elements is altogether typical, the way they are woven together virtually always being the sign of a split in the subject, a tearing apart, or the presence of suffering.

- Finally, there are long intermediary phrases, more thematic or melodic in nature, but which could actually be shown to collapse, or break, as it were, like waves on the underground ocean of the low orchestration.

This set of four things is very distinctive, and it shows once again, I firmly believe, that it is really the *music* that is responsible for constructing the split subject. Of course, the dramatic situation is a given, but what makes it *present*, what enables Tannhäuser's suffering to be restored to us intact, so to speak, in the present moment on the stage, and not merely dissolved in becoming, are these particular operators, not the overall story Tannhäuser tells.

When you listen to this version of *Tannhäuser*, you get the very odd sensation of something massive – there is a subjective massiveness that stands out – and at the same time of something detotalized and cracked, like a cracked monument. This is only an analogy, but I think that the techniques Wagner used all come together to create this feeling we get of detotalized massiveness or of a cracked sonic monument, which clearly can only be resolved by being destroyed. The monument is there, of course, but it is so obviously cracked that we know it cannot survive. That's why I find the stage set in this version, which features a ruined monument, fitting, metaphorically appropriate to what we actually see; namely, that Tannhäuser is *himself* a ruined monument who is going to break apart and be destroyed right in front of us. Everything is leading up to Tannhäuser's collapse and death.

I think that in Wagner, and in this sense especially, suffering is indeed a being-there. It is integrated into the narrative to the extent that the narrative explores the destructive consequences of the non-dialectical split. That would be my abstract definition of Wagnerian suffering: a textual and musical construction of the destructive consequences of the non-dialectical split. It is completely erroneous to say that we are dealing with no more than a crafty instrument for reconciliation; I really do not believe that that is the impression produced at all. On the contrary, the impression of monumentality is undeniable, and I think it constitutes one of the rare examples in which the affect of suffering is presented in a monumental guise. In fact, I think that it is precisely on account of this monumentality that the idea was put forward that it was not suffering that was involved but annihilation or redemption instead. What is really involved, however, is a monument to suffering per se. Suffering is monumental in a certain sense for the subject; he is himself like a cracked, broken-down monument. There are other possible versions of suffering, but in Wagner its presence is really tantamount to the presentation of the destructive consequences of the non-dialectical split in the subject.

7. The drama of difference

Is Wagner's dramatic and musical strategy of composition dialectical in the sense that it is entirely subordinated to a terminal figure of reconciliation and that the finale serves both to resolve and to unify all the differences that have been built up within the opera? Some absolutely classic examples of this exist. The best known, in *Tristan und Isolde*, is strictly a matter of harmony: the overall system of theoretical dissonances merely postpones the fact that the chord nevertheless comes in at the end. The return to the key of A-flat at the end of *Parsifal* is even more exemplary: ultimately, the redemption of the Redeemer amounts more or less to the A-flat.

Once again we note that, in support of these criticisms that would to some extent make of Wagner an impostor as regards difference and, when all is said and done, a belated Hegelian – someone who resolves everything in the conclusion and does not usher in a new age – there are some undeniable technical arguments that can be brought to bear. Nevertheless, I have the feeling (which I will attempt to defend without losing sight of these indisputable facts) that every Wagner opera actually represents the exploration of a possibility, that is to say, the exploration of a possibility of an ending, in keeping with the progressive dimension of the nineteenth century. Marx, Darwin and others in the nineteenth century, not only Wagner, put forward great visions or theories about the evolution of species or the evolution of history and humanity, and these great systems of thought coincided with a sort of political eschatology, a theory of progress, or things of that sort. Wagner was the contemporary of all this, and to my mind opera was for him a compendium for exploring widely divergent possibilities of an ending. In Wagner there is no one single, unifying pole towards which the music is somehow oriented as such, but rather an exploration of diverse possibilities.

This, then, is how I interpret the striking fact that every Wagner opera has a musical colour scheme that can be instantly identified. Each one is different in its own individual way. You can instantly recognize *Parsifal*'s colour scheme; it is utterly different from that of *Die Meistersinger*, for example. So there is always a distinctive colour scheme that cannot be attributed solely to the skilful variation of the instrumentation – although it naturally has to do with that, too – nor to the appropriation of the music to dramatic ends. The fact of the matter is that the *hypotheses* treated differ from one opera to the next, and the colour scheme, the thematic structure, the overall rhythm, and so forth, in each opera are all in the service of that opera's own particular hypothesis. That is the first issue I wanted to raise and make a case for.

The second is that the fact that each opera's hypothesis may be just one among several, as opposed to a specific theoretically validated or well-developed point, accounts for our sensing in Wagner a difficulty in concluding rather than any certainty. Getting to the finale was a difficult process for him, one marked by hesitation, and he had a tendency to leave several interpretations or hypotheses open. There is actually a distinctly Wagnerian brand of hesitation, which clearly exists alongside what may be a sort of superficially bombastic ending. Indeed, a number of artists have observed that Wagner had trouble making a choice, not unlike Tannhäuser, who had a hard time choosing between Venus and the Virgin Mary. Wagner was similarly torn. In fact, more generally speaking, one finds in Wagner a hesitation regarding what it really means to conclude. I would like to deal with this issue in connection with three endings, each of which, as is immediately apparent, derives from a very different hypothesis: the endings of *Götterdämmerung*, *Die Meistersinger* and *Parsifal*.

1. The ending of Götterdämmerung

The ending of *Götterdämmerung*, which is also the ending of the Ring Cycle as a whole – in other words, the ending of an extraordinarily complex, monumental project – is encapsulated in a post-revolutionary, very 'nineteenth-century' hypothesis. It reminds us of the fact that Wagner took part in the Dresden uprising, that he was a friend of Bakunin, that his formative experience in 1848 was incontestably his alliance with the revolutionaries, and that he was tracked down and persecuted for a long time on account of this.

The hypothesis he put to the test in *Götterdämmerung* involved a certain hesitation: as a well-known anecdote would have it, he took out the most resolutely revolutionary part of the final text and did not set it to music. This has been alleged as proof that, although Wagner had been a revolutionary in his youth, by the time he wrote *Götterdämmerung* he had already lost a lot of his illusions, not unlike most people when they get older, so he removed that particular sequence. In fact, contrary to what has been claimed, his revolutionary attitude did not change. Once again, my interpretation, which is perfectly defensible, is that the final text is in some respects *more* revolutionary than the text he originally intended to publish. Yet it does not really matter, because we are still left with the hypothesis that after the gods comes humanity. You can twist it around as much as you like, but the fact still remains that that is how it all ends, and the responsibility for the world formerly ruled by Wotan, the gods, the treaties or the contracts now falls to humanity, represented by the crowd, without its being said exactly what this responsibility consists of.

Patrice Chéreau's famous staging of the opera, at the end of the 1970s in Bayreuth, is superb in this respect because it ends on an interrogative, as it were. In fact, I'm inclined to say that this ending consists in the fate of the world being handed over to *generic* humanity, since no specific nation is mentioned. Neither Germany nor anything else of the sort is involved. Instead, it is really humanity, stripped of all transcendence and left to its own devices, that will have to take responsibility for its own fate. This hypothesis is put forward in *Götterdämmerung* only after much trial and error and many partial revisions, and it ultimately boils down to this: after the gods comes humanity, regarded in a revolutionary sense, an utterly generic, not specific, sense.

2. The ending of Die Meistersinger

In *Die Meistersinger* we get a completely different hypothesis, which has to do with the essence of Germany. Here, on the contrary, we move from generic humanity to something completely specific inquiring about the true nature of Germany: What is Germany? As you are aware, this is an old question for the Germans, who can be defined as the people for whom the question of Germany is critical. This is hardly the case with the French! The French never interrogate themselves about France. The French can be defined as those who claim to know what France is, while the Germans can be

defined as those who do not know what Germany is. That is why
the great German philosophers are all philosophers who explain that
the only thing that matters, when all is said and done, is the question
of Germany. Wagner is of this school, too – you can't be German
without being of this school, unless you claim that Germany should
simply be eliminated, which was in fact Thomas Mann's stance after
the war. Germany should just disappear. Europe is a hypothesis
of this sort, about whether Germany can be dissolved into it. But
dissolving Germany is not as easy as all that.

Wagner wonders about this at the end of *Die Meistersinger*,
whose full title, *Die Meistersinger von Nürnberg*, specifically refers
to Germany. This point should be taken seriously inasmuch as
Wagner puts to the test the hypothesis that there is really no
possible political essence of Germany, in the sense of a German
destiny. This is something that needs to be taken literally: the
essence of Germany is German art; it is *not* an aestheticization
of politics. The idea is that no political definition of Germany,
strictly speaking, is possible. The text says as much: even if there
were no longer any Holy Roman Empire, or if there were no
longer to be a German state, there would still be German art.
And the purpose of art is not to configure a politics but to define
Germany. We could say that in *Götterdämmerung* the hypothesis
about art's role is that art serves to bring about generic humanity, humanity seized by its own fate, while in *Die Meistersinger*
the hypothesis is that art can be a specific essence. This is the
case with Germany, whose universality, in the final analysis, has
no hope whatsoever of being realized either politically or impe-
rially; it resides and subsists in German art. This is an entirely
different hypothesis, and it is put forward in the music, music
that is completely different from that of *Götterdämmerung*.

3. *The Ending of* Parsifal
Finally, in *Parsifal*, we have a more overtly metaphysical or ontological hypothesis about whether there exists something beyond

Christianity. The question in *Götterdämmerung* is: What happens once the gods are dead? What happens is that humanity arrives on the scene. The question in *Die Meistersinger* is: What is the essence of Germany, given that it cannot be a historical or political essence? The answer is: high art. And the third question, in *Parsifal*, is: Is there something beyond Christianity?

The latter question, as you know, was also posed by Nietzsche. Opinions on this issue differ: is it really possible to break with Christianity? I'm inclined to say that Wagner's answer amounts to claiming that what is beyond Christianity is actually the full affirmation of Christianity itself. But it is important to understand what this means. It does *not* mean neo-Christianity or a heresy of any particular sort. On the contrary, it means that Christian figurality can be recovered and reaffirmed as a matrix ultimately constituting a world or universe that will be beyond Christianity. This world or universe will both save Christianity and in a way abolish it, since all the assumptions constitutive of Christianity will disappear through this affirmative operation and be replaced by a synthetic affirmation whose guiding principle will be 'Redemption to the Redeemer'.

'Redemption to the Redeemer' means: Christianity has ceased being a doctrine of salvation, and it is only through the figural or aesthetic reaffirmation of the Christian totality, which in a certain way de-Christianizes and de-idealizes it, that something beyond Christianity can be found. In other words, this is a very strange – Nietzschean, all in all – treatment of Christianity. But, where Nietzsche advocated a total break (his final slogan, don't forget, was 'to break the history of the world in two', and that meant in regard to Christianity) and in the end got bogged down and lost in his project of an absolute fracturing of the history of the world, Wagner, on the contrary, proposed a *positive* treatment. *Parsifal* is the eternal return applied to Christianity. Christianity returns, but it does so in an aesthetically affirmed mode, that of the 'Redemption to the Redeemer', as though it had to return as something different from, yet based on, itself.

4. The musical structure of the three endings

If we deal with each of these three examples in detail, we are faced with the problem of determining what it all implies in terms of the music, in terms of the techniques Wagner employed to realize these reaffirmations.

i. *Götterdämmerung* concludes with an enormously long speech combined with the destruction of the gods. Staging this is quite complicated, not only to bring off but also to understand, because it involves a speech taking place against a backdrop of disaster. After Siegfried's death, Brünnhilde delivers a big speech announcing that the world of the gods is over. She also retells certain elements of the story – Wagner never misses a chance to tell a story everyone is already familiar with all over again, which makes of him a true disciple of Aeschylus. Telling is essential, of course, but *retelling* is no less so, and Wagner never tires of telling the same story yet again. But here what we are actually dealing with is a speech. I will come back later to this fundamental issue of the Wagnerian character as a declaratory character whose essence is speech.

So we have a big speech announcing the destruction of the gods and turning the future over to the sole survivors, namely humanity. In the furious dispute between the gods of the upper and lower regions over the gold, humanity must learn to live, if possible, without gold. The Rhine gold has been returned to the Rhine: a non-mercantile humanity must now arise out of the twilight of the gods. The way this finale is structured is absolutely stunning.

I'd like to come back to the meaning of the finale from the standpoint of the music's composition. Humanity gazes out over the scene of destruction, especially its non-human elements. One after another we see: the ring being returned to the Rhine Maidens, hence to its natural element; then Hagen, the last representative of the lower, or dark, gods, diving into the water in vain to retrieve the ring; and finally Valhalla itself going up in flames and disappearing. All of the non-human elements are thus either destroyed or restored to their original natural state, and all that is left is humanity. In the Chéreau–Boulez production, we are afforded an absolutely staggering theatrical gesture: the crowd of men and women on stage slowly stands up, turns to face the audience, and in essence asks: 'What about *you*? Here is where we stand now, you and we both.' It is an exceptionally powerful gesture, implying self-denial on the part of the conductor in not having the last word, since the image persists for quite a while after the music has ended.

In no way does this finale recount the creation of a new mythology; on the contrary, it relates the destruction of *all* mythologies since even Wotan's attempts to create a free hero who would rescue mythology are a total failure, as I will discuss in a moment. The end of *Götterdämmerung* is really the twilight of the gods, the death of the gods; mythology can no longer be the solution. The only thing left, then, is humanity's gazing out over the scene of destruction, over the end of mythology. Everything will have to be begun anew starting from this gaze. This is how I interpret the fact that the only musical theme remaining is effectively the theme that has been called *redemption through love*, although, frankly, it is impossible to see what the figure of redemption is in any of this business. All there is is human solitude, nothing else. So it is actually the theme of *love* – let's call it that – that provides the only clue, the only injunction. Humanity remains, and so does the possibility for love that hovers above it.

This theme, mind you, was used only once before in the entire Ring Cycle, in Act III of *Die Walküre*, where it was sung by Sieglinde as an annunciation of sorts. Even so, it is not one of the themes included in the basic themes (*Grundthemen*); it is superfluous, as it were. It was evoked only once before, yet now it comes in as the theme of the finale, which, as this makes clear, is in no way merely a synthesis of the previous material. It floats above, and this theme is really treated, even orchestrally, as something hovering above musical material that, for its part, bears witness to the destruction of mythology, namely the Valhalla theme (the gods' castle has burned down) and the Rhine Maidens theme (nature and the gold have been partly reunited). So all we have left is this theme, about which I think Adorno was completely wrong when he judged it to be sentimental and trite, and a very weak musical conclusion to Wagner's enormous tetralogy.[3] As a matter of fact, this theme is not weak at all; it is actually a floating theme, one that has come, in a way, out of nowhere and that bears witness to the fact that that gaze without a fixed content is an element hovering above the destruction of everything.

I must stress the fact that this conclusion is not really a conclusion at all to the colossal edifice that is Wagner's tetralogy, that relentless story of the obsolete nature of all mythologies, even the 'replacement' mythology that poor Siegfried might have been, which led only to a pathetic disaster – that's the truth of the matter. Besides, among what I call the 'debris motifs' (because they are motifs that have been reduced to a state of death and debris) the Sword motif is heard, and it is treated in the same way as the Valhalla theme is, the same way as Hagen is. That entire world is over and done with now. Mythologies and heroes are no more. The only thing remaining is humanity, left to its own devices.

ii. In *Die Meistersinger*, the finale is also a group finale owing to the fact that the chorus plays a crucial role in it, just as it did in *Götterdämmerung*. But I think something else altogether is involved in the finale of *Die Meistersinger* because, in direct contrast with what we see in *Götterdämmerung*, the ending of *Die Meistersinger* is based on the necessity of a synthesis. In *Götterdämmerung* the ending implies that no synthesis is possible: everything has been destroyed and there is an enigmatic sort of hovering over the scene of destruction.

Die Meistersinger is Wagner's only comedy, and it has a highly distinct colour scheme, with a finale that comes across as the

---

3   Theodor Adorno, 'Wagner's Relevance for Today', *Essays on Music*, trans. Susan H. Gillespie, ed. Richard Leppert. Berkeley: University of California Press, 2002, pp. 598–9.

necessity of a synthesis, ultimately a synthesis between rupture and rules. The classic problem of art is posed: What is art's position, between creative genius, formal rupture and so forth on the one hand, and rule-bound tradition, on the other? In the opera, rule-bound tradition is embodied by the master singers, who are in a certain way split between conservatives and liberals. They are open, to a greater or lesser degree, to innovation, and – since we are dealing with an academy or a guild, after all – they also stand for tradition. Innovation is represented here by Walther with his free-form, life-affirming song. What will trigger the ending, for certain, is the necessity of a synthesis in connection with this issue.

The plot is as simple as can be. With the unanimous acclaim of the audience, Walther wins the prize for his song. There are always song contests in Wagner, and naturally he always puts *himself* on stage and wins the contest – such is the wonderful naïvety of great artists. Vitez always claimed that Claudel's *Soulier de satin,* that enormous work, is really just about Claudel's need to rationalize how he was duped by a hysterical young Polish woman he met aboard a ship in 1900 and how he behaved towards her. He made a big deal about it, and although the end result was brilliant, it nevertheless all took off from this incident. There is a bit of the same in Wagner: he always makes himself a contestant in the singing competition, too. So Walther wins the contest and Sachs suggests that he becomes a master singer, hence that he who won the contest on the basis of new ways of doing things, of artistic innovations, nonetheless joins the academy of tradition. The master singers woo Walther obnoxiously, but he turns them down.

The finale is a speech Sachs makes explaining why Walther shouldn't disdain the master singers but rather agree to become one of them. Sachs proposes a synthesis between innovation and tradition in the realm of aesthetics, a synthesis between remaining within and breaking with tradition. His speech is a plea for this sort of synthesis. Why is it necessary? Because it is what defines art's power historically: art's power must always be grounded in an incorporation of the past. It cannot lie solely in the sheer anarchy of formal rupture. Although Walther is enormously gifted and his singing is superb, he has to have the courage to declare that art's historical power also requires something other than just this capacity for pure innovation.

This debate is an interesting one for us today. Can art be entirely grounded in formal subtraction, that is, in a break with the past, radically new creation, irreducible originality? The master singers in the opera are very wise because they hail the latter: Walther is effectively the innovator, opposed to the traditional ways. But art is also historicity; it cannot consist solely in breaking with the past. How can it incorporate this historicity, though? Only by acknowledging that innovation is innovation on the basis of something that *isn't* new, and that it is this dialectic that must be sanctioned by art, that creates art's power. If art is capable of such power, if it is able to incorporate historicity into the new – not through an eclectic synthesis but through an immanent acknowledgement instead – then and then alone can it represent a people or a nation. Here is where the German themes come in. Holy German art is an art that has achieved such a synthesis, thereby turning Germany into a power unaffected by historico-political vicissitudes. Even if there is no longer any empire, German art will live on as the universal power of which the Germans proved themselves capable by realizing such a synthesis.

A very important theme that can always be observed in Wagner is that what must be thought is what survives in the hypothesis of destruction: what is it that hovers or somehow remains above the scene of destruction? Of course, we saw this sort of thing in *Götterdämmerung*, but the same idea is apparent here in *Die Meistersinger* as well. The great final chorus expresses it: Let the Holy Roman Empire disappear; the holy realm of German art will live on! And that is why Walther must agree to be decorated with the insignia of Master.

We can make out another idea as well, however. The person who sacrifices himself for the new synthesis is actually Sachs, not Walther. It is Sachs who goes on renouncing and in a way sacrificing himself in order for the synthesis I mentioned to become operative. In reality, it is *he* who is the master: through his very renunciation he becomes the master. Indeed, the ultimate conclusion of the opera is 'Long live our new master Sachs!', with Sachs having virtually become a monarch reigning over the people.

This is an interesting point. Sachs is the master of the people because he is the master of art. That is why the title *Die Meistersinger* (*The Mastersingers*, in English) is really polysemic. He who truly achieves mastery in the realm of art is the one who is capable of sacrificing himself in order to bring about the synthesis between old and new. Walther may become the master much later on, when he, too, is capable of sacrificing himself. But for the time being, Sachs is the real master, because he is the one who brings about the new synthesis that endows art with historical power; he is the one who was able to acknowledge the new from within the old. This is a doctrine of intra-artistic sovereignty, although it is hardly Carl Schmitt's. It is not 'the sovereign is he who decides on the state of exception' but a different doctrine, doubtless also a German one: The master of art is he who is able to sacrifice himself in a timely manner so that the new can be incorporated into the old, so that artistic innovation can be synthesized with tradition. It is consequently he who becomes the *people's* master precisely because he is the master of art.

This is an interesting doctrine because it hinges on the fact that artistic mastery cannot be reduced to genius. Rather, it is a dialectic of genius and mastery in the realm of art, as is very clear here. There are three main character types in *Die Meistersinger*:

- The genius, Walther, who introduces something new into singing.
- The typical reactionary, Beckmesser. He is the Jew, when you come right down to it – Meyerbeer, in actual fact. The

hatred Wagner felt for Meyerbeer played a big part in warp-
ing his judgement.

- And finally, the master, who occupies a singular position
  that, rather than coinciding with genius, is a position in which
  genius is accepted, acknowledged, and incorporated into the
  synthetic power of art.

This ending has often been summed up with the claim that it is
all just a hymn to the glory of Germany. But it is infinitely more
complicated than that, even though the signifier *Germany* does
remain centrally present.

iii. And now, *Parsifal*. The issue of renunciation will serve as a
springboard to this third example. In *Parsifal* the issue is also one
involving the passing on of powers or the advent of a new type
of mastery. Let me explain where the finale of *Parsifal* comes in.
The old Christianity – the point of departure – is moribund, in the
guise of old Titurel, who is definitely dead, and his son Amfortas,
who is scarcely any better off. Amfortas has a disgusting, oozing
fatal wound, owing to the fact that he could not resist temptation.
But let's leave aside the sexual business, which, though important
in Wagner, is not necessarily crucial.

Why is the old Christianity moribund? Because it became too
focused on survival. As the old Christianity became increasingly paro-
chial, with an increasingly negative, defensive dimension, its slogan
was 'we must survive and ensure that Christianity survives'. This
speaks volumes about the situation today: Christianity's only remaining concern is to continue to survive as long as possible. But when
survival is the only thing that matters, you are defenceless against
the insistence of the sexual drive. You are devastated by it, by the
Real, and defenceless against the *jouissance* that is symbolized here by
Amfortas's utterly obscene wound, aptly filmed by Syberberg with
terrifying obscenity as a vagina displayed on a cushion. When the only
thing that matters is survival, you are defenceless against the obscene.

Parsifal, who will put an end to this moribund Christianity,
will have to suggest a new approach, then: the reaffirmation of

Christianity, as I have called it, or the redemption of the Redeemer. Something other than a focus on mere survival or self-preservation will have to be proposed, hence something other than self-concern. All concern with survival is actually a form of *self*-concern, which explains why it does not protect us from the obscenity of *jouissance*. The old patriarch, Titurel, constantly demands that the Grail be uncovered just so he can go on surviving; otherwise he might drop dead. Lying in a tomb, on his last legs, he urges his son: 'Perform the ceremony, because if you don't, I'll die!' If the only thing the uncovering of the Eucharist is good for is enabling Titurel to go on living for a little while longer, it is easy to see how Christianity, reduced to this alone, has become terribly moribund. Amfortas, on the other hand, *wants to die*, so he does not want to perform the ceremony.

There is ultimately a very interesting symmetry here. One of them wants to survive at any cost, and to that end the ceremony must take place, while the other does not want to perform it because *he* wants to die. It is all a matter of self-concern. So the positive solution will have to be one of self-denial. The compassion/self-denial or compassion/unselfishness pair – absolute concern for the other and lack of self-concern – that Parsifal embodies will in my opinion be proposed not as a kind of all-purpose ethical formula (not, at any rate, in that era) but rather because if it is true that Christianity has become merely about survival, then this alone is the solution that can ensure its redemption.

In the music, the pairs compassion/self-denial and Christianity/survival are presented, on the one hand, through the theme of Amfortas and his wound, and, on the other, through the theme of Parsifal, which is practically understated, barely phrased in the brass, and a little elusive, even though Parsifal is in principle the main hero. The pairing of the lyrical, fearsome theme of Amfortas's suffering with Parsifal's very understated theme truly represents the pair comprised by dying Christianity – sensual, obscene and deathly all at once – and the hypothesis of its rescue or redemption.

In terms of the music, I would say that this whole finale, concerned as it is with replacing moribund, narcissistic, deathly Christianity with a new, reaffirmed Christianity around the idea of a central, innocent self-denial, will attempt to represent what I would call the evaporation of sovereignty into gentleness, or the transmutation of sovereignty into gentleness. That is what I think is really at stake in the music of the finale. Whether it succeeds or not is partly a question of analysis and taste. Although we might agree with Boulez, who was somewhat uncomfortable with the saccharine aspect of this ending of *Parsifal*, we should nevertheless not lose sight of what is at stake, which is the following: If what I am claiming is really the meaning of this ending, in which Parsifal arrives with the Spear, heals Amfortas, and takes over from him, then this cure is actually a kind of *death*. The new Christianity must no longer be in thrall to the self-serving, survivalist type of sovereignty symbolized by Amfortas and Titurel but on the contrary should be about the humble, innocent self-denial represented by the redemption of the Redeemer. The music must consequently transmute power into gentleness, and I think that it is this metamorphosis, once again, that Wagner is attempting to convey in the ending of *Parsifal*.

I want to make just a few remarks now about Syberberg's production. First of all, it is not a stage play but an utterly extraordinary *film* that accordingly makes use of all the resources of cinema. I highly recommend it as an approach to *Parsifal*. The set is actually an enormous replica of Wagner's death mask, and *Parsifal* is performed inside its skull as a cranial drama, so to speak. It has a deliberately over-the-top aspect to it that reveals the extent to which this world is a dying one, effectively given over to obscenity.

As for Parsifal, he is played by two different actors: he is both a young man and a young woman, as if only either by combining the two sexes or showing that there is no difference between them or that they are hard to tell apart could represent the redemption of the deathly sensuality and obscene *jouissance* in which the Christianity of the past has exhausted itself. There is a wonderful scene in Act II in which Parsifal has to put his capacity for self-denial to the test by resisting temptation. (In the theatre, resisting temptation is the only way to portray a character's capacity for self-denial.) Temptation here takes the form of the seductress Kundry, who has already seduced Amfortas, along with everybody else, long ago, and will manipulate Parsifal at the most visceral level by making his mother appear to him in an almost incestuous way. She will tell him his mother is dead and turn in part into the lascivious ghost of the mother. So we get an utterly Oedipal scene, with the seduction of the innocent son by a kind of weird mother who is both dead and alive, a sexual vampire of sorts. Parsifal will go pretty far, yielding as he does to Kundry's kiss. But then, right in the middle of the kiss, he starts to feel Amfortas's wound. So he pulls away, then he flees and wanders around endlessly again, like all Wagner's heroes, until at last he happens upon the forgotten road leading to the Christian fortress where Amfortas lies dying.

What is fascinating in Syberberg's production is that it is precisely at the moment of the kiss, the moment when the kiss both takes place and is broken off, that we get the doubling of Parsifal as an adolescent boy replaced by an adolescent girl, as if we were somehow witnessing the heralding of a new sexuation. Christianity's renewal is also a sexuation about which nothing is said except this one astonishing and absolutely convincing, remarkable thing: a girl replacing a boy in the test of sexuality itself. In the denouement, the two of them will become as one. Initially, it is a matter of substitution, then, at the end, of combination, because we really get the pairing of an adolescent boy and an adolescent girl.

Syberberg, too, thought it necessary to end with an enigmatic look. It is as if all these endings, which are about an indistinct future, be it humanity's or Christianity's, somehow demanded to be treated visually by a questioning look or a look addressed as a kind of question to the audience.

The final chorus is about the redemption of the Redeemer, coming after we have seen Parsifal taking power and the new couple, who are a little like a new Adam and Eve in Syberberg's interpretation, representing a new beginning for humanity through a new kind of innocence. It is the possibility for Christianity to be an allegory of vital innocence rather than of the continuation of ailing sovereignty; it is the replacement of ailing sovereignty by the affirmative possibility for a vital innocence. We have also seen how the Pope's skull is used in this film to show that Christianity is in fact really finished, really dead.

There is a theme close to Jean-Luc Nancy's heart – the deconstruction of Christianity – which he regards as an essential task for us today, one that has yet to be accomplished.[4] As far as I'm concerned, *Parsifal* is just such an attempt to deconstruct Christianity. Whether it succeeds or fails is another story, but it is really a question of an attempt at deconstruction, if by *deconstruction* we mean something that reaffirms in a different way what took place and is not merely a critique of Christianity, since reaffirmation is much more radical than mere critique.

The question is whether Christianity might not be more resilient than that, though. In his preface to *Parsifal*, Marcel Beaufils, the translator, argues that, in the end, Wagner mistakenly imagined that Christianity could be dealt with in the same way as the pagan gods, but *Parsifal* proved that it was really Wagner who was taken in by Christianity, not the other way around.[5] In short, Wagner's redemption of the Redeemer did not work because the time for a pure and simple mythologizing of Christianity had not yet come about. The deconstruction of Christianity could

4   Jean-Luc Nancy, *Dis-Enclosure: The Deconstruction of Christianity*. New York: Fordham University Press, 2008.

5   Richard Wagner, *Parsifal*, trans. and pref. by Marcel Beaufils. Paris: Aubier, 1964.

not yet be undertaken because – even as mythological material – Christianity was still too deeply rooted in people's minds for it to be manipulated in such a way. Yet I think that Wagner really did intend to perform the same operation on Christianity as he did on the gods of Germanic mythology and to show that Christianity could be transcended by virtue of a singular reaffirmation of its availability.

Perhaps it was more difficult a task than it seemed; perhaps *Parsifal* should not have been called a sacred drama since we are obviously in the presence of the sacred *beyond* the sacred; perhaps it was foolhardy of Wagner. Issues like these are all matter for discussion.

8. Music and Theatricalization

We have now come to the fourth issue, concerning the question of an underlying rational framework and the subjection of the music to the text – the idea that beneath the music's apparent continuity there supposedly lurks a kind of Wagnerian alchemy that, when all is said and done, privileges the narrative and subordinates the musical aims to it.

There is a rather odd yet convincing argument to the effect that Wagner would write the text first and would usually not change a single line of it thereafter. The music had to come afterwards. That is an undeniable fact. If there was already a lot of text, it had to be sandwiched into the music, as if Wagner were in a way taking orders from the text, which the music had to follow. But this idea is counterbalanced by another completely different, and in my opinion crucial, factor. Wagner firmly believed that the essence of the dramatic subject is *speech* and it is this that accounts for the subject's growth into a 'larger than life' character. It is because the subject goes on and on about the ins and outs of his situation, about what he is going to do, what he is going to decide, the obstacles he faces, and so on, that he expands, or comes to fill up the stage.

In this regard, I think Wagner is a genuine disciple of Aeschylus inasmuch as Agamemnon and Clytemnestra ultimately proceed no differently.

It is common knowledge that in the nineteenth century the Germans – Nietzsche first and foremost – were all obsessed with the idea of rivalling Greek tragedy. My thesis, however, is that Wagner was quite successful at it. He was a real disciple, a peer, of Aeschylus, since he managed to expand the dramatic subject spectacularly through the use of techniques that are in the final analysis techniques of speech. Action in Wagner is sporadic and most of the time very brief. Between a few long drawn-out speeches, three people are killed in a matter of minutes, and that's it for the plot incident. More broadly speaking, the action sequences are admittedly never the most inspired ones in terms of the music. Setting duels to music has always posed a problem for opera. There are nevertheless lots of duels; people are always running each other through – in Wagner's operas as well, of course – but it is not an easy thing to pull off and Wagner may have been right to get it all over with as quickly as possible. In effect, it is not the action that is interesting; it is the characters' speech, or, in other words, what creates subjective possibility: the possibility of a new subjectivity, of which the ins and outs of the plot are merely its result or ornament. It is what is *said* about the action, its subjective aspect, that is crucial, not the plot incident or the action itself. This is a very important point.

The subject's declaratory essence always constitutes a proposition about the generic meaning of existence; it is a far-reaching declaratory proposition regarding 'Who am I in the overall situation of the world, in terms of the meaning it may have for me and for everyone else?' It is never merely an expression of self, let alone an expression of a combination of identities of the sort I mentioned earlier with respect to operatic ensembles. It is truly a proposition or a hypothesis, conveyed by a character, about the overall meaning of the situation and his own project as regards this situation, his chances of success or failure.

That is why – just as in Aeschylus, in my opinion – there is a propensity for always telling the story one more time, a propensity that has been widely ridiculed. Wagner never tires of retelling what has happened before; he does it over and over again, in many different guises. For example, one character will ask questions that another character will answer by retelling everything that has happened up to that point. But I maintain that this is not in the least just a convenient solution – besides, what would be so convenient about it? Wagner was well aware that the repeated tellings of the story were somewhat cumbersome. However, telling the story is part and parcel of the character's speech. The character's subjective position can only be clarified by his running through the telling of the story, and each of these accounts is a unique one that illuminates the story from a new subjective point of view. So it is not really a simple matter of repetition. Granted, we hear something we already know about; we are told yet again about the Nibelungs and the gods, how they fought over the gold, how the giants appeared on the scene, and so on. Of course we know the story, but that is not the point. This reiteration of the story within the story constitutes the subject's declaratory essence, because the subject is not speaking about himself or his own personal faculties but about the *story itself* and the part he thinks he is playing in it. He therefore tells it again from that point of view, and in my opinion these are *powerful*, not weak, passages, which must be understood musically and dramatically as such.

As a result, the music, as I have already mentioned, will be a music of metamorphosis, in which we see how a subject, through the telling of the story, completely transforms his situation or delivers a speech and changes his situation. The music is what changes the story of the world into the subject's deadlock. I propose to examine a very interesting excerpt from *Die Walküre,* in which the music serves just such a function. In this excerpt, we are afforded a narration of the story of the world musically structured in such a way that, through its very temporality, it will morph into the

subject's deadlock. It is not merely an additional telling of the
story; it is something else altogether. We already saw this to some
extent in Sachs's monologue, and we have a typical example of it
in Wotan's monologue in Act II of *Die Walküre*.

First, though, a word about where this monologue comes in. It
is an absolutely pivotal moment in the tetralogy as a whole because
it is the moment when Wotan realizes he is going to go down in
defeat and that ultimately his only true desire is the desire for
the end. The monologue takes the shape of an account he gives
his daughter Brünnhilde of everything that has occurred so far.
(Father–daughter love is one of *Die Walküre's* true subjects and
the opera moreover concludes with a heart-rending farewell scene
between them.) That he should tell Brünnhilde the whole story
right from the start is incidentally rather odd. We have every
reason to believe that, like us, she is already familiar with it: she is
in a way our stand-in as the auditor of Wotan's narrative. All of us
are acquainted with the story, then, but we have to hear it all again.

Wotan has essentially two things to say about his downfall.
First, that in reality he is not free, since he is bound by the treaties. He is a man bound by the law and as such he cannot do what
he wants to. In particular, he is not really free to act fully on his
desire. Remember the previous scene, when his wife Fricka comes
and tells him he is a man bound by the law and that consequently
he cannot flout their nuptial agreements or create problems with
his incestuous children. His wife's role is to remind him that he
is not free. We thus become aware of a very important issue in
the Ring Cycle as a whole: the critique of the law. The law, in the
sense we are dealing with it here – the treaties or the contracts – is
a world of enslavement, in which desire lacks any genuinely creative force.

Wotan expresses as much, declaring that the scheme he devised
to get around this issue – his idea of creating an utterly free hero,
a hero not bound by the law, who could handle the problem and
win the ring back in his name while not being dependent on him

– is unworkable because it is forbidden him by the law. Creating an utterly free hero to do the job he himself cannot do because he is bound by the law amounts to a crude trick, which Fricka has immediately sniffed out. What's more, she has arrived on a chariot drawn by her rams and made a terrible scene – the longest conjugal scene in the opera, in fact – as a result of which, seeing that he has been found out, Wotan admits the truth to her.

The theme of the god's inability to create a free hero without it either contradicting or negating his own divinity had a lot of potential. Sartre, for example, used it in *The Flies*. In that play, the free man ends up telling Zeus to stop complaining, that it is his own fault for having created him free. Something along the same lines happens here, too, since the free hero will break Wotan's spear. Poor Wotan will have no alternative then but to go back to Valhalla, as we saw a little while ago, and sit around dejectedly awaiting the final disaster.

These will be Wotan's two philosophical themes: First, in the world of the law, desire cannot be acted on with respect to its changing objects; and second, creating freedom is not a genuine option. So the only thing left to do is to wait for the end, for his downfall, to come. This parable of the end, of the process by which the end will come about, is narrated in the excerpt I am referring to.

Once again, it is Chéreau's production that I have chosen. The set consists of an enormous clock, a sort of Foucault's pendulum that symbolizes time's passing. There is also a large mirror symbolizing Wotan's subjective narcissism. Thus, the gap between objective law, expressed by the passing of time, and the narcissistic reflection in the mirror is clearly shown. The scene plays out between these two things, and at the very end, just when time is really about to win out, Wotan will stop time.

It is easy to see how the scene is constructed. It starts out almost like something Wotan confides to himself, which is particularly evident in Chéreau's totally inspired idea of staging it like a conversation Wotan is having with his own reflection in the mirror. Then, as the music mounts towards the theme of dereliction at the end, it can be seen, on closer inspection, to consist of an extremely deliberate, calibrated, and altogether extraordinary orchestral upsurge reaching its climax through successive stages, which, although hard to distinguish, really constitute an absolutely amazing example of musical art.

The story it tells is an important one where Wagner is concerned, namely, the moments when power and impotence are in equipoise, when the two are interchangeable. The sentence expressing this idea is stated explicitly: 'Since by my treaties I rule, by those treaties I am enslaved.'[6] Moments like these (and other examples could be given), when an equivalence between power and impotence is revealed, were always a spur to creativity for Wagner.

9. Music and waiting in vain

One of Adorno's criticisms of Wagner, as we have seen, was that waiting in Wagner is a rigged sort of waiting because it is entirely dictated by its ultimate resolution, by the outcome of the waiting. Adorno refers to a passage from Berg's *Wozzeck* in which there is a famous crescendo that absolutely incarnates waiting in vain. He contrasts Wagner to Beckett, as far as this issue is concerned, since Beckett, as I mentioned earlier, was the exemplary modernist insofar as he was capable of representing, beyond form, waiting in vain as such, that is, waiting as pure waiting, rather than as something fulfilled by an end result. Adorno accused Wagner of being incapable of treating waiting this way on account of his teleology and his latent dialectical Hegelianism.

To this it can be objected that the lengthiest wait in the entire history of art is, without question, Tristan's in Act III of *Tristan*

---

6 Richard Wagner, *The Ring of the Nibelung*, trans. Andrew Porter. New York: W.W. Norton and Company, 1976, p. 109.

und Isolde. True, some will retort, but size doesn't always constitute a proof. Still, it is indisputably the most excessive artistic material of waiting ever: everything will be quickly wrapped up (Isolde
arrives; Tristan dies as soon as she gets there; King Mark arrives,
then Isolde dies of love, and the opera is over), yet a full three-
quarters of the act consists of nothing but waiting, the wounded
Tristan waiting for Isolde to come.

The objection, though, is that Isolde *does* in fact come. I maintain that the fact that Isolde finally arrives in no way determines
the musical, operatic or dramatic manner in which the waiting
occurs; it is really presented as waiting as such. I will argue this
point in more or less the same terms as I argued the issue of suffering earlier: just because, at a given moment, healing or redemption occurs does not mean that the reality of the thing, as far as its
artistic presentation is concerned, is thereby disproved. Especially
because, even though Isolde does arrive, her arrival is in a certain
way *beyond* all the waiting since the only thing Tristan can do then
is die. All he says is 'Isolde' and he dies. It is a little like a *supplement* to the waiting, rather than its resolution; it is by no means the
beginning of something else but merely the fact that, beyond the
waiting and as though in excess of it, there is effectively this ultimate figure of Tristan's death in Isolde's arms. But the waiting as
such is a structuring presented for its own sake.

It would be interesting to show from an analytic point of view
how this waiting is constructed throughout the entire act. If space
allowed, we could do a macro-structural analysis of it. There are
actually three successive sequences, three rebirths, as it were, each
one of which comes to an end when Tristan loses consciousness,
after which he begins waiting all over again. The futility of the
waiting is demonstrated by the fact that the exaltation bringing
Tristan back to life is each time presented as being utterly in vain.

The production I now have in mind is one by the great German
dramatist Heiner Müller that took place in Bayreuth. Müller had
read Adorno and knew that he had contrasted waiting in Wagner

with waiting in Beckett. But for the actor, as far as Müller was concerned, the waiting in *Tristan* was identical to Beckett's waiting in vain. Consequently, he directed this third act exactly as if he were directing Beckett. The set is an apocalyptic, dust-ridden one, and the characters are covered in ash just as in Beckett's plays. Even the shepherd, who plays a very sad, nostalgic song on his flute, is an utterly Beckettian character – blind, wearing dark glasses, sitting on the ground. One of the ironies Heiner Müller brought out was to show that staging *Tristan* like Beckett would really hold up, that a Beckettian adaptation of Tristan's waiting was possible.

I don't think it can be said that any of this business was shaped from within by an underlying redemption; on the contrary, it is the *dereliction* of the waiting, and heightened absence, that is presented, and each of the sequences concludes only with the character's death or loss of consciousness. No other finale is possible, precisely because what is developed within is simply the amplification or the augmentation of the unbearable nature of the waiting.

It must have required a lot of care and talent on Heiner Müller's part to have succeeded in drawing such a thing out of an operatic tenor. There is a kind of dramatic energy, a special sort of heart-break associated with waiting, which you can expect to find in the theatre, but it is a very hard job to obtain the same thing in opera.

10. Music and new forms of time

To conclude now, if it is really possible to do so, we come to what in some respects is the most important question: the essence of Wagner's music as gauged by its capacity to create an experience of time. Wagner announced that he was abandoning the formalism of individual arias, but he also eventually gave up his allegiance to the saturated endless melody. The issue thus hinges on evaluating his capacity for creating an experience of time, which is linked to

Adorno's objection that, since the kind of form he aspired to – form that would be nothing but its own disintegration – was lacking in Wagner's music, Wagner was guilty of not having developed the possibility for a new experience of time.

I shall suggest, on the contrary, that Wagner can be credited with creating not just an original experience of time but three distinct types of time that were signature conceptions of his, that were truly invented by him and are paradigmatic in his music.

- I would call the first one *the time of disparate worlds.* It is the time of transition from one world to another, a time created by a spacing out of worlds. It could also be called the time of transit or the time of wandering, which is such an important phenomenon in Wagner.

- A second kind of time, derived from the first but altogether different from it, is *the time of the period of uncertainty.* Here, we are dealing with a decision or a plot incident, with subjectivity, with an in-between kind of time when the creation of a possibility has not yet actually taken shape and so there is something spinning uncertainly around.

- Finally, there is *the time of the tragic paradox.*

I think these three kinds of time, as well as the way they are all interwoven, are exemplary creations of Wagner's that render the criticisms levelled against him about the length of his work irrelevant. The truth of the matter is that, in view of the fact that he creates these types of time, whether his music is long or short is of little account: what matters is that it always occurs within this new experience of time. So I think the objection cannot be sustained that, since Wagner is long and intrinsically so, no genuine experience of time can really be found in his music. Let me just say a word about these three different types of time now.

1. The time of transition from one world to another

In the case of the first type of time, that of the transition from one world to another, the music is made to serve as the medium for the transition from one site, or world, to another. This type of time is constructed by the music. Wagner usually goes about it in the following way. Into a very affirmative, controlled thematic construction he introduces a *different* construction that is seemingly a distant derivative of the first one, but he brings it in from within the first one. Something like a quadratic periodic structure is established, and, from within it, something creating a feeling of distance vis-à-vis this structure is introduced, although there is always a certain undecidability between the quadratic periodic structure and what is derived from it, or what shapes or unfolds it from within. This truly creates a time of transition.

The best example of this is clearly the interlude in Act I of *Parsifal*. Here there is a transition – a march, strictly speaking, a march anticipating the knights' processional that comes shortly thereafter. We move from outside to inside, from narrative to ceremony, from potential life to imminent death; in other words, we are afforded a host of transitions from one symbolic world to another. We go from an explicit theme at the beginning introducing the march to a sort of holy pealing of bells at the end, which in fact heralds another march, that of the entry of the knights. Listening to this passage, you get a very powerful feeling of an experience of time being created, which is expressed directly in the sonic figure.

In Syberberg's film this whole passage is very ornamental, because Syberberg interprets this experience of time in part as a slow expedition across Germany, which is symbolized by a collection of provincial and national flags. What's more, the Nazi flag is seen, not at the end but at the beginning, as a sort of send-off, because this expedition is actually a march towards a dying Germany, inasmuch as Syberberg equates moribund Christianity with the feeling that Germany is sick and rotting. Parsifal's initiator, Gurnemanz, who is one of the knights, the local good guy, so to speak, is taking him to the ceremony, and their walk takes place in a kind of passageway that is basically the passageway of Germany heading towards its own demise.

This experience of time is constructed by the music, the ground bass of which, moreover, is effectively a march, a march symbolizing the transition from one world to another. The subject of this transition is Parsifal, since, in terms of both the music and the characters, it is not Gurnemanz, who already knows all about this, for whom this temporality is something new. It is instead Parsifal who serves as the medium for the transformation, who must undergo it; it is he who comes to discover this German passageway between nature without and sickness within.

2. The time of the period of uncertainty

I called the second type of time an in-between time or a time of uncertainty. It is essentially the time of possibilities that have not yet come about, the time when the creation of something possible is still in abeyance, when it is on the agenda but has not yet been put into effect. Incidentally, there is one aspect of this type of time that is quite interesting insofar as it may be closely related to our own circumstances today. It is a time when something has occurred that is no longer practicable but when what is to come is still in the offing.

This is exactly the situation Ibsen portrayed in his play *Emperor and Galilean*. The main character, the Emperor Julian, is the Roman emperor who wanted to restore paganism to the Christian empire. His position is precisely that of someone claiming that the old beauty of the past is dead while the new truth has not seen the light of day, since Christianity in the Roman Empire is nothing but hypocrisy. We are suspended between the world or the enigma of beauty and the Christian world of truth. This temporal situation could be compared to the articulation between the twentieth and twenty-first centuries in which we currently find ourselves.

The musical procedure corresponding to this temporal mode can be found in many fairly concise passages of Wagner's that are instances of in-between time. The technique he uses to achieve it is a sort of thematic uncertainty combined with an effect of dispersion, a scattered orchestral frothiness. In other words, we don't know exactly what the dominant theme is or will be, and the orchestration, instead of coming together in an organic affirmation, tends to stray a bit. I personally find these passages of Wagner's to be very interesting and innovative. Not to exaggerate the similarities, but they do sometimes sound a bit like Debussy. Found precisely in intervals such as these, they are Debussy-like moments in Wagner which ultimately don't take root.

An example that, albeit only an approximation, nonetheless involves this phenomenon, can be found in the Prelude to Act III of *Tannhäuser*. In Act II, Tannhäuser has gone off to see the Pope, and in Act III he returns, devastated. Between the two acts, though, we do not have a very clear idea of what has happened because the opera does not provide us with any news of him. Elisabeth is praying constantly; she doesn't know whether Tannhäuser has finally been reconciled or not. Thus, as far as Tannhäuser's fate is concerned, we are in an in-between time, suspended between his departure and his return. This state is what the Prelude to Act III describes, and that is why it is ambiguous, even as it prepares us for a lengthy monologue, Elisabeth's great prayer.

The passage I'm referring to is purely orchestral. We are afforded an experience of time constructed by a unique sort of thematic interweaving. Its rhythm is not ascendant or anything of that sort; it is instead a kind of temporality that is closed up on itself since what is involved is a figure of waiting, albeit a waiting different from Tristan's: we are really dealing with a figure of uncertainty about what has happened.

3. The time of the tragic paradox

The third type of time, that of the tragic paradox, is a time that essentially spreads open the appearance of how the facts unfold – it creates a kind of gap in it – so as to disclose behind it a much more extensive temporality in conflict with it.

The tragic, as you know, is precisely such a conflict. The tragic is always the conflict between the appearance of things and something far more extensive, which is revealed in a gap in this appearance and which has been secretly influencing its fate for a long time. The disclosure of this vast, hidden temporality holding sway over appearance is the time of tragic paradox. When Wagner wants to produce this kind of time, he goes about it by playing off the discourse or the explicit theme, or even the melody at times, against deep, subterranean layers of the music, usually orchestrated in the low register. Such is the very essence of Wagner's orchestral and metric innovations, namely, his capacity for creating, in contrast to an established melodic discourse, this sort of upward surge of the music's deep underlying layer, which is like a kind of unsuspected inner ocean suddenly revealed to us in a gap.

The example I'd like to suggest to illustrate this phenomenon occurs in Act I of *Götterdämmerung*. It is the monologue of Hagen, the demigod Alberich's son. These gods are all obsessed with bearing sons and fighting one another through them. That's how it works in war, after all: it is the sons who get sent to the front. It is no different here. One of the gods produces Siegfried, and the other, Hagen. Thus, the last act of *Götterdämmerung* is to some extent about a confrontation between these two sons. Neither of them, incidentally, is particularly fond of his father. There is a terrifying scene in the opera between Hagen and Alberich, just as in *Siegfried* there is a scene involving a direct confrontation between Wotan and Siegfried, who breaks his spiritual father's spear. Of course, since both these sons are more or less independent of their fathers, the underlying paternal influence manifests itself in the fact that each of them has problems with his father. The two sons face off, and Hagen, that sombre, pallid, gloomy son, hatches sinister plots to get hold of the ring, because Siegfried had given it to Brünnhilde after wresting it from Fafner the dragon. The ring is at once the ring of omnipotence and the symbol of mercantile society utterly in thrall to gold.

In his monologue, Hagen himself describes tragic time even as he is simultaneously its instrument, in keeping with the declaratory dimension of the characters. Hagen is ugly and despised, and Siegfried, the golden boy, regards him as a loathsome worm. Yet it is Hagen who is actually creating Siegfried's unwitting fate, and it is *he* who will ultimately get hold of the ring and triumph. The hideous gnome declaims his own triumphant destiny precisely at the same time as Siegfried's journey down the Rhine is taking place, that is, at the time when the hero's bright future seems assured.

For the sake of anecdote, I'll just mention that in Chéreau's production the man singing Hagen was himself a kind of neo-Nazi. He had a lot of trouble because he profoundly despised all the French singers and couldn't understand what they were even doing in Bayreuth in the first place! He was a major pain in the neck, surly and furious – just like Hagen – and that may have contributed to the unusual force of his performance. As a result, on the DVD there is an absolutely terrifying close-up of this fellow at the end.

I would like to mention in passing that what we have here is an example of a very important technique of Wagner's. It is what I would call one theme's subjection by another. At the end of Hagen's monologue, when he has finished singing, we hear both the Sword motif associated with Siegfried and the motif of Wotan's power, but this time around they are entirely submerged in the orchestration that is imposed, so to speak, by the fateful character of Hagen. The leitmotifs thus no longer serve to identify the characters with whom they are usually associated but rather to express the fate being engineered by Hagen now.

The possibility that a given theme might be not only playing a narrative or subjective role but also serving as material for another theme – as though it actually *were* another theme – is an utterly amazing faculty linked to Wagner's harmonic and orchestral virtuosity. It is in the low brass instruments that one can really hear this phenomenon, especially the Sword motif, which is usually played in a higher register. Although it is in principle a heroic motif, it is played here in an utterly ominous register, so that we truly enter into the mind of Hagen, who, as he himself admits, knows full well that he is engineering everything against that fine fellow, the hero. This is expressed in the music, inasmuch as Siegfried's heroic theme takes on the dark colouring and the sound of lapping water underlying it all, which is truly the sign of Hagen.

11. Conclusion

I would like to conclude with a theme I mentioned at the outset, the theme of high art, because everything we have been discussing can really be subsumed under the rubric of what Wagner can teach us about this question of high art, not in terms of any nostalgia about its disappearance but perhaps in terms of its presence on our horizon.

I think we need to make a distinction between what Wagner saw as his own greatness (there are a host of explicit pronouncements and intentions to this effect) and the place where his greatness really lies, namely, in the accomplishments that *we* can discern today. I should point out that this kind of updating is just as timely for someone completely different from Wagner, his French rival Mallarmé. I think Mallarmé, too, demands a very complex effort to bring up to date his message about poetic greatness, which is a bit different from what he himself thought it was, that is, the creation of a new religion. The latter idea was ubiquitous in the nineteenth century – Wagner, Hugo and many others were haunted by it – but we definitely have to distinguish what was really accomplished in Mallarmé's poems or Wagner's operas from ideological saturation of that sort.

In other words, what is at stake is not a mythological assertion with a view towards creating a new myth, although that obviously exists, nor is it the reconfiguration of the German people or the totalization of the arts. This can all be found in Wagner's explicit statements, but it is no longer meaningful for us today because it no longer affords us the potential materials for greatness. I think what we can extract from Wagner are five rules – I'm not sure what to call them, perhaps five directions, or five clues – concerning what greatness, as distinct from totality or from messianic will, might be.

1. Creating a possibility

The first rule has to do with the sense of creating a possibility. In Wagner, there is an exemplary sense of the approach that can be taken by art to make the creation of a possibility explicit. Many examples of this can be found in his music. There is a Wagnerian strategy as far as this issue is concerned, but it is hardly a Hegelian or dialectical one. It consists in showing, *as it is occurring*, how a new subjective possibility can emerge, and I have tried to demonstrate that it involves a musical process rather than a narrative or a story.

2. The multiplicity of hypotheses

The second rule is that a multiplicity of hypotheses can always be tolerated in the work of art and in Wagner's conception of it (he was not after some ultimate, unifying, final hypothesis or purpose that would take in all the others) and this multiplicity of hypotheses can be tolerated to the point where one hesitates to choose among them. For art to be great, it must venture to the limits of hesitation with regard to the multiplicity of possibilities it accounts for or causes to exist.

3. Tolerating a split subject in the present

The third rule has to do with the subject's inner split as constituting the subject's essence in the present. The subject is not a structure that becomes actualized nor a particular plot incident;

instead, the split in the subject is the essence of the subject in the present, which, for Wagner, includes suffering. Consequently, to the extent that art has to do with the question of the subject in a non-illustrative way, the question of the actuality of the presentation of an irresolvable split (not a split presented merely so that its resolution can be provided) is raised. This is the question of tolerating a split, and more broadly speaking, of tolerating the heterogeneous, provided that a form can be found for it. As we saw in Tannhäuser's monologue, the split subject in Wagner's music is tantamount to the proposal of a form for the split.

4. The non-dialecticity of resolutions
The fourth rule concerns the non-dialecticity of resolutions, that is, the possibility that a resolution may not necessarily be the reprise, the sublation, the condensation of, or the solution to, the differences set up in the artistic process. This amounts to accepting that resolutions may be non-dialectical without necessarily being, or having to be, instances of arbitrary stopping. (This is the major, very contemporary problem of the temptation to substitute an interruption for a resolution in order to avoid any appearance of a dialectical resolution.) I think that Wagner's approach – and again, I'm not saying he always succeeded, that is not at all my intention – is to seek figures of resolution that are not interruptions of the music as such but neither do they necessarily consist in imposing a unilateral possibility or a single idea. There is always an element of hesitation involved too.

5. Transformation without finality
The last rule has to do with the notion of transformation without any finality as the principle of development, in the sense that the giving of a form to the development can be found in the resources of transformation.

I believe that, with these five rules – and others can no doubt be found – Wagner invented musical resources, which he provided not for us to imitate or replicate, of course, but as a possible direction for us. At their heart I think there lies an incomparable mastery of the transformations whereby local cells are capable of configuring a global situation.

Ultimately, I would say that the most important thing we can learn from Wagner is, in this way, topological: it resides in the relationship of the local to the global, concerning which I believe he really contributed some significant, innovative ideas. These can be found in every aspect of his work, from the writing of the dramatic text to details of the orchestration. That is why I have always considered that the fact that he allowed the overall configuration of his work to be linked to transformations of local cells, even if there was occasionally a little gimmickry – he was a crafty man, it's true – necessarily made him the founder of something new and not just someone who brought something to a close.

In this connection, I can't help thinking of someone whom it might seem strange to compare with Wagner, namely Haydn. In Haydn's music the systematic use of the plasticity of short cells is in actual fact more important, when all is said and done, than their strictly methodical arrangement. There is something similar to this in Wagner, who, no doubt on a somewhat broader scale, could be considered the Haydn of Romantic opera. As you know, Haydn was in many respects a founder of the classical style, and I'm convinced that in Wagner's case there was something like the invention of a new style that was abandoned.

Somebody (I think it was Barraqué) said that Wagner was an isolated case and I found this statement very striking. It is paradoxical, because Wagner's impact was enormous – everyone was influenced by him – but in another way I think that in certain essential respects it is true that he had no heirs, since there was a long stretch of time during which it was considered important, or even necessary, to sideline him. But this does not amount to nostalgia for what might have happened if things had been different. Rather, what I wanted to discuss was the hypothesis that, all the evidence to the contrary notwithstanding, Wagner still represents a music for the future. So, to return to some very basic things, I would say that Wagner's connecting of leitmotif and totality, of leitmotif and 'endless melody' (since – the description is not completely erroneous – this is how Wagner's lesson about first replacing the operatic set numbers with 'endless melody' and then weaving it all together with leitmotifs is often summed up), is nevertheless a step in the direction of totality-free greatness. The most important thing for us is precisely that path, namely, the possibility that he was the last to aspire to greatness, to dispensing with totality in what was nevertheless his strongest suit.

Lesson 5

The Enigma of Parsifal

The question I want to pose is the following: what is the real subject of *Parsifal*, when all is said and done?

Right off the bat you'll wonder, as I myself do, what a question about an opera's subject can mean. How can we ask what an opera's subject is if by *subject* is meant the particular modality of the Idea's constitution, the particular way in which the Idea itself comes to be constituted (since my point of view is not that art is the descent of the Idea into the artistic materials but rather that the assemblage of the artistic materials itself constitutes the locus of the Idea)?

The question of the subject is an especially difficult one when it comes to those art forms that are the most impure, such as cinema, for example. There has been much debate – to which I myself have contributed – about the subject in cinema. Cinema is a composite art form, with extremely complex, overlapping materials, and the question as to how the Idea comes to be constituted within it is an especially tricky one. Even before the advent of cinema, however, opera was already an extremely impure art form. It was actually like a fantastical, nineteenth-century proto-cinema. That is incidentally why the connections between opera and cinema virtually amount to a separate question in and of themselves.

The trouble with impure art forms is that the particular way in which the Idea is constituted is the moment when the impure becomes pure; that is to say, it is a matter of detecting, within the extremely impure, complex composition that is an opera, the moment when the immanent purity of this very impurity emerges, or, in other words, of determining how something pure is crafted out of the impure. Thus, the question clearly has to do with the fact that the assemblage of the Idea's artistic materials, the way the Idea is materially constituted, actually occurs within a heterogeneous multiplicity, or at any rate within a seemingly heterogeneous multiplicity.

If we approach the issue of an impure art form from this angle, the question then becomes: What is a heterogeneous multiplicity? A multiplicity might be said to be heterogeneous when it is composed of chance and nothingness, or when it is exposed to material contingency (the often heterogeneous combination of the various artistic sources or materials it mixes together) and, on account of this, it exposes the purity of the Idea precisely to nothingness, to disappearing beneath the contingency of its materials.

This combination of chance and nothingness characteristic of heterogeneous multiplicity in art forms that are the most impure was noted specifically in regard to *Parsifal*, and thus was born a tradition that François Nicolas has astutely analyzed and dissected, a tradition of denigrating *Parsifal*. In fact, the idea that *Parsifal* is not Wagner's best opera but rather the work of a worn-out old man has been around for a very long time. *Parsifal* has been underestimated, greatly underestimated, according to Thomas Mann.[1]

So now, what can be said about chance? Chance is what has consistently sparked critical attacks on *Parsifal*'s laughter-provoking scenic and symbolic hotchpotch. Poking fun at *Parsifal* is very easy to do; I myself am not above doing so on occasion.

---

1   Cf. François Nicolas's presentation 'Écoutez *Parsifal!*' and Isabelle Vodoz's presentation 'De *Parȥival* à *Parsifal*' at the *Parsifal* conference held on 6 May 2006 at the École Normale Supérieure: www.diffusion.ens.fr/index.php?res=cycles&idcycle=282.

- In the first place, there are all the queer Christian trappings: the Grail, redemption, the Mass, the sin of the flesh, and so forth.

- Then, there are whiffs of racialism – there's no getting around that. For instance, it was even alleged that 'Redemption to the Redeemer' meant that Christ himself needed to be redeemed because he was Jewish. But even without going that far, there are things in *Parsifal* having to do with blood, with the question of the purity of the blood, that are effectively part of an ideological hotchpotch.

- There is also a dubious sexual symbology and, in the final analysis, Nietzsche was not altogether wrong when he claimed that it is hard to tell the apology of chastity apart from the apology of sensuality in *Parsifal*. It is all very interchangeable, just like *to serve* and *to corrupt*. And although the Flower Maidens scene may be admirable as far as the music is concerned, the claim has often been made that it looks a lot like a Bavarian brothel!

- And then there is Amfortas's wound. It is the *Thing* – Slavoj Žižek has written some absolutely brilliant things about this[2] – the Thing that is exhibited almost like a piece of meat in Syberberg's film and that bears some obvious similarities with female genitalia.

So all this stuff is jumbled up together in *Parsifal,* and the opera can in fact be regarded as one big grab bag, an extremely dubious mishmash. So much for chance, then. Now what about

---

2   Slavoj Žižek, 'The Politics of Redemption. Why is Wagner Worth Saving?,' *Journal of Philosophy and Scripture*, vol. 2, no. 1 (Fall 2004). See also his presentation '*Parsifal*, une pièce du théâtre didactique brechtienne' at the *Parsifal* conference cited above.

nothingness? Nothingness, too, has given rise to effects that account for *Parsifal*'s supposedly being incapable of really producing the purity of the Idea.

- Thus, the opera has often been taken to task for its inordinate expansion of time. It has been objected that the system of leitmotifs, which in Wagner's previous operas had been one of transformation, became a system of expansion, if not plain succession, in *Parsifal*, particularly since a good deal of *Parsifal*'s themes are long ones, rather than segmentary cells that can be quickly combined or transformed.

- It has also been claimed that there was a kind of decorative affectation about *Parsifal*. Precisely in order to conceal the opera's inaptitude for transformation, the old Wagnerian witchcraft was put into play, but it was slapped on like a coat of paint.

- Another objection was that, although the sublime was present in the opera, it was a kitschy, somewhat sugary sort of sublime. Even Boulez could never really bring himself to like the ending of *Parsifal*. He said that there is no getting around the fact that it is sentimental.

So, if that is what *Parsifal* really boils down to, then this means that it has failed in the two struggles constitutive of the Idea where impure art forms are concerned: the struggle against chance and the struggle against nothingness, the two effects of heterogeneous multiplicity. How, then, can chance and nothingness be combated, if combating them is indeed what is at stake when it comes to evaluating *Parsifal*? In this connection, there is an absolutely explicit ethics of art in Mallarmé and, for reasons that will later become clear, I will be making use of a comparison between Mallarmé's enterprise and Wagner's in *Parsifal*.

In reality, the problem has to do with changing chance into the infinite and nothingness into purity. This does not imply eliminating either of them, strictly speaking, but rather changing them. Both are mentioned in an extremely forceful way at the end of Mallarmé's *Igitur* manuscripts. First, with respect to the act in *Igitur*, Mallarmé writes that 'it reduces chance to the *Infinite*'.[3] That's the first struggle. Then, the last sentence of the *Igitur* manuscripts reads, 'Nothingness having departed, there remains the castle of purity.'[4] We might then say that, in the case of impure works of art, which are particularly exposed to the pernicious effects of chance and nothingness or to a combination of the two, the subject would be the moment when the castle of purity encounters its dis-closure, or its infinite dis-enclosure, the moment when purity, as it were validating nothingness, also becomes dis-enclosure. In other words, it becomes an open castle: the open castle of purity.

That is actually a tentative description of *Parsifal*. In any event, Parsifal – the name Parsifal, the character himself – does indeed symbolize all this. The character of Parsifal really stands for this question of open purity, of purity as dis-enclosure, rather than closure. It should be noted, however, that Parsifal is not really a *character* at all. As soon as you try to imagine him as a character you run into trouble. The fact is that this story of a virgin seduced by the image of his mother in Act II, who then gets lost for an indefinite period of time (no one is really sure why, incidentally), does not add up to much. Ultimately, Parsifal does not do much of anything; in fact, he basically does nothing at all. He says 'no' at a certain moment, and that's about it. As a character, he is flat. What's more, he has very little singing to do. He sings for a total

3   Stéphane Mallarmé, *Oeuvres Complètes*. Paris: Gallimard, 1945, p. 442: 'il réduit le hasard à l'*Infini*'. English translation by Mary Ann Caws in *Stéphane Mallarmé: Selected Poetry and Prose*, ed. Mary Ann Caws, New York: New Directions, 1982, p. 100.

4   Ibid., p. 443: 'Le Néant parti, reste le château de la pureté.' English translation by Caws, op. cit., p. 101.

of twenty minutes in the whole opera – he could almost have done it all in one go. Moreover, you have to admit that playing Parsifal is very hard, a real bear, as a rule, especially when the singer is a big tub of a 65-year-old. He has an even harder job of it than a fat Siegfried, and that is already hard enough to pull off! Syberberg came up with an inspired, remarkable solution, but he had the advantage, it's true, of lip-synch.

So I think the idea of Parsifal as a character should be entirely abandoned and he should actually be regarded as a *signifier*. The '*Rein*', or 'pure', signifier is what he embodies. *He* is the castle of purity. His symbolic arc – the play of his signifier – begins at pure innocence, or, in other words, purity as innocence, or the purity of '*der reine Tor*' ('the pure Fool'): purity almost as a kind of madness, then, purity that was in fact heralded by a prophecy. His symbolic arc will proceed from this mad purity, this pure innocence as prophecy, all the way to his speech at the end of the opera, which is actually a performance since a speech is a performative speech act. But then, right at the moment this speech occurs, something like the opposite phenomenon becomes involved: purity alone remains, but its status has completely changed; it has now become '*reinsten Wissens Mach*', 'purest wisdom's might'.[5] Parsifal's arc thus goes from the powerlessness of purity's ignorance to purity as power or force, purity as a force of knowledge.

This is an important point: *pure* is an invariant, *purity* is an invariant, because it is ultimately the name of the Idea – just as the subject in a certain sense must be – but its *attributes* change. The opera is essentially the story of the changes in the attributes of invariant purity. In other words, we go from purity as non-knowledge to purity as a force of knowledge: that is the story of

---

5   Richard Wagner, *Parsifal*, trans. Andrew Porter. English National Opera Guide #34, London: John Calder, 1986, Act III, scene 2. (Translator's note: '*Wissen*' is here translated poetically as 'wisdom', rather than 'knowledge'. However, since Badiou translates '*Wissen*' more faithfully as '*savoir*', I will henceforth use the term 'knowledge'.)

Parsifal. So it is clear that we are dealing here with the construction of the castle of purity.

Now, in contrast to this is the other castle, the *Burg*, Montsalvat. The problem with *this* castle is precisely that it is turned in on itself, on its own closure, and has lost all capacity for the infinite; it is closed up. And it is closed up under the signifier of *the Father* because, even though Amfortas is partly to blame for it, Titurel bears the major share of responsibility. Titurel thinks that it is the Grail that allows him to go on living although he is dead. He is lying in his tomb, still alive, and, provided that he is given his Grail periodically, he can go on. Since this is a somewhat self-centred use of the Grail's transfigurative symbolism, however, it is Titurel, when you come right down to it, who is responsible for instigating the disappearance and decline of the community. Parsifal's purity, as an invariant proceeding from non-knowledge to knowledge, will thus be structured around this closure in such a way as to constitute its opening. So we do indeed find in the *Parsifal* story a logic linking purity and the infinite together as the working through, and reworking, of heterogeneous, impure material, hence as a constitutive struggle against chance and nothingness.

'Redemption to the Redeemer', the opera's final words, is the name for that struggle. *Redeemer*, when all is said and done, means that which has attained its closure. It must therefore be redeemed. There must be a redemption of the Redeemer himself, meaning the infinite reopening – by means of a nothingness transformed into purity, by means of the arc of an invariant purity – of that which has closed up on itself. The story thus truly inscribes *the infinite* and *purity* in the epic of *Parsifal* as constitutive of the character of Parsifal himself.

Then there is a contrasting symbolism, in the Titurel–Klingsor couple, the couple of the closed. (Interestingly enough, the characters of *Parsifal* can all be divided up into small groupings, and almost any combination of them can work, which is really quite remarkable. At any given moment you can say Titurel and Klingsor stand for one and the same thing. But Klingsor and Amfortas are also related. Kundry and Klingsor work together, too, but so do Kundry and Amfortas. As for Parsifal, he goes with everyone, naturally, since he is the universal signifier.) The symbolism opposite to that of the inscription of the infinite and purity in the *Parsifal* epic is embodied in the Titurel–Klingsor couple, which in reality encloses the Amfortas–Kundry couple: Amfortas is Titurel's son while Kundry is Klingsor's slave. So the Amfortas–Kundry couple inside the Titurel–Klingsor couple is what will have to be dis-enclosed; it will have to be opened up in such a way that the work of purity can be revealed as infinite.

This having been said, it is clear that, though I may have solved the problem of the subject strictly in terms of the story, I have by no means done what I set out to do, because the story is, after all, peripheral to what an opera really is. An opera obviously cannot be reduced to its story. So what I have just been discussing is only a first, abstract level. It exists, but it does not resolve the issue, the problem of the opera's subject. To put it another way: Where in the opera is the connection between the infinite and purity as an index of the Idea, as the struggle against the contingency of the material and the nothingness of its effects, expressed?

I am therefore going to suggest that the subject of the opera is revealed at the moment when the structuring of the music is indistinguishable from the opera's dramatic effect, that is, when we truly have a distinct, palpable impression of indistinguishability, into which we become incorporated, between the structuring of the music and the dramatic effect. It is in this phenomenon of indistinguishability perceived as a specific moment that the subject of the opera – as immanent cohesion (or, to use my own philosophical vocabulary, as a transcendental registration of the opera or as a transcendental of the world of the opera) – is revealed and will from that moment onward be diffused throughout the opera as such. The method by which such moments are diffused throughout the opera as a whole is a very important analytic problem in and of itself.

So we might say that the opera's subject can be identified on the basis of moments of indiscernability between the structuring of the music and the dramatic effect such that there are moments when the impurity is not abolished per se but is actually *synthesized:* its various components are neither done away with nor cancelled out but instead persist as an effect of indiscernability. That would be one general theory.

Let me now provide two examples that might serve as an introduction to this idea.

Suppose we ask what the subject of Mozart's *Don Giovanni* is – something that has always been hotly debated. Now, if we apply the foregoing criteria, we would have to say that, when all is said and done, the subject of *Don Giovanni* is not seduction, women and so forth at all. (The opera is actually a borderline pathetically comic opera: the hero, Don Giovanni, really fails at everything he undertakes; it is one long string of disasters.) I think the subject is a very 'eighteenth-century' subject: the idea that the supernatural can be defied, that this is a possibility. Such a possibility was introduced by the figure of critique in the eighteenth century.

The subject here is both delayed and anticipated. It is *delayed* because it is actually only announced in the penultimate scene of the opera, when Don Giovanni in fact defies the statue of the Commander and finally accepts and risks his own death. The supernatural can be defied, although that doesn't necessarily mean it *should* be. However, the subject is also *anticipated,* since the musical material of this scene is already present in the Overture. Thus, the subject is both announced beforehand and delayed. How, then, is it diffused throughout the opera? I think it is diffused by means of a very peculiar form of nocturnal anxiety that binds everything together and permeates the opera as a whole (even when it is comical), a nocturnal anxiety framed by the imperatives of the Overture and by the penultimate scene as a possibility, as this particular possibility: if the supernatural can be defied, then all human ventures are imbued with suspense and anxiety.

Now let's turn to another example. Suppose we ask what the subject of Debussy's *Pelléas et Mélisande* is. I would say, as regards *Pelléas et Mélisande*, that I have always been struck by the fact that the success or failure of any performance of this opera hinges on a few extremely brief moments. For instance, the way Mélisande says to Pelléas, 'Why are you leaving?'[6] I have always thought that the interpretation of Mélisande hinges entirely on the way this one line is spoken.

There are other such moments in the opera, too, always ones involving Mélisande. For example, later on, there is the way she will say, 'I'm so unhappy!'[7] or, at the very end, the way she will say, 'Oh, oh, I have no more courage! I have no more courage!'[8] These things are incredibly difficult, almost impossible, to speak or to sing, and the opera, in an extremely succinct way, stakes its subject on these very moments. Why should this be so? Because, in my opinion, the subject of *Pelléas et Mélisande* is *the effects of the unspoken in love*. And indeed, the moment at which we are dealing with something that involves speaking the unspoken – which is the case in all three of these examples – is the moment when the subject is revealed. Therefore, instead of something delayed or anticipated, we get suspended, allusive forms in which the music is absolutely stripped down to the level of what is being said.

So perhaps these examples can go a little way toward justifying this theory of the subject in operas other than *Parsifal*. Now, if we apply the theory to *Parsifal*, we can take a new approach to the question of the subject, by seeking the moment. First of all, I think that in *Parsifal* the subject is not announced or supported by the singing or by verbal utterance per se. Rather, it will be found

---

6 Claude Debussy, *Pélleas et Mélisande*, trans. Hugh Macdonald. English National Opera Series Guide #9, London: John Calder, 1982, Act I, scene 3.

7 Ibid., Act II, scene 2.

8 Ibid., Act IV, scene 4.

elsewhere. What is explicitly stated is not a direct guide to the subject of *Parsifal*. I see two proofs or examples of this, one at the beginning of the opera and the other at the end.

The opera is in fact framed, for obvious reasons, by Gurnemanz's lengthy narrative and by Parsifal's concluding speech. Now, Gurnemanz's narrative, which is magnificent, patently displays what François Nicolas calls its medium [*support*]. It is a synthetic piece in which the synthesis is overt. If its various components are moved ever so slightly apart, their radical heterogeneity can be seen.

As for Parsifal's speech at the end, I think our interpretation of Parsifal will depend a good deal on what we think or feel in relation to this speech. I personally think it is music devoid of any effect of meaning. Whereas Brünnhilde's final speech in *Götterdämmerung* is a true speech of conclusion, Parsifal's is a sort of elusive one: it conveys very little meaning, which proves that it is not on the level of speeches, proclamations or narratives that the problem of *Parsifal*'s subject will be resolved.

Nor will it be resolved, as far as I am concerned, in terms of the contrasting features that have traditionally been brought to bear: the world of the sacred vs the world of the profane, the world of reality vs the world of appearance, the world of purity vs the world of sensuality, or the masculine world vs the feminine world. All these major oppositions have been trotted out for *Parsifal*, and the list could go on: the intelligible vs the sensible, the castle vs the forest (or even a macrobiotic or a vegetarian diet), pure vs impure blood, Jews vs non-Jews, you name it – absolutely any classical opposition that at one moment or another is involved in the analysis of *Parsifal* as a way of explaining it. The most convincing one, I think, is probably the opposition between appearance and reality because it is at work in the dramatic heart of Act II, which is the story of the dissipation of appearance. But even though this may clarify the dynamics of Act II, it does not account for the structure of the opera as a whole.

Thus, it is neither in these dialectical oppositions nor in the question of Christianity as it was elaborated by Nietzsche that *Parsifal*'s subject can be found. But let me put it another way: it is absolutely obvious that in *Parsifal* the crucified Christ is a *problem* rather than a solution. The crucified Christ is the very *opposite* of Christianity. What will enable us to find the solution to the problem of the condition to which the original Christian redemption has been reduced, namely to nothing at all, is not the reaction to it, which is why the basic idea of *Parsifal* – and this is a crucial point – is not that there has to be a restoration of Christianity, although it often comes very close to that. It is not, strictly speaking, a matter of regenerating Christianity as such; that is not the solution. In fact, with respect to this issue of Christianity, the limit point proposed by *Parsifal* is suspended in its infiniteness: it is not a dialectical sublation in the sense of its being something that has been accomplished. Instead, all we are afforded is a point suspended in its infiniteness that simply announces that the infinite and compassion are connected. Compassion is the instrument that makes it possible to open closure to the infinite. Compassion is required in order to disenclose what is closed, including within Christianity itself. And for this reason Parsifal, in his speech at the end of the opera, will speak of 'compassion's highest power'.[9]

So the foregoing approaches are of no avail. Where, then, will we find the dramatic figure that matches the expansion of time in the music, that is coextensive with its tonal colour and is also connected with the layering of sound in the music (what François Nicolas calls the 'cloud effect' in *Parsifal*)? Where will we find the moments when there is really an attempt to make harmony and counterpoint indistinguishable, the moments when the interweaving of the horizontal and vertical dimensions is really brought about through the use of new techniques? Where does this occur?

---

9   Richard Wagner, *Parsifal*, Act III, scene 2, trans. Derrick Everett, www.monsalvat.no/trans3.htm.

I think it occurs most forcefully in the two scenes involving the ceremony in the castle. There are two great ceremonial moments in the opera: the second scene in Act I and the second scene in Act III, both of which are introduced by some exceptionally beautiful orchestral music. There is thus a deliberate symmetry. Accordingly, I will suggest that the *subject of* Parsifal *is the question as to whether a modern ceremony is possible.* The subject is the question of ceremony, and this question is intrinsic to *Parsifal.* It is distinct from the question of religion. Why? Because a ceremony can be said to be a collectivity's or even a community's mode of self-representation, but transcendence is not an essential condition of it. In fact, we could say that the question posed by *Parsifal* is whether a ceremony *without* transcendence is possible.

Thus, the question is also distinct from that of the sublime, from the aesthetics of the sublime, to which it has sometimes been reduced. In the aesthetics of the sublime, the ceremony, including the one in *Parsifal,* is actually only a means, a formal support for the sublime. Wagner did his best to make us view it this way, inasmuch as the ceremony in the opera is ascendant, with one choir at the base of the dome, another halfway up it, and a third all the way at the top (the voices of the angelic children). The ceremony thus seems to be built upon a principle of ascension that would imply transcendence. I don't think this is actually the case, however. The question still remains: what is a ceremony without transcendence, a ceremony that is therefore not a means to something but *the thing itself,* the representation of the community in and of itself?

You've got to remember that in the late nineteenth century the question of ceremony was being raised on all sides and it became an end in itself. The issue was not ceremony as a means of transcendence but rather ceremony as a *possibility.* Was a ceremony possible, the implicit thesis being that it was indeed no longer possible, that modern times were characterized precisely by the fact that ceremony had become an impossibility. As Mallarmé remarked, it would be difficult to regard the sessions of Parliament as a ceremony!

I'm obviously taking up my Mallarmé thread here: the question of ceremony is an explicit, even fundamental, question in Mallarmé. Let me remind you that *Le Livre* – the famous *Livre* which never materialized – was actually a protocol for a ceremony. Quite a few of its manuscripts are devoted to questions about how the chairs were to be set out, where the celebrant would stand, how much it would cost; it is mostly about things of that sort. *Le Livre* was a ceremonial protocol, intended to be read and distributed at a great mass meeting. From this perspective, the whole 'Religious Services' section in *Variations on a Subject* can serve as a reference. As I will attempt to show, these texts are extremely enlightening as regards *Parsifal*.

In them, Mallarmé examined various figures of ritual or ceremony, inevitably leading up to the Mass, the holy service, as the prototype of a ceremony. The first thing he looked at were concert overtures, about which he said: 'Music declares itself to be the last and most complete human religion.'[10] That was certainly the case then. Now, however, music has become a solitary religion. At big rock concerts the yearning for ceremony is blatant. You feel it intensely when you see how young people of all stripes share this deep yearning for ceremony. Except that it is a parody; it never manages (as *Parsifal* might not; I'll come back to this later) to get beyond parody, yet that is clearly what it is attempting to do. Music was once the 'the last and most complete human religion', but it has turned out to be a human religion in as sorry a state as the Brotherhood of the Knights in Act I of *Parsifal*. It has ended up being about having earphones in your ears – portable music players! Obviously nothing could be further removed from a ceremony than a portable music player. The ceremony is a meeting in a specific place; it is the constitution of a place, whereas the portable music player is music devoid of place.

---

10   Mallarmé, *Oeuvres Complètes*, p. 388: 'La Musique s'annonce le dernier et plénier culte humain.' English translation by Rosemary Lloyd in Heath Lees, *Mallarmé and Wagner: Music and Poetic Language*. Hampshire: Ashgate, 2007, p. 18; translation slightly modified.

Mallarmé turned next to the Mass, which he said was affirmed 'in the consecration of the host'[11] because, like Wagner, he was immersed in Christian metaphors and symbolism. In Mallarmé, it is a matter of the host, not the Grail, but it is nevertheless the *Thing*, which is affirmed as the prototype of the ceremonial object. The Catholic Mass, for Mallarmé, was the prototypical ceremony. So you can see that in this respect, too, Wagner was dealing with the same general material.

Finally, the third hypothesis Mallarmé put forward was the *mise en scène* of State – or political – religion: 'devotion to one's Country . . . requires a religion', if it is to be imbued, he claimed, with a certain 'exultation', which is hardly something self-evident. For that you would need a religion.[12] In this connection, Mallarmé's titles are highly significant: 'Sacred Pleasure' and 'Catholicism' are the titles of the passages in which he explored the issue of ceremony. He concluded with what I regard as a very contemporary statement when he wondered whether modernity wouldn't actually consist in the new ceremony's having to be secular [*laïque*] in nature. After examining the issue, he said 'Nothing . . . will prove to be exclusively secular because the latter word has no precise

---

11   Ibid., p. 394: 'Notre communion ou part d'un à tous et de tous à un, ainsi, soustraite au mets barbare que désigne le sacrement – en la consécration de l'hostie, néanmoins, s'affirme, prototype de cérémonials, malgré la différence avec une tradition d'art, la Messe.' English translation by Grange Woolley in *Stephane Mallarmé: 1842–1898: A Commemorative Presentation including Translations from his Prose and Verse with Commentaries.* Madison, NJ: Drew University, 1942, p. 129: 'Our communion or part of one to all and of all to one, thus, liberated from the barbarous meal that the sacrament designates – in the consecration of the host, is nonetheless affirmed, prototype of ceremonials, in spite of its difference from an art tradition, the Mass.' Translation slightly modified.

12   Ibid., p. 397: 'cela ne demeurera pas moins, que le dévouement à la Patrie, par exemple, s'il doit trouver une sanction autre qu'en le champ de bataille, dans quelque allégresse, requiert un culte: étant de piété.' English translation by Eric Gans: 'it will nevertheless remain true that devotion to one's country, for example, if it is to find a basis elsewhere than on the battlefield, in some form of exultation, needs a religion, being of the order of piety.'

meaning.'[13] I couldn't agree with him more about this point. 'Secular' is a word that has no precise meaning and it consequently precludes the possibility that a place for the presentation of the collectivity as such might be represented or constituted in its name.

So that leaves only one solution, and it is the one Wagner, too, was forced to choose: to go beyond religion. It is impossible to eradicate or abolish religion. We have to go beyond it; it must therefore be sublated by means of a relationship that, for Mallarmé, will be one of *analogy*. It will in no way *be* religion. The analogy with religion is the strict Mallarméan equivalent of 'Redemption to the Redeemer'. There is something analogous in the solution to the problem if one wishes to maintain – and Mallarmé is profoundly convinced that it must be maintained – a modern ceremony.

There is a well-known sentence of Mallarmé's, 'A magnificence, of one sort or another, will unfold, analogous to the Shadow of yore.'[14] That sentence could serve as the epigraph to *Parsifal*. 'The Shadow of yore' refers to the exhausted nature of nineteenth-century Christianity. 'Magnificence' means the sublation – via the invention of a modern ceremony – of everything implied by this exhaustion. 'Of one sort or another' indicates that we are in the age of democracy and therefore that this magnificence that is to unfold cannot be tied to religious particularity; it must tolerate the 'of one sort or another'. This – in terms of my own interests – can obviously be expressed as: the question hinges on knowing whether a ceremony of the generic is possible. Can there be a ceremony of the generic? That is exactly what Mallarmé is talking about.

In 1895 Mallarmé writes, 'A magnificence *will* unfold'. So he is still speaking – cautiously – in the future tense, whereas Wagner thinks he has already made it happen in 1882, that being the year *Parsifal* was first performed. Wagner's thesis, therefore, is: the

---

13   Ibid., p. 397: 'Rien, en dépit de l'insipide tendance, ne se montrera exclusivement laïque, parce que ce mot n'élit pas précisément de sens.'
14   Ibid., p. 394: 'Une magnificence se déploiera, quelconque, analogue à l'Ombre de jadis.'

ceremony, the *new* ceremony, exists. But in what way, we might ask, does it actually exist? It exists as a *theatre* for the ceremony. This is a very complicated business, however, because the theatre is obviously Bayreuth. Bayreuth is the place where the ceremony takes place, that is, the place where *Parsifal* is performed. But what actually *is* the ceremony here? Is it the ceremony as it is performed in Bayreuth or is *Bayreuth itself* the site of the ceremony? Is it the *audience* of *Parsifal* that is gathered together for the purposes of a specific ceremony or is the aforementioned ceremony the one whose genealogy and history are in effect recounted in *Parsifal*?

In actual fact, Wagner is fundamentally ambivalent about this. He did indeed propose that Bayreuth be a ceremonial site, and he proposed it specifically for *Parsifal,* since, as you know, he thought that *Parsifal* could, and should, be performed only in Bayreuth. And because it was a ceremony, he thought that there should be no applause at the end, that it should be exempt from the usual theatrical conventions, that the performance and spectacle aspect should be, so to speak, done away with, in favour of the purely ceremonial dimension. Yet he couldn't get around the fact that the *content* of the ceremony, if it was indeed Bayreuth, was the *performance* of the ceremony and that therefore the ceremony was a ceremony of ceremony! So that was the hitch, a sort of admission that he couldn't be sure that the ceremony had actually taken place. Mallarmé may therefore have been right to say that 'a magnificence *will* unfold': in *Parsifal* it does unfold, but in something that, to the extent that it is a representation of representation – or a ceremony of ceremony – might well reinstate closure.

Now, what does Mallarmé mean by 'analogous'? Mallarmé's thesis is that the new ceremony will be 'analogous' to the 'Shadow of yore'. What is so remarkable is that Wagner had actually already set out to demonstrate that it would be analogous. He endeavoured to demonstrate that the new ceremony of the future is analogous to the old one insofar as it is the sublation of the latter. It is analogous in a scenic and even a musical sense because the parallels between the two ceremonies in *Parsifal* are blatantly obvious, and the whole point is precisely to determine the exact occurrence of the difference between the old ceremony and the new one, the ceremony in the second scene of Act I and the ceremony in the second scene of Act III.

So the subject of *Parsifal*, to get back to that now, has to do with *re*presenting as a ceremony the transition from the 'Shadow of yore' (I'm using Mallarmé-ese here) to the new ceremony. Wagner will display or turn into a ceremony (in the second sense of the word, i.e., a self-reflexive or self-representative ceremony) a subject matter that has to do with the transition from 'the Shadow of yore' – the old ceremony, in other words – to the new one. That is his thematics.

This obviously leads us to the question of how this subject exists in terms of its sensible, musical, etc. components. What are the differences – in the work itself and in the connection or indiscernability between music, story, decor, texts, and so forth – between the second ceremony and the first one, between the ceremony performed by Parsifal and the previous one performed by Amfortas acting under orders from Titurel, who wants to be served a meal in his tomb?

This is really where all the difficulty begins, because these differences amount to a rather enigmatic problem. Moreover, you can see that what is at stake is a fundamental, wholly contemporary problem for us, namely, can we pursue the possibility of a new ceremony that would not be a restoration, that would not actually be the nostalgic project of preserving or reproducing the old ceremony? Now, if we look at *Parsifal*, at those moments of ceremony that are in my opinion moments when the dramatic and musical effects absolutely cannot be told apart, hence moments when the Idea is definitely entering the materials (not that the Idea itself shouldn't be interrogated: it may well be an Idea of restoration), then we must inquire as to what the differences between the two scenes are.

We notice that the setting, the structure of the site, is unchanged. We are still in the castle. Directors, incidentally, often alter the setting: they present the castle in ruins, or even a dilapidated old blockhouse with abandoned railroad tracks, or other things of the sort. Such changes are indefensible unless they are in the service of the Idea itself. The fact is, the setting remains unchanged, and the best evidence we have for this is when Gurnemanz tells Parsifal: 'Yes, yes, you have indeed returned to the same place.' Parsifal's whole problem is to return to the same place after having retrieved the Spear.

The *formal* protocol of the ceremony is the same as before: the Grail must be shown. The objects are the same: the Grail and the Spear. Ultimately, uncovering the Grail is the essence, the absolute crux of the ceremony. But this is what Amfortas no longer wants to do, since every time he uncovers the Grail, he ends up writhing in pain on the ground. (Incidentally, Amfortas's groaning is not the weirdest thing in the opera – everyone's taste will differ – but you really do feel like giving him some ibuprofen!) Since Amfortas, wracked with pain, just can't do it anymore, Parsifal will succeed him as king. In fact, Parsifal was declared king prior to the ceremony. He himself had demanded of Gurnemanz, 'Make me king!' and Gurnemanz had replied 'Sure, of course.' So Parsifal has become the king, and now he arrives on the scene. And what does he do? Exactly the same thing as before! *Formally*, he does exactly the same thing: he uncovers the Grail and shows it to the Knights. The setting is therefore unchanged and the formal protocol remains the same, too.

What does this formal protocol require? This is a very interesting point. The formal protocol, too, is very Mallarméan. It requires a celebrant, a crowd and certain symbolic objects, all in all a very simple, bare-bones affair: you've got two symbolic objects (the Grail and the Spear), one chief celebrant, and a crowd. The celebrant's task is to show the objects to the crowd. It is in fact very Mallarméan in its simplicity because the whole issue hinges on what it means *to show* and *who is able to show*. Apparently, some extraordinary conditions must be met. Apparently, Amfortas can no longer do it, and apparently no one else can either, otherwise it would be hard to understand why any old guy couldn't just say, 'If you don't want to do it, I will!' Apparently, that's not possible. Poor Gurnemanz, for example, cannot imagine himself uncovering the Grail; it is just not possible. And yet Gurnemanz is a good guy. Right from the start we can tell that *he* is not going to be corrupted: he is already too old. So, couldn't just anyone do it? No, some rigorous – albeit doubtless quite obscure – conditions have to be met in order to be the celebrant at the ceremony. In Mallarmé, the celebrant of the future is the poet. He explicitly says as much. The poet will be the priest of the ceremony of the future.

So you need a celebrant, a crowd and certain objects, and, as far as what takes place at the end of the opera is concerned, we have the same objects, a celebrant, and even the same crowd, the knights. However, at this point, the problem becomes focused on the change of celebrant. The transformation from the previous ceremony to this one – hence the possibility of a modern ceremony – has to do with the fact that there is a new celebrant. The opera thus tells the story of *the change of celebrant*.

Celebrant can be understood in the broadest sense of the term. Perhaps the new celebrant, when all is said and done – and I think Syberberg was right about this – is something like the Parsifal–Kundry duo. But it doesn't really matter. There is a new celebrant, and the fact that, for the first time, a woman can enter the castle is significant. That is part of the novelty: women can now participate in the service. (Kundry may have only come there to die, but at least it's a start!) What, then, does the change of celebrant involve, when all is said and done? What is the content of this change of celebrant, of the transition from Amfortas to Parsifal, or, shall we say, from Titurel–Amfortas to Parsifal–Kundry?

Well, now we are getting to the crux of the matter, to the problem of the Idea itself, because this change in the content is brought about in terms of the drama by the substitution of one person for another. There is a new king, Parsifal, and he tells Amfortas: 'I'm taking over your functions now. You're healed, I've closed up your wound. But you can forget about being king from now on!' – the cure doesn't come without a price – '*I'm* the king now!' Although, in terms of the drama, this occurs by way of Parsifal's taking the place of the ailing Amfortas, the substitution is itself obscure. What I mean is, it is obscure in terms of the *difference* it produces, since, *formally*, the action continues to be the same.

The substitution is also signified in the music, through Parsifal's speech. And it is true that, at that precise moment, the subject is revealed. However, as I see it, the problem is that, dramatically, the substitution may have taken place, but it is nevertheless not really *signified* because it is a *substitution* (whose formal gestures are the same). And musically, it may be signified – as the opening of a new, infinite register of dis-enclosure of the castle – but the musical material of Parsifal's speech and what follows perhaps signifies this musically, too, simply through the striking contrast between the manner of Amfortas's and Parsifal's utterances, between Amfortas's howling and Parsifal's extremely fluid, soothing music. Parsifal's proclamation is one in which triumph is restrained. However, precisely because this musical material, which is a fluid, soothing kind of music, is very restrained, it in no way really clarifies the meaning of the disjunction.

Ultimately, and almost in conclusion, I would say the following. If we agree that the subject of *Parsifal* is the great question about the possibility of a new ceremony raised at the end of the nineteenth century – where and how will the new ceremony take place, in which the collectivity will represent itself to itself without transcendence? – if this is indeed the subject of *Parsifal*, then we have to admit that there is a certain indeterminacy between restoration and innovation with respect to the realization of the Idea. I'm not saying that restoration prevails over innovation but rather that there is an undecidability between the two. It is perhaps precisely *this* that is the subject, all things considered. It is the idea that, concerning the question of the new ceremony, there is no clear distinction between restoration and innovation, or between nostalgia and the creation of something new.

I see yet another possible indication of this, incidentally, in the fact that the concluding formula, 'Redemption to the Redeemer', is essentially the fulfilment of the prophecy announced at the beginning. But when something is the fulfilment of a prophecy, then there is instantly an absolute indeterminacy between restoration and innovation, since, if something has been prophesied and its fate is to come true, then the order of necessity or law has actually taken precedence over the order of rupture or discontinuity.

This introduces a question that preoccupied the twentieth century (and it may still be the case today): Can a ceremony really be *new* in essence? Can there really be a modern form of ceremony that would exist by virtue of true *creation* rather than the mere indeterminacy between restoration and innovation?

As you are well aware, politics in the twentieth century was obsessed with the question of ceremony. This is one of the reasons why Wagner was accused of being a proto-Nazi and why someone as intellectually sophisticated as Lacoue-Labarthe could still fundamentally argue that the question of the new ceremony consists in imposing on the masses a mythical configuration reiterating their closure. The theory of the mythical essence of Wagner's œuvre holds that Wagner was nothing but an artistic precursor of the aestheticization of the masses, that is, a precursor of the need for imposing a mythical figure on the masses, which in fact periodically takes on the guise of a ceremony. Thus, the great mass rallies in Nuremburg and Moscow were ceremonies, ceremonies in which the people were in fact summoned to self-representation, but not as a reflection of their infinite potential, only as a massive new closure that was mythical in nature. The ceremonial visibility of the masses that haunted the twentieth century is supposedly in line with Wagner's enterprise, and with Mallarmé's as well, in fact, since, as we have seen, there is no major difference between them concerning this issue.

Yet I don't think this is the case at all, because I don't think that Wagner's solution involved imposing a myth on the masses. Wagner explored the problem. He attempted to make it the subject of an opera, which is a very difficult thing to do. I believe that the real conclusion of the work – assuming we agree that the conclusion, in terms of artistic greatness, realizes the subject or makes it come into being – is that in fact, at that particular juncture, making a choice between restoration and innovation wasn't an easy thing to do, and the decision between nostalgia and the creation of something new had to remain suspended.

Thus, Nietzsche's quarrel with Wagner is relevant here, too: Nietzsche may have had good reason to say that Wagner was ultimately a failure. But what type of break did Nietzsche himself propose? He proposed becoming the tortured subject of madness *himself*. What's more, he even said as much: '*I* am breaking the history of the world in two,' he said. But he brought in the word 'I', and he paid for it with his life. He brought in that 'I' precisely at the point of the impossible ceremony.

The idea that, with reference to an impossible ceremony, in its stead, something like dereliction occurs, is without question an essential theme of *Parsifal*: Kundry can in this sense be regarded as the opera's heroine. Kundry is no doubt the one who knows that, in the end, it is impossible to decide. Her extraordinary musical virtuosity – her undecidable vocal range (the well-known problem concerning whether she is a mezzo-soprano or a soprano), her remarkably jagged musical line, the amazing variations in pitch she is capable of producing – all this perhaps suggests that we are dealing with a historical mutability that renders a ceremonial approach unworkable or at any rate undecidable. This may just be the way things are.

This would then imply that *democracy, by definition, is the failure of ceremony*. Mallarmé wondered if this wasn't the case. Many arguments can obviously be marshalled to prove that any time there was a ceremony or an attempt at a ceremony, totalitarianism reared its head. But are such arguments tenable? Can humanity really do without ceremony? Can politics do without ceremony?

I obviously do not think it is possible in the long run. The infinite circulation of goods does not constitute a sustainable model of human relations, and the question consequently remains unanswered. It is in this sense that *Parsifal* is contemporary, even if its conclusion was all in all a realistic one – I'm not talking about Wagner himself; Wagner himself is beside the point. Wagner himself came to such a conclusion, because if he hadn't, he would not have tried to make a ceremony out of the ceremony. He would not have had to say, 'Not only is *Parsifal* about the new ceremony but on top of that I created a ceremony in Bayreuth.' Just think, with all the gussied-up bourgeois from around the world who were in attendance, the ceremony was ultimately pathetic! No one applauded at the end, everyone walked out of the theatre without a word, and then they all went out for sauerkraut – what else was there to do? – commenting that 'the tenor wasn't so great'. It is also possible to say that the priest wasn't very good when Mass is over; that doesn't diminish the ceremonial nature of the ceremony as such. But it is clear that, in the case of *Parsifal*, the self-reflexive nature of the ceremony (the ceremony of the ceremony) discredited or passed judgement on the validity of the ceremonial proposition as such, the supposedly universal proposition of a sublation of Christianity without transcendence. That was what the proposition was.

Thus, even if Wagner's conclusion was one of undecidability, the question still remains relevant because the question as to whether the Crowd declares itself, as Mallarmé puts it, cannot be exclusively recapitulated in collective figures of revolt. The people's declaration, the declaration of the Crowd, somehow cannot be satisfied with anarchic revolt alone. It must also put forward, examine and produce its own consistency.

And so, as I firmly believe, ceremony is necessary. It is probably both necessary *and* impossible today, but that is not a serious problem; that is the way things often are. Genuine problems are like that, both necessary and impossible. And possibility arrives right when you no longer expect it. That is what an event is. It could be said that an event today would be something that would make a ceremony possible. In this sense, *Parsifal* is prophetic in its own way: Will an event occur that will make a ceremony possible? That is what happens in *Parsifal*, but in my opinion it does not succeed, from a formal point of view, in changing the ceremony into something new, in really displacing the new ceremony.

So there you have it, and that is why I am really going to conclude now, by citing Mallarmé again. Mallarmé said that, at least in our imagination, we should practice 'the intrusion into future celebrations'.[15] Intruding into future celebrations is what *Parsifal* invites us to do: at least to be able to get ready to intrude into future celebrations, that is, to anticipate or have the necessary prerequisites for the future celebration. That is why I would say that the nostalgia in *Parsifal* – which I acknowledge, which does exist, which is counterbalanced by innovation – is only the reverse, or the flip side, or the necessity for, this intrusion into future celebrations.

We are therefore poised between nostalgia and intrusion, but 'the intrusion into future celebrations' is nevertheless a little more than mere restoration. It is the historical state of the question of ceremony as Mallarmé and Wagner set it out it for us.

---

15   Ibid., p. 392: 'l'intrusion dans les fêtes futures'.

Afterword:

Wagner, Anti-Semitism and 'German Ideology'

Slavoj Žižek

My Israeli friend Udi Aloni told me the story of an incident which demonstrates better than anything else the partial character of Wagner's anti-Semitism. A couple of decades ago, he belonged to a group of radical cultural provocateurs who, in order to defy the prohibition on publicly performing Wagner's music in Israel, announced in the daily newspapers that they would show the full video of Wagner's *Ring* in their club. They, of course, planned the evening as a drinking party with wild dancing, but something strange happened that prevented this. As the hour of the performance approached, increasing numbers of old Jews, both men and women, dressed in the ridiculously old-fashioned, solemn way of pre-Hitler Germany, appeared in the club: for them, a public performance of Wagner was, more fundamentally than the Nazi misuse of his music, a reminder of the good old Weimar Germany where Wagner's operas had once been a crucial part of their cultural experience. It goes without saying that, out of respect for these unexpected guests, the provocateurs renounced their wild partying and allowed the event to turn into an evening of restrained musical appreciation.

In 1995, at a conference on Wagner at Columbia University in New York, after the majority of participants outdid each other

in the art of unmasking the anti-Semitic and proto-fascist dimension of his art, a member of the public asked a wonderfully naïve
question:

> So if all you are saying is true, if anti-Semitism is not just Wagner's
> personal idiosyncrasy, but something which concerns the very
> core of his art, why, then, should we still listen to Wagner today,
> after the experience of the Holocaust? When we enjoy Wagner's
> music, does this stigmatize us with complicity in or, at the very
> least, acquiescence, to the Holocaust?

The embarrassed participants – with the honourable exception of one honest, fanatical anti-Wagnerite who really meant it
when suggesting that we stop performing Wagner – replied with
confused versions of 'No, of course we didn't mean that, Wagner
wrote wonderful music . . .' – a totally unconvincing compromise,
even worse than the standard aestheticist answer: 'Wagner as a
private person had his defects, but he wrote music of incomparable
beauty, and in his art there is no trace of anti-Semitism.' Is our
passionate attachment to Wagner to remain an obscene secret to
be disavowed in public academic discourse?

The problem is a more general one, concerning the core of
German ideological identity. It is popular to assert that there
are two Germanys, the ascetic-military 'Prussian' Germany,
focused on ruthless discipline and dedicated service to the
State, and the more friendly, southern Austrian–Bavarian–
Schwabian Germany focused on *Kultur*, on art, and spiritual-
ized *joie de vivre*. When, in his late years, Goethe witnessed the
retreat in Germany of *Kultur* and the rise of German political
nationalism, he was horrified by the prospect of the dangers
that this engendered. (One can claim that the very duality of
the Federal Republic of Germany and the German Democratic
Republic in the second half of the twentieth century expresses
this opposition. The 'Prussian' character of the GDR was often
noted.) From this perspective, Nazism predictably appears as

the climactic point of 'Prussian' Germany. Might Goethe have presciently perceived the shadow of the Nazi threat at its very source? One should reject this conclusion.

It is not an accident that in the finale of his *Meistersinger*, Wagner, whom the Nazis perceived as their predecessor, celebrated the survival of German art following the decline of the German *Reich*; it is no accident that Hitler was Austrian, fanatically devoted to Wagner and in thrall to German *Kultur* much more than to Prussian militarism; and it is no accident that the dominant motif of the conservative defence of Germany in the First World War (starting with Thomas Mann's 'Reflections of an Unpolitical Man' in 1918) was the defence of German *Kultur* against French and Anglo-Saxon civilization. (This, incidentally, allows us to propose a succinct definition of barbarism which covers Nazism as well as today's Islamic and Christian fundamentalisms: barbarism is not the opposite of culture, but rather, it is pure culture – culture without civilization.) Nazism was not 'Prussian'. Rather, it enacted the synthesis of two Germanys: the full appropriation of the 'Prussian' Germany by the Germany of *Kultur*. Here, one might follow Philippe Lacoue-Labarthe, who detected the source of Nazism in the post-Kantian *aestheticization of the political*, which began with Schiller and the conservative Romantics.

To return to Wagner now: despite the triumph of the Stuttgart Opera's *Ring* several years ago, this production – along with Patrice Chéreau's groundbreaking centenary staging at Bayreuth – exhausted the options for providing a clear interpretive key to Wagner's work. Two of the most representative post-Chéreau Wagner stagings, Ruth Berghaus's Frankfurt Opera *Ring* (1985–1987) and Hans-Jürgen Syberberg's film *Parsifal* (1982), both stand under the post-Sontag marquee 'against interpretation'. At a glance, the two versions could not be more different. Berghaus performs a postmodern, deconstructive reading, undermining the *Ring*'s aesthetic unity, rendering visible and playing with the inconsistency of all signs and ideological motifs. The living unity of the work is denounced as a montage of incoherent multiplicity; characters are like dolls enacting different clichés. Berghaus, a pupil of Brecht, extraneates the *Ring*, but without providing a firm interpretive background: all that remains is the endless play of inconsistent signifying fragments.

Syberberg, on the contrary, is thoroughly opposed to Leftist ideologico-critical readings: he wants to resuscitate the mythic impact of Wagner's work, not by abstracting it from history, but by incorporating history itself into a mythic texture. The surprising fact is how similar these two versions are despite their points of difference. Syberberg's *Parsifal*, too, is overfilled with inconsistent symbols which lack a firm interpretive grid. Too much meaning destroys coherence, so all that remains is the general impression that there is some deep, unfathomable, mythic meaning.[1] Thus, we have the same inconsistent multiplicity of signs: first in the extraneated artificial, meaningless mode of the *combinatoire*, and secondly in the deeper, meaningful mode of unfathomability.

Syberberg is right to reject historicist readings that yearn to elucidate the true meaning of Wagnerian tropes (Hagen as a masturbating Jew, Amfortas's wound as syphilis, and so on). Wagner, so the argument goes, was mobilizing historical codes known to everyone in his own time: when a person stumbles, sings in cracking high tones, or makes nervous gestures, 'everyone knew' this was a Jew. However, do we really learn anything salient in this way? What if such historicist contextualization were not only superfluous, but an active obstacle? What if, in order to properly grasp a work like *Parsifal*, one needs to *forget* all this historical paraphernalia? Historicist reductionism and abstract aestheticism are two sides of the same coin. A work is eternal not against its historical context, but through the way it answers the challenge of its historical moment.

---

1   See a detailed overview in Patrick Carnegy, *Wagner and the Art of Theatre*. New Haven and London: Yale University Press, 2006.

One needs to abstract from historical trivia, to *decontextualize* the work, to tear it out of the context in which it was originally embedded. There is more truth in *Parsifal's* formal structure, which allows for different historical contextualizations, than in its original context. Nietzsche, Wagner's great critic, was the first to perform such a de-contextualization, proposing a new figure of Wagner: no longer Wagner as the poet of Teutonic mythology, of bombastic heroic grandeur, but the 'miniaturist' Wagner, the Wagner of hystericized femininity, of delicate passages, of bourgeois family decadence.

Therein resides one of the achievements of Alain Badiou's groundbreaking study of Wagner, which reasserts the artistic-political unity of *the event called Wagner*. Beyond all historical paraphernalia, Wagner's opus embodies a certain vision of and answer to the deadlock of European modernity, a vision and an answer which can in no way be dismissed as proto-fascist. Was there an artist who questioned more radically the very fundaments of power and domination? Instead of seeing in Wagner's Hagen a masturbating Jew, is it not much more productive and urgent to see in him the first clear depiction of a Fascist populist leader? Instead of dismissing the Grail brotherhood as a homoerotic, elitist, male community, is it not much more productive and urgent to discern in it the contours of a new post-patriarchal revolutionary collective?

The battle for Wagner is not over: today, after the exhaustion of the critical-historicist and aestheticist paradigms, it is entering its decisive phase. In order to clarify the stakes of this battle, one must reach back to Mozart, and perhaps, even, to the very beginnings of opera.

Mercy and its transformations

It rarely happens that a (relatively) unpopular work like Mozart's *La clemenza di Tito* plays such a crucial structural role in the history of music. As we shall see, what makes it unpopular is not its archaic character, but, on the contrary, its uncanny contemporaneity: it directly addresses some of the key issues of our time.

Clemenza has to be located in the series which begins with the very beginning of opera. Why was the story of Orpheus *the* topic for opera or in the first century of its history, when almost one hundred versions of it existed? The figure of Orpheus asking the gods to bring back his Eurydice to him stands for an intersubjective constellation which provides as it were the elementary matrix of the opera, or more precisely, of the operatic aria: the relationship of the Subject (in both senses of the term: autonomous agent as well as the subject of legal power) to his Master (Divinity, King, or the Lady of courtly love, *die Minne*) is revealed through the hero's song (the counterpoint to the collectivity embodied in the chorus), which is basically a supplication addressed to the Master, a call to him to show mercy, to make an exception, or otherwise forgive the hero his trespass. The first, rudimentary, form of subjectivity is this voice of the Subject beseeching the Master to suspend, for a brief moment, his own Law. A dramatic tension in subjectivity arises from the ambiguity between power and impotence that is expressed in the gesture of grace by means of which the Master answers the Subject's entreaty.

As regards the official ideology, grace expresses the Master's supreme power, the power to rise above one's own law: only a really powerful Master can afford to dispense mercy. What we have here is a kind of symbolic exchange between the human Subject and his divine Master: when the Subject, the human mortal, by way of his offer of self-sacrifice, surmounts his finitude and attains the divine heights, the Master responds with the sublime gesture of Grace, the ultimate proof of his humanity. Yet this act of grace is at the same time branded by the irreducible mark of a forced empty gesture: the Master ultimately makes a virtue out of necessity, in that he promotes as a free act what he is in any case compelled to do – if he refuses clemency, he takes the risk that the Subject's respectful entreaty will turn into open rebellion.

Crucial here is the move from Monteverdi's *Orfeo* to Gluck's

Orfeo ed Euridice: what Gluck contributed was a new form of subjectivization. In Monteverdi we have sublimation at its purest: after Orpheus turns around to glance at Eurydice and thus loses her, the Divinity consoles him. True, he has lost her as a flesh-and-blood person, but from now on, he will be able to discern her beautiful features everywhere, in the stars in the sky, in the glistening of the morning dew . . . Orpheus is quick to accept the narcissistic benefit of this reversal: he becomes enraptured with the poetic glorification of Eurydice that lies ahead of him. To put it succinctly, he no longer loves *her,* what he loves is the vision of *himself* displaying his love for her.

This, of course, throws a different light on the eternal question of why Orpheus looked back and thus screwed things up. What we encounter here is simply the link between the death drive and creative sublimation: Orpheus' backward glance is a perverse act *stricto sensu;* he loses Eurydice intentionally in order to regain her as the object of sublime poetic inspiration (this is an idea that was developed by Klaus Theweleit[2]). But shouldn't one go even a step further here? What if Eurydice herself, aware of the impasse of her beloved Orpheus, intentionally provoked his turning around? What if her reasoning was something like: 'I know he loves me; but he is potentially a great poet, this is his fate, and he cannot fulfil that promise by being happily married to me. So the only ethical thing for me to do is to sacrifice myself, to provoke him into turn-ing around and losing me, so that he will be able to become the great poet he deserves to be' – and then she starts gently coughing or something similar to attract his attention.

Examples here abound. Like Eurydice who, by sacrificing herself (that is, by intentionally provoking Orpheus to turn his gaze towards her and thus send her back to Hades) delivers his creativity and sets him free to pursue his poetic mission, Elsa in

2   See Klaus Theweleit, *Buch der Koenige, Band I: Orpheus und Euridike.* Frankfurt: Stroemfeld und Roter Stern, 1992.

Wagner's *Lohengrin* also intentionally asks the fateful question
and thereby delivers Lohengrin, whose true desire, of course, is to
remain the lone artist sublimating his suffering into his creativity.
Wagner's Brünnhilde, that 'suffering, self-sacrificing woman', is
the ultimate example here: she wills her annihilation, but not as a
desperate means to compensate for her guilt; she wills it as an act
of love destined to redeem the beloved man, or, as Wagner himself
put it in a famous letter to Franz Liszt:

> The love of a tender woman has made me happy; she dared to
> throw herself into a sea of suffering and agony so that she should
> be able to say to me 'I love you!' No one who does not know all her
> tenderness can judge how much she had to suffer. We were spared
> nothing – but as a consequence I am redeemed and she is blessedly
> happy because she is aware of it.

Once again, we should descend here from the mythic heights into
everyday bourgeois reality: the woman is aware of the fact that, by
means of her suffering which remains invisible to the public eye,
of her renunciation *for* the beloved man and/or her renunciation
of him (the two are always dialectically interconnected, since, in
the fantasmatic logic of the Western ideology of love, it is for the
sake of her man that the woman must renounce him), she rendered
possible the man's redemption, his public social triumph, like
Traviata, who abandons her lover and thus enables his reintegration into the social order.

In the case of Gluck, however, the denouement is completely
different: after looking back and thus losing Eurydice, Orpheus
sings his famous aria 'Che faro senza Euridice', announcing his
intention to kill himself. At this precise point of total self-aban-
donment, the goddess of Love intervenes and gives him back his
Eurydice. This specific form of subjectivization – the intervention of Grace not as a simple answer to the subject's entreaty, but
as an answer which occurs at the very moment when the subject

decides to put his life at stake, to risk everything – is the twist added by Gluck. What is crucial here is the link between the assertion of subjective autonomy and the 'answer of the Real', the mercy shown by the big Other: far from being opposed, they are dependent on each other. The modern subject can assert its radical autonomy only insofar as it can count on the support of the 'big Other', only insofar as its autonomy is sustained by the social substance. No wonder this gesture of 'autonomy and mercy',[3] of mercy intervening at the very moment of the subject's assertion of full autonomy, is discernible throughout the history of opera, from Mozart to Wagner. In *Idomeneo* and *Seraglio,* the Other (Neptune, Bassa Selim) displays mercy at the very moment when the hero is ready to sacrifice his/her life, and the same happens, twice, even, in *The Magic Flute* (the magic intervention of the Other prevents both Pamina's and Papageno's suicide); in *Fidelio,* the trumpet announces the Minister's arrival at the very point when Leonore puts her life at stake to save Florestan; and finally, in Wagner's *Parsifal,* Parsifal himself intervenes and redeems Amfortas precisely when Amfortas asks to be stabbed to death by his knights.

What occurs between Monteverdi and Gluck is thus the failure of sublimation: the subject is no longer ready to accept the metaphoric substitution, to exchange 'being for meaning', that is, the flesh-and-blood presence of the beloved for the fact that he will be able to see her everywhere, in the stars and the moon, and so on. Rather, he prefers to take his own life, to lose it all, and it is at this point, to fill in the refusal of sublimation, of its metaphoric exchange, that mercy has to intervene to prevent a total catastrophe. And still today we live in the shadow of this failed sublimation.

Michel Houellebecq's novels[4] are interesting in this context. He endlessly varies the motif of the failure of sublimation in

3 See Ivan Nagel's outstanding *Autonomy and Mercy.* Cambridge: Harvard University Press, 1991.
4 For example, Michel Houellebecq, *The Possibility of an Island.* New York: Knopf, 2006.

contemporary Western societies characterized by 'the collapse of religion and tradition, the unrestrained worship of pleasure and youth, and the prospect of a future totalized by scientific rationality and joylessness'.[5] Here is the dark side of the sexual liberation of the 1960s: the full commodification of sexuality. Houellebecq depicts the morning after the sexual revolution, the sterility of a universe dominated by the superego injunction to enjoy. All of his work focuses on the antinomy of love and sexuality: sex is an absolute necessity, to renounce it is to wither away, so love cannot flourish without sex. Simultaneously, however, love is impossible precisely because of sex: sex, which 'proliferates as the epitome of late capitalism's dominance, has permanently stained human relationships as inevitable reproductions of the dehumanizing nature of liberal society; it has, essentially, ruined love.'[6] Sex is thus, to put it in Derridean terms, simultaneously the condition of the possibility and of the impossibility of love. The miracle of sublimation is precisely to temporarily resolve this antinomy: through it, love continues to transpire in the very imperfections of the sexual body in decay.

In Catherine Breillat's *Romance*, there is a fantasmatic scene which perfectly stages this radical split between love and sexuality. The heroine imagines herself lying naked on her belly on a small, low table divided in the middle by a partition with a hole just big enough for her body. With the upper side of her body, she faces a nice, tender guy with whom she exchanges gentle loving words and kisses, while her lower part is exposed to one or more sex-machine studs who penetrate her wildly and repeatedly. However, the true miracle occurs when these two series momentarily coincide, when sex is 'transubstantiated' into an act of love. There are four ways to disavow this impossible/real conjunction of love and sexual enjoyment: (1) the celebration of asexual 'pure' love, as if the sexual desire for the beloved demonstrated love's inauthenticity; (2) the

---

5   Nicholas Sabloff, 'Of Filth and Frozen Dinners', *The Common Review*, Winter 2007, p. 50.

6   Ibid., p. 51.

opposite assertion of intense sex as 'the only real thing', which reduces love to a mere imaginary lure; (3) the division of these two aspects, their allocation to two different persons: one loves one's sweet wife (or the idealized inaccessible Lady), while one has sex with a 'vulgar' mistress; (4) their false immediate merger, in which intense sex is supposed to demonstrate that one 'truly loves' one's partner, as if, in order to prove that our love is a true one, every sexual act had to be the proverbial 'fuck of the century'.

All four of these stances are wrong, an escape from assuming the impossible/real conjunction of love and sex; a true love is enough in itself, it makes sex irrelevant. But precisely because 'fundamentally, it doesn't matter', we can fully enjoy it without any superego pressure. Love and sex are not only distinct, but ultimately incompatible, they operate at thoroughly different levels, like *agape* and *eros*: love is charitable, self-erasing, ashamed of itself, while sex is intense, self-assertive, possessive, inherently violent (or the opposite: possessive love versus generous indulging in sexual pleasures). However, the true miracle occurs when (exceptionally, not 'as a rule'), these two series momentarily coincide, when sex is 'transubstantiated' into an act of love, an achievement which is real/impossible in the precise Lacanian sense, and as such is marked by an inherent rarity. This miracle is the miracle of sublimation: the object of love is not idealized, it is accepted with all its imperfections: it is in and through it, in its imperfections, that the absolute Thing transpires. This is why Scottie's obsessive love for Madeleine in Hitchcock's *Vertigo* is fake: if his love were true, he should have accepted the full identity of (the common, vulgar) Judy and (the sublime) Madeleine. It is in this identity of the incongruous opposite, of the sublime and the ridiculous, that resides the comedy of love, or, as Fernando Pessoa put it: 'All love letters are comical. They would not be about love, if they were not comical.'

Mozart as a critic of postmodern ideology

The Fast Runner, a unique film retelling an old Inuit (Eskimo) legend, was made by the North Canadian Inuits themselves. The authors decided to change the ending, replacing the original slaughter, in which all the participants die, with a more conciliatory conclusion. They claimed that such an ending was more fitting for today. The paradox is that this readiness to adapt the story to today's specific needs attests to the fact that the authors were still part of the ancient Inuit tradition: such 'opportunistic' rewriting is a feature of pre-modern culture, while the very notion of 'fidelity to the original' signals that we are already in the space of modernity, that we have lost immediate contact with tradition.

One should bear in mind this fundamental paradox when dealing with numerous recent attempts to stage classical operas not only by transposing them into a different (most often contemporary) era, but also by changing some basic facts of the narrative itself. There is no a priori abstract criterion that allows us to judge the success or failure of such attempts. Every such intervention is a risky act and must be judged by its own immanent standards. Such experiments often misfire ridiculously – not always, however, and there is no way to tell in advance, so one has to take the risk. One thing is certain: the only way to be faithful to a classic work is to take such a risk: avoiding it, sticking to the traditional letter, is the safest way to betray the spirit of the classic. In other words, the only way to keep a classical work alive is to treat it as 'open', as pointing towards the future; or, to use the metaphor evoked by Walter Benjamin, to act as if the classic work were a film requiring a chemical for development which is invented after the fact. In this manner, it is only today that we can get the full picture.

There are changes (or interpretations) which, even if they appear both 'daring' and well-founded, are clearly wrong. Take, for example, one of the ways to stage the finale of *Così fan tutte*. Since the libretto does not specify who the couples reunited at the end are (are they the same as at the beginning, or do we get an exchange of partners?), *Così* is sometimes staged in such a way that the partners are exchanged. The problem with this change is in its very psychologically convincing character: it is as if, at the beginning, the partners were mismatched, and, through the ridiculous masquerade, they discovered their true amorous attachments. However, by way of this re-inscription of *Così* into the standard plot of the discovery of true love, the unsettling premise of the plot – the idea that the first love attachment is no less mechanically produced than the alternate one, since all love attachments are 'artificial' – is obliterated.

Among the cases of successful changes, two stand out: Jean-Pierre Ponnelle's Bayreuth version of *Tristan*, in Act III of which Tristan dies alone (Isolde stays with her husband, King Marke, and her reappearance at the opera's end is merely the dying Tristan's hallucination) and Syberberg's *Parsifal* (in which Amfortas's wound is a partial object, a kind of continually bleeding vagina carried on a pillow outside his body; plus, upon gaining insight into Amfortas's suffering and rejection of Kundry, the boy who plays Parsifal is replaced by a cold young girl). In both cases, the change possesses a tremendous power of revelation: one cannot resist the strong temptation to believe that this is how it really should be.

Along these lines, imagine – my own personal dream – a *Parsifal* taking place in a modern megalopolis, with Klingsor as an impotent pimp running a whorehouse. He uses Kundry to seduce members of the 'Grail' circle, a rival drug gang. 'Grail' is run by the wounded Amfortas, whose father Titurel is in a constant delirium induced by an excess of drugs; Amfortas is under terrible pressure from the members of his gang to 'perform the ritual'; that is, to deliver the daily supply of drugs to them. He was 'wounded' (infected by AIDS) by Kundry, his penis bitten while Kundry was giving him fellatio. Parsifal is the young, inexperienced son of a single, homeless mother who does not get the point of drugs; he 'feels the pain' and rejects Kundry's advances while she is performing fellatio on him. When Parsifal takes over the 'Grail' gang, he establishes a new rule for his community: free distribution of drugs.

A similar sort of scenario could be imagined for *Tristan*: the action would be transposed into a conflict between two patriarchal, Sicilian gangster-fishermen families, a kind of *Tristan* transposed into *Cavalleria rusticana*. The *capo* of one of the families (Marke) sends his nephew (Tristan) across the bay to the other family to bring him Isolde. The marriage is arranged to end a family feud. On the boat, the two recall their past encounter and, afterwards, the servant accompanying Isolde gives her a placebo drink instead of poison.

In recent stagings of Mozart, it is Peter Sellars's version of *Così fan tutte* (available on video and DVD) that succeeds triumphantly in the exercise of subtle narrative change. Apart from the convincing transposition of the action to a contemporary setting (a US naval base, with Despina as a local bar owner, and the two gentlemen – naval officers – returning not as 'Albanians', but as purple- and yellow-haired punks), its main premise is that the only true, passionate love is the one between the philosopher, Alfonzo, and Despina, who experiment with the two young couples in order to act out the deadlock of their own desperate love. This reading hits at the very heart of Mozartian irony, which is to be opposed to cynicism. To simplify it to the utmost, if a cynic fakes a belief that he privately mocks (publicly you preach sacrifice for the fatherland, privately you amass profits), ironically, the subject takes things more seriously than it appears: he secretly believes what he publicly mocks. Alfonzo and Despina, the cold philosophical experimenter and the corrupt, dissolute servant-girl, are the true passionate lovers, using the two pathetic couples and their ridiculous erotic imbroglio as instruments to confront their own traumatic attachment.

What makes *Così* the most perplexing, traumatic even, of Mozart's operas is the very ridiculousness of its content: in terms of our psychological sensitivity, it is almost impossible to suspend our disbelief and accept the premise that the two women do not recognize their own lovers in the Albanian officers. No wonder, then, that throughout the nineteenth century the opera was performed in an adapted version in order to render the story plausible. There were three main versions of these changes, all of which fit perfectly the main modes of the Freudian negation of traumatic content: (1) the staging implied that the two women knew the true identity of the 'Albanian officers' all along: they just pretended not to know in order to teach their lovers a lesson; (2) the couples reunited at the end are not the same as at the beginning; they change their places diagonally, so that, through the confusion of identities, the true, natural love links are established; (3) most radically, only the music was used, with a wholly new libretto telling a totally different story.

Edward Saïd drew attention to Mozart's letter to his wife Constanze from 30 September 1790, the time when he was composing *Così*. After expressing his pleasure at the prospect of seeing her again soon, he went on: 'If people were to be able to see into my heart, I would have to be almost ashamed of myself . . .' At this point, as Saïd perspicuously perceives, one would expect the confession of some dirty private secret (sexual fantasies of what he will do to his wife when they finally meet again, etc.). However, the letter goes on: 'everything is cold to me – cold like ice'.[7] It is here that Mozart enters the uncanny domain of 'Kant avec Sade', the domain in which sexuality loses its passionate, intense character and turns into its opposite, a 'mechanical' exercise in pleasure executed by cold distance, like the Kantian ethical subject doing his duty without any pathological commitment.

Isn't this the underlying vision of *Così*: a universe in which subjects are determined not by their passionate engagements, but by a blind mechanism that regulates their passions? What compels

---

7   See Edward W. Saïd, '*Così fan tutte*', in *Lettre international* 39 (Winter 1997), pp. 69–70.

us to establish a parallel between *Così* and the domain of 'Kant avec Sade' is its very insistence on the universal dimension already indicated by its title: 'they are *all* doing the same thing', determined by the same blind mechanism. In short, Alfonzo, the philosopher who organizes and manipulates the game of changed identities in *Così*, is a version of the figure of the Sadean pedagogue educating his young disciples in the art of debauchery. It is thus oversimplified and inadequate to conceive of this coldness as that of 'instrumental reason'.

The traumatic core of *Così* resides in its radical 'mechanical materialism' in the Pascalian sense, as advice to nonbelievers: 'Act as if you believe, kneel down, follow the rite, and belief will come by itself!' *Così* applies the same logic to love: far from being an external expression of the inner feeling of love, love rituals and gestures *generate* love. So, act as if you are in love, follow the procedures, and love will emerge by itself. Apropos of Molière's *Tartuffe*, Henri Bergson emphasized how Tartuffe is funny not on account of his hypocrisy, but because he gets caught in his own mask of hypocrisy:

> He immersed himself so well into the role of a hypocrite that he played it, as it were, sincerely. This way and only this way he becomes funny. Without this purely material sincerity, without the attitude and speech which, through the long practice of hypocrisy, became for him a natural way to act, Tartuffe would be simply repulsive.[8]

Bergson's precise expression 'purely material sincerity' fits perfectly with the Althusserian notion of Ideological State Apparatuses, that is, of the external ritual which materializes ideology: the subject who maintains his distance towards the ritual is unaware of the fact that the ritual already dominates him

---

8   Henri Bergson, *An Essay on Laughter*. London: Smith, 1937, p. 83.

from within. This 'purely material sincerity' of the external ideological ritual, not the depth of the subject's inner convictions and desires, is the true locus of the fantasy which sustains an ideological edifice. Moralists who condemn *Così* for its alleged frivolity thus totally miss the point: *Così* is an ethical opera in the strict Kierkegaardian sense of the 'ethical stage'. The ethical stage is defined by the sacrifice of the immediate consumption of life, of our yielding to the fleeting moment, in the name of some higher universal norm.

If Mozart's *Don Giovanni* embodies the Aesthetic (as was developed by Kierkegaard himself in his detailed analysis of the opera in *Either/Or*), the lesson of *Così* is ethical. Why? The point of *Così* is that the love that unites the two couples at the beginning of the opera is no less 'artificial', mechanically brought about, than the second falling in love of the sisters with the exchanged partners dressed up as Albanian officers that results from the manipulations of the philosopher Alfonzo: in both cases, we are dealing with a mechanism that the subjects obey in a blind, puppet-like way. Therein consists the Hegelian 'negation of negation': first, we perceive the 'artificial' love, the product of Alfonzo's manipulations, as opposed to the initial 'authentic' love; then, all of a sudden, we become aware that there is actually no difference between the two – the original love is no less 'artificial' than the second. So, since one love counts as much as the other, the couples can return to their initial marital arrangement. This is what Hegel has in mind when he claims that, in the course of a dialectical process, the immediate starting point proves itself to be something already mediated, its own self-negation: in the end, we ascertain that we always-already were what we wanted to become, the only difference being that this 'always-already' changes its modality from In-itself into For-itself. Ethical is in this sense the domain of repetition qua symbolic: if, in the Aesthetic, one endeavours to capture the moment in its uniqueness, in the Ethical a thing only becomes what it is through its repetition.

This perspicuous example compels us to complicate Pascal's 'Kneel down and you will believe!' a little bit, adding an additional twist to it. In the 'normal' cynical functioning of ideology, belief is displaced onto another, onto a 'subject supposed to believe', so that the true logic is: 'Kneel down and you will thereby make someone else believe!' One has to take this literally and even risk a kind of inversion of Pascal's formula: 'You believe too much, too directly? You find your belief too oppressing in its raw immediacy? Then kneel down, act as if you believe, and you will get rid of your belief – you will no longer have to believe yourself, your belief will already exist objectified in your act of praying!' That is to say, what if one kneels down and prays not so much to regain one's own belief but, on the contrary, to *get rid of* one's belief, of its over-proximity, to acquire a breathing space of a minimal distance towards it? To believe – to believe 'directly', without the externalizing mediation of a ritual – is a heavy, oppressing, traumatic burden, which, through performing a ritual, one has a chance of transferring onto an Other.

If there is a Freudian ethical injunction, it is that one should have the courage of one's own convictions: one should dare to assume fully one's identifications. And exactly the same goes for marriage: the implicit presupposition (or, rather, injunction) of the standard ideology of marriage is that, precisely, there should be no love in it. The Pascalian formula of marriage is therefore not 'You don't love your partner? Then marry him or her, go through the ritual of shared life, and love will emerge by itself!', but, on the contrary: 'Are you too much in love with somebody? Then get married, ritualize your love relationship in order to cure yourself of the excessive passionate attachment, to replace it with boring daily custom – and if you cannot resist passion's temptation, there are always extra-marital affairs.'

This insight brings us back to the power of Sellars's staging, enabling us to formulate the difference between the two couples and the additional couple Alfonzo–Despina. The first two exemplify

Henri Bergson's 'purely material sincerity'. In the great love duets of Act II of *Così*, the men, of course, hypocritically fake love to test the women; however, in exactly the same way as Tartuffe, they get caught in their own game and 'lie sincerely'. This is what the music renders, this sincere lie. However, with Alfonzo and Despina, the situation is more complicated. They enact, through others, the rituals of love for the sake of their own love, but in order to get rid of its direct traumatic burden. Their formula is: 'We love each other too much, so let us stage a superficial love imbroglio involving the two couples in order to acquire a distance towards this unbearable burden of our own passion.'

What all this implies is that Mozart occupies a very special place between pre-Romantic and Romantic music. In Romanticism, music itself – in the very substantial, 'passionate' rendering of emotions celebrated by Schopenhauer – not only can lie, but *lies in a fundamental way, about its own formal status*. Let us take the supreme example of music as the direct rendering of the subject's immersion into the excessive enjoyment of the 'Night of the World', Wagner's *Tristan*, in which the music itself seems to perform what words helplessly indicate, the way the amorous couple is inexorably drawn towards the fulfilment of their passion, the 'highest joy' (*hoechste Lust*) of their ecstatic self-annihilation. Is this, however, the metaphysical 'truth' of the opera, its true ineffable message? Why, then, is this inexorable sliding towards the abyss of annihilation interrupted again and again through the (often ridiculous) intrusion of fragments of common daily life? Let us take the most extreme case, that of the finale itself: just prior to Brangaene's arrival, the music could have moved straight into the final Transfiguration, two lovers dying embraced. Why, then, the rather ridiculous arrival of the second ship which accelerates the slow pace of the action in an almost comic way: in a mere couple of minutes, more events happen than in the entire opera up to that point (the fight in which Melot and Kurwenal die, etc.), in similar fashion to Verdi's *Il trovatore*, in which in the last two minutes a whole slew of things happen. Is this simply Wagner's dramatic weakness? What one should bear in mind here is that this sudden hectic action does *not* just serve as a temporary postponement of the slow but unstoppable drift towards orgasmic self-extinction; this hectic action follows an immanent necessity, it has to occur as a brief 'intrusion of reality', permitting Tristan to stage the final self-obliterating act of Isolde. Without this unexpected intrusion of reality, Tristan's agony of the impossibility of dying would drag on indefinitely. The 'truth' does not reside in the passionate drift towards self-annihilation, the opera's fundamental affect, but in the ridiculous narrative accidents/intrusions which interrupt it – again, the big metaphysical affect lies.

Catherine Clément was therefore right: one should reverse the standard notion of the primacy of music in opera: the idea that words (the libretto) and stage actions are just a pretext for the true focus, the music itself, so that the truth is on the side of the music, and it is the music which delivers the true emotional stance (say, even if a lover complains and threatens, the music delivers the depth of his/her love which belies the aggressivity or, rather, shows it in its true light). However, what if the opposite were true – what if the music were the emotional, phantasmatic envelope whose function was to render palpable the bitter pill delivered by the words and actions (women getting killed or abandoned, and so on)? One might thus read opera as Freud proposes to read a dream, to treat the basic emotional tone as a lie, a screen obfuscating the true message, which resides within the action on stage. Wagner was wrong when he advised a friend in Bayreuth in the midst of the performance of *The Flying Dutchman*: 'Just close your eyes and enjoy the music.' It is absolutely crucial to bear in mind what happens on stage, to listen to the words also.

This brings us back to *Tristan*: crucial for *Tristan* is the gap between this opera's 'official ideology' and its subversion through the work's texture itself. This subversion in a way reverses the famous Mozartian irony, where, while the person's words display the stance of cynical frivolity or manipulation, the music renders their authentic feelings. In *Tristan*, the ultimate truth does not reside in the musical message of passionate self-obliterating love-fulfilment, but in the dramatic stage action itself which subverts the passionate immersion into the musical texture. The final shared death of the two lovers abounds in Romantic operas; suffice it to recall the triumphant 'Moriam' insieme' from Bellini's *Norma*. Against this background, one should emphasize how in Wagner's *Tristan*, the very opera which elevates this shared death into its explicit ideological goal, this, precisely, is *not* what effectively happens: in the music, it is as if the two lovers die together, while in reality they die one *after* the other, each immersed in his/her own solipsistic dream.

Along these lines, one should read Isolde's ecstatic death at the end of *Tristan* as the ultimate operatic prosopopea: Tristan can only die if his death is transposed onto Isolde. When Tristan repeats his claim that death could not destroy their love, Isolde provides the concise formula of their death: 'But this little word "and" – if it were to be destroyed, how but through the loss of Isolde's own life could Tristan be taken by death?' In short, it is only in and through *her* death that he will be able to die. Doesn't Wagner's *Tristan* then offer a case of the interpassivity of death itself, of the 'subject supposed to die'? Tristan can only die insofar as Isolde experiences the full bliss of lethal self-obliteration for him, in his place. In other words, what 'really happens' in Act III of *Tristan* is *only* Tristan's long 'journey to the end of the night' with regard to which Isolde's death is Tristan's own fantasmatic supplement, the delirious construction that enables him to die in peace. Now we can formulate the uniqueness of Mozartian irony. Although music is already fully autonomized in it with regard to words, *it does not yet lie*. The Mozartian irony is the unique moment when the truth really speaks in music, when music occupies the position of the Unconscious rendered by Lacan's famous motto, '*Moi, la vérité, je parle.*' And it is only today, in our postmodern time, allegedly full of irony and lacking belief, that the Mozartian irony reaches its full actuality, confronting us with the embarrassing fact that – not within us, but in our acts themselves, in our social practice – we believe much more than we recognize.

At first blush, of course, things cannot but appear exactly inverted. Romanticism stands for music that, in a direct, non-lying way, renders the emotional core of the human being (that is, it tells the truth much more directly than words). Meanwhile, the uncanny and disturbing lesson of Mozart's *Così* is precisely that music *can* lie. For example, although the two Albanians' seduction arias and ensuing duets are phoney – each pretends to be madly in love in order to seduce the other's fiancée – the music is absolutely 'convincing' in rendering the emotion of love. The answer to this counter-argument is that it misses the point of Mozartian irony. Of course the individuals think that they are faking love, but their music bears witness to the fact that they 'fake to fake' – that there is more truth in their declarations of love than they are aware of. In Romanticism, on the contrary, the very pretence of rendering the emotional truth directly is phoney – not because it does not accurately render the individual's emotion, but because this very emotion is in itself already a lie.

Clemenza strengthens this Mozartian irony even further. Gioachino Rossini's great male portraits, the three from *Barbiere* (Figaro's 'Largo al factotum', Basilio's 'Calumnia' and Bartolo's 'Un dottor della mia sorte'), plus the father's wishful self-portrait of corruption in *Cenerentola*, enact a mocked self-complaint, where one imagines oneself in a desired position, being bombarded by demands for a favour or service. The subject twice shifts his position: first, he assumes the roles of those who address him, enacting the overwhelming multitude of demands which bombard him; then, he feigns a reaction to it, the state of deep satisfaction in being overwhelmed by demands one cannot fulfil. Let us take the father in *Cenerentola*: he imagines how, when one of his daughters is married to the Prince, people will turn to him, offering him bribes for a service at the court, and he will react to it first with cunning deliberation, then with fake despair at being bombarded with too many requests. The culminating moment of the archetypal Rossini aria is this unique moment of happiness, of the full assertion of the excess of Life which occurs when the subject is overwhelmed by demands, no longer being able to deal with them. At the high point of his 'factotum' aria, Figaro exclaims: 'What a crowd/ of the people bombarding me with their demands/ Have mercy, one after the other (*uno alla volta, per carità!*)', referring therewith to the Kantian experience of the Sublime, in which the subject is bombarded with an excess of data that he is unable to comprehend.

And do we not encounter a similar excess in Mozart's *Clemenza*, a similar sublime/ridiculous explosion of mercies? Just before the final pardon, Titus is himself exasperated by the proliferation of treasons which oblige him to proliferate acts of clemency:

> The very moment that I absolve one criminal, I discover another. [. . .] I believe the stars conspire to oblige me, in spite of myself, to become cruel. No: they shall not have this satisfaction. My virtue has already pledged itself to continue the contest. Let us see, which is more constant, the treachery of others or my mercy. [. . .] Let it be known to Rome that I am the same and that I know all, absolve everyone, and forget everything.

One can almost hear Titus complaining: 'Uno alla volta, per carità!' – 'Please, not so fast, one after the other, in the line for mercy!' Living up to his task, Titus forgets everyone, but those whom he pardons are condemned to remember it forever:

> SEXTUS: It is true, you pardon me, Emperor; but my heart will not absolve me; it will lament the error until it no longer has memory.

> TITUS: The true repentance of which you are capable, is worth

more than constant fidelity.

This couplet from the finale blurts out the obscene secret of *Clemenza*: the pardon does not really abolish the debt; rather, it makes it infinite: we are forever indebted to the person who pardoned us. No wonder Titus prefers repentance to fidelity: in fidelity to the Master, I follow him out of respect, while in repentance, what attaches me to the Master is the infinite indelible guilt. In this, Titus is a thoroughly Christian master.

One usually opposes rigorous Jewish Justice to Christian Mercy, the inexplicable gesture of undeserved pardon: we, humans, were born in sin, we can never repay our debts and redeem ourselves through our own acts; our only salvation lies in God's Mercy, in His supreme sacrifice. In this very gesture of breaking the chain of Justice through the inexplicable act of Mercy, of paying our debts, Christianity imposes on us an even stronger debt: we are forever indebted to Christ, we can never repay him for what he has done for us. The Freudian name for such an excessive pressure which we can never remunerate is, of course, *superego*. (One should not forget that the notion of Mercy is strictly correlative to that of Sovereignty: only the bearer of sovereign power can dispense mercy.)

Accordingly, it is Judaism which is conceived of as the religion of the superego (of man's subordination to the jealous, mighty and severe God), in contrast to the Christian God of Mercy and Love. However, it is precisely through not demanding from us the price for our sins, through paying this price for us Himself, that the Christian God of Mercy establishes itself as the supreme superego agency: 'I paid the highest price for your sins, and you are thus indebted to me forever.' The contours of this God as the superego agency, whose very Mercy generates the indelible guilt of believers, are discernible up to Stalin. One should never forget that, as the (now available) minutes of the meetings of the Politburo and Central Committee from the 1930s demonstrate, Stalin's direct interventions were as a rule those of displaying mercy. When younger CC members, eager to prove their revolutionary fervour, demanded the immediate death penalty for Bukharin, Stalin always intervened and said 'Patience! His guilt is not yet proven!' or something similar. Of course this was a hypocritical attitude – Stalin was well aware that he himself generated the destructive fervour, that the younger members were eager to please him – but, nonetheless, the appearance of mercy is necessary here.

And the same holds for today's capitalism. Referring to Georges Bataille's notion of the 'general economy' of sovereign expenditure, which he opposes to the 'restrained economy' of capitalism's endless profiteering, Peter Sloterdijk provides (in *Zorn und Zeit*) the outlines of capitalism's split from itself, its immanent self-overcoming: capitalism culminates when it 'creates out of itself its own most radical – and the only fruitful – opposite, totally different from what the classic Left, caught in its miserabilism, was able to dream about'.[9] His positive mention of Andrew Carnegie shows the way: the sovereign self-negating gesture of the endless accumulation of wealth is to spend this wealth on things beyond price, and outside market circulation: public good, arts and sciences, health, and so on. This concluding 'sovereign' gesture enables the capitalist to break out of the vicious cycle of endless expanded reproduction, of gaining money in order to earn more money. When he donates his accumulated wealth to the public good, the capitalist negates himself as the mere personification of capital and its reproductive circulation: his life acquires meaning. It is no longer just expanded reproduction as self-goal.

Furthermore, the capitalist thus accomplishes the shift from *eros* to *thymos*, from the perverted 'erotic' logic of accumulation to public recognition and reputation. What this amounts to is nothing less than elevating figures like George Soros or Bill Gates to personifications of the inherent self-negation of the capitalist process itself: their work of charity, their immense donation to public

---

9   Peter Sloterdijk, *Zorn und Zeit*. Frankfurt: Suhrkamp, 2006, p. 55.

welfare, is not just a personal idiosyncrasy, whether sincere or hypocritical; it is the logical concluding point of capitalist circulation, necessary from the strictly economic standpoint, since it allows the capitalist system to postpone its crisis. It re-establishes balance – a kind of redistribution of wealth to the truly needy – without falling into a fateful trap: the destructive logic of resentment and enforced statist redistribution of wealth which can only end in generalized misery. (It also avoids, one might add, the other mode of re-establishing a kind of balance and asserting *thymos* through sovereign expenditure, namely wars.)

This brings to mind a chocolate laxative available in the US, publicized with the paradoxical injunction: 'Do you have constipation? Eat more of this chocolate!' In other words, eat the very thing that causes constipation in order to be cured of it. This structure of a product counteracting its own essence, containing the agent of its own containment, is widely visible in today's ideological landscape. Soros stands for the most ruthless financial speculative exploitation combined with its counter-agent, the humanitarian worry about the catastrophic social consequences of the unbridled market economy. Even his daily routine is marked by a self-eliminating counterpoint: half of his working time is devoted to financial speculation, and the other half to humanitarian activities such as providing funds for cultural and democratic activities in post-Communist countries and writing essays and books, which ultimately combat the effects of his own speculations. The two faces of Gates parallel the two faces of Soros. The cruel businessman destroys or buys out competitors, aims at virtual monopoly, employs all the tricks of the trade to achieve his goals. Meanwhile, the greatest philanthropist in the history of mankind quaintly asks: 'What does it serve to have computers, if people do not have enough to eat and are dying of dysentery?' The ruthless pursuit of profit is counteracted by charity: charity is the humanitarian mask hiding the face of economic exploitation. In a superego-blackmail of gigantic proportions, the developed countries 'help' the undeveloped with aid, credits and so on, and thereby avoid the key issue, namely, their complicity in and co-responsibility for the miserable situation of the undeveloped. This paradox signals a sad predicament of ours: today's capitalism cannot reproduce itself on its own; it needs the extra-economic mercy in order to sustain the cycle of social reproduction.

How, then, does *Clemenza* fit into the series of Mozart's operas? The entire canon of Mozart's great operas can be read as the deployment of the motif of pardon, of dispensing mercy, in all its variations: the higher power intervenes with mercy in *Idomeneo* and *Seraglio*; in *Le nozze di Figaro*, the subjects themselves pardon the Count who refuses mercy, and so on. In order to grasp properly the place of *Clemenza* in this series, one should read it together with *The Magic Flute*, as its mocking shadowy double. If *The Magic Flute* is mercy at its most sublime, *Clemenza* turns this sublimity into a ridiculous excess. The ridiculous proliferation of mercy in *Clemenza* means that power no longer functions in a normal way, so that it has to be sustained by mercy all the time: if the Master has to show mercy, it means that the law has failed, that the legal state machinery is not able to run on its own and needs an incessant intervention from the outside. (One witnessed the same situation in state-socialist regimes: when, in a mythical scene from Soviet hagiography, Stalin takes a walk in the fields, meets a driver there whose tractor has broken down, and helps him to repair it with some wise advice, what this effectively means is that not even a tractor can function normally in state-socialist economic chaos.)

The obverse, the truth, of the continuous celebration of mercy, the wisdom and mercy displayed by Titus, is therefore the fact that Titus as a ruler is a fiasco. Instead of relying on the support of faithful subjects, he ends up surrounded by sick and tormented people condemned to eternal guilt. This sickness is reflected back onto Titus himself. Far from radiating the dignity of the severe but merciful rulers from Mozart's early operas, Titus's acts display features of hysterical self-staging: Titus is playing himself all the time, narcissistically fascinated by the phoney generosity of his own acts. In short, the passage from Bassa Selim in *Seraglio* to Titus in *Clemenza* is the passage from the naïve to the sentimental. And, as is usual with Mozart, this phoniness of Titus's position is rendered by the music itself which, in a supreme display of the much-praised Mozartean irony, effectively undermines the opera's explicit ideological project.

Perhaps, then, the fact that *Clemenza* was composed in the midst of Mozart's work on *The Magic Flute* is more than a meaningless coincidence. *Clemenza*, composed to honour the investiture of the conservative Leopold II after the death of the progressive Joseph II, stages the obscene reactionary political reality that underlies the reinvented fake 'magic' of the universe of *The Magic Flute*. Back in the 1930s, Max Horkheimer wrote that those who do not want to speak (critically) about capitalism should also keep silent about fascism. *Mutatis mutandis*, one should say to those who detract *Clemenza* as a failure in comparison with the eternal magic of *The Magic Flute*: those who do not want to engage critically with *The Magic Flute* should also keep silent about *La clemenza di Tito*.

The fourth choice

Does this mean that, with regard to Mozart, Wagner opened up the path that ends up in later neo-Romantic kitsch – the claim repeated over and over by Adorno? There are signs that point in this direction. When, a couple of years ago, Plácido Domingo accepted the post of Artistic Director of the Los Angeles Opera, he immediately announced his intention to bring it closer to the popular Hollywood film industry (using digitalized, cinematic special effects, and so on). It is little wonder that his first project was to stage a 'Hollywood *Ring*': Wagner's tetralogy cut down from its awesome fourteen hours to a collection of big numbers, ornamented with all the technoglitz. Cultural critics in the Adornian vein were quick to note that this was not simply a vulgar profanation of Wagner's 'high art'.

The cinematic nature of Wagner's *Ring* itself has often been noted. The stage instructions to Act III of *Die Walküre* (Valkyries riding on clouds, and so on), for example, can be followed only on film – even more so, perhaps, in today's digitally manipulated cinema, in the style of *The Lord of the Rings* (no wonder that Tolkien's novel effectively takes its title from Wagner: in *Rheingold*, Alberich is literally designated as 'lord of the ring'), another example of how an old art form can develop notions which call for a new art form that arises out of technological inventions. Wagner's cinematic nature is then used to argue for the kitsch aspect of his music. It is no wonder that a leitmotif-like technique was widely used in classic Hollywood composition. Did Wagner really accomplish the first step towards the kitschy 'fetishization' of music that reaches its apogee in classical Hollywood?

But what if the original sin had already been committed by Beethoven? Undoubtedly his music often verges on kitsch – suffice it to mention the over-repetitive exploitation of the 'beautiful' main motif in the first movement of his Violin Concerto, or the rather tasteless climactic moments of the *Leonore* Overture No. 3. How vulgar are the climactic moments of *Leonore* No. 3 (and No. 2 is even worse, an utterly boring version) in comparison with Mozart's Overture to *The Magic Flute*, where he still retains what one might call a proper sense of musical *decency*, interrupting the melodic line before it reaches the full orchestral climactic repetition by jumping directly to the final staccatos? Can one imagine this overture rewritten in Beethoven's *Leonore No. 3* style, with the bombastic repetition of the melodic line? Perhaps Beethoven himself sensed it, writing another, final, overture – the brief and concise, sharp *Fidelio*, Op. 72c, the very opposite of *Leonore* No. 2 and No. 3. (The true gem, however, is the underestimated *Leonore* No. 1, Op. 138, whose very date is uncertain. It is Beethoven at his best, complete with its beautiful climactic rise, without any embarrassing excess.)

Is Wagner, then, really the kitsch extension of what is worst in Beethoven? No: Wagner's true achievement was precisely to provide *a proper artistic form for what, in Beethoven, functions as kitschy excess*. (This is exemplary in *Rheingold*, the key Wagner opera, the zero-level 'music drama', which clears the slate and thus renders possible the return of 'transubstantiated' operatic elements from Act I of *Die Walküre* onwards, culminating in the *Götterdämmerung* revenge trio.) There is nonetheless a feature which (some of) Wagner's operas share with (some) popular films: the narrative progresses towards the final moment as its big culminating gesture – among films, it suffices to mention Chaplin's *City Lights* and Peter Weir's *Dead Poets' Society*. It is little wonder, then, that one sign of unresolved antagonisms in Wagner's work is the failure of his big finales. Here, a special place belongs to the finale of *Götterdämmerung* – the biggest of them all, the mother of all finales. It is not only, as is well known, that Wagner oscillated between different words in the finale; the final version of the opera in a way even has *two* finales, Siegfried's death and the following *Trauermarsch*, and Brünnhilde's self-immolation.

Finding an appropriate conclusion for the Ring Cycle caused Wagner immense difficulty. His ideas for the end changed several times as his political and philosophical views evolved. The story of these changes is so well known that only a brief summary is necessary. The *Ring*'s trajectory begins with his first written project, 'The Nibelung Myth as Sketch for a Drama' (1848), in which Siegfried and Brünnhilde rise above Siegfried's funeral pyre to Valhalla to cleanse Wotan of his crime and redeem the gods; there is no suggestion that the gods will or ought to suffer annihilation. In a new version written a year later as 'Siegfried's Death', Brünnhilde's final oration also stresses the cleansing effect of Siegfried's death:

> Hear then, you mighty Gods. Your guilt is abolished: the hero takes it upon himself. The Nibelungs' slavery is at an end, and Alberich shall again be free. This Ring I give to you, wise sisters of the watery deeps. Melt it down and keep it free from harm.

In 1851, Wagner developed the story backwards, by adding a vast 'prequel' (consisting of the events staged in *Das Rheingold* and *Die Walküre*) and expanding the role of Wotan, who became the central figure. In the new ending, the gods achieve redemption, but only in their death. Brünnhilde's final speech now reads: 'Fade away in bliss before the deed of Man: the hero you created. I proclaim to you freedom from fear, through blessed redemption in death.' The next version, written a year later, shows the traces of Wagner's passionate debates with Bakunin, as well as his study of Ludwig Feuerbach. Here, the Bakuninian notion of the purifying role of radical destruction (which clears the field for a new beginning) is combined with two basic insights from Feuerbach: gods are merely a product of the human imagination, and among all human acts, sexual love is the greatest. In this 'Feuerbachian' ending, Brünnhilde proclaims the destruction of the gods and their replacement with a human society ruled by love:

> Not goods or gold, nor glittering Gods; Not house, nor hall, not splendid displays; not broken bonds of treacherous treaties, nor arrogant custom's adamant law: blissful in gladness and sorrow – love alone shall endure.

Finally, in 1856, Wagner again rewrote the ending under the influence of his discovery of Schopenhauer and his reading of Buddhist texts. This 'Schopenhauerian' ending, which focuses on resignation vis-à-vis the illusory nature of human existence and on self-overcoming through the negation of the will, found its most concise expression in Brünnhilde's new lines:

> Were I no more to fare to Valhalla's fortress, do you know whither I fare? I depart from the home of desire, I flee forever the home of delusion; the open gates of eternal becoming I close behind me now: To the holiest chosen land, free from desire and delusion, the goal of the world's migration, redeemed from incarnation, the

enlightened woman now goes. The blessed end of all things eternal, do you know how I attained it? Grieving love's profoundest
suffering opened my eyes for me: I saw the world end.

After much deliberation, Wagner nonetheless decided not to
set the Schopenhauer-inspired words to music (although they
appeared in some published versions of the libretto). Why? As a
rule, this omission is interpreted not as a sign of Wagner's abandoning Schopenhauer, but as proof of his artistic sensibility. By
the end of his composition of the *Ring* (in 1874), Wagner realized
that the music itself, not the words, should deliver the final message
of the cycle. Is this, however, really the case?[10] Does this standard
reading not rely on a rather primitive aesthetic rule (that the work's
message should not be stated explicitly, but arise 'organically' out of
the depicted content)?

Let us recapitulate the problem again. As far as its ideological content is concerned, the ending of *Götterdämmerung* oscil-
lates between three main positions best designated by the names
Feuerbach, Bakunin and Schopenhauer: the reign of human love;
the revolutionary destruction of the old world; resignation and
withdrawal from the world. Because of these oscillations, it is not
clear how we are to conceive of the crowd of men and women who,
'in deepest emotion', bear witness to the final destruction in fire
and water – who are they? Do they really embody a new, liberated society? The change from early revolutionary to 'mature'
Schopenhauerian Wagner is usually conceived as a shift from
humanistic belief in the possibility of the revolutionary transformation of existing social reality – in other words, from the belief that
our reality is miserable due to contingent historical reasons – to the
more 'profound' insight into how reality *as such* is miserable, and
that the only true redemption resides in withdrawing from it into

---

10   See Philip Kitcher and Richard Schacht, *Finding an Ending. Reflections on
Wagner's* Ring. Oxford: Oxford University Press, 2004.

the abyss of the 'night of the world'. It seems easy to denounce this shift as the most elementary ideological operation, that of elevating a contingent historical obstacle into an a priori transcendental limitation. So, again, is the Schopenhauer ending really the ending we get in the opera? What Alain Badiou says about Wagner holds here especially: one should not take his general programmatic proclamations at face value; rather, one should make the effort of testing them against a detailed analysis of what Wagner is actually doing.

It is a well-known fact that, in the last minutes of *Götterdämmerung*, the orchestra performs an excessively intricate cobweb of motifs, basically nothing less than the recapitulation of the motivic wealth of the entire *Ring*. Is this fact not the ultimate proof that Wagner himself was not sure about what the final apotheosis of the *Ring* 'means'? Not being sure of it, he took a kind of 'flight forward' and threw together *all* of the motifs – the ultimate musical smorgasbord, as it were. This rather vicious hypothesis was proposed by Adorno (in his *In Search of Wagner*) as well as some other critics: Wagner did not know how to end the cycle, so he merely spun together a few obvious motifs; Adorno added that the final bars of the *Ring* (the 'redemption through love' motif) were used simply because they were the most beautiful sounding – beautiful in the sense of kitsch, not of authentic artistic beauty, since, as George Bernard Shaw noted with derision apropos this motif, 'the gushing effect which is its sole valuable quality is so cheaply attained that it is hardly going too far to call it the most trumpery phrase in the entire tetralogy.'

One is effectively tempted to paraphrase the ending with this beautiful motif as something like the sentimental wisdom: 'What does it matter if all of this is a mess – the important thing is that we love each other!' So the culminating motif of 'redemption through love' (a beautiful and passionate melodic line which previously appears only in Act III of *Die Walküre*) cannot but make us think of Joseph Kerman's acerbic comment about the last

notes of Puccini's *Tosca* in which the orchestra bombastically recapitulates the 'beautiful' pathetic melodic line of the Cavaradossi's
'E lucevan le stelle', as if, unsure of what to do, Puccini simply
desperately repeated the most 'effective' melody from the previous score, ignoring all narrative or emotional logic.[11] And what if
Wagner did exactly the same thing at the end of *Götterdämmerung*?
Not sure about the final twist that should stabilize and guarantee
the meaning of it all, he resorted to a beautiful melody whose effect
is something like 'whatever any of this may mean, let us make sure
that the concluding impression will be that of something triumphant and uplifting in its redemptive beauty . . .' In short, what if
this final motif enacts an *empty gesture*?

However, in the very last seconds of *Götterdämmerung* it is
not only that out of all the chaos of destruction we still hear the
'redemption through love' motif: three additional, subordinate
motifs are heard, that of the Rhine Maidens, celebrating the innocent playfulness of the natural world; that of Valhalla, rendering
the dignified majesty of the rule of law; and that of Siegfried, the
free hero. 'These themes are preceded by the soaring melody of
Sieglinde's expression of wonder, and they lead back to it, as in the
very last measures of the orchestral score that melody is extended
to a new resolution, a final triumph a final peace.'[12] Do these final
moments not imply a subjective position that, as Badiou suggests,
is paradigmatically feminine, as the three motifs are coloured –
transfigured – by the fourth, by love? Sublime as they are, even
the most intense natural beauty, the rule of law and the most heroic
acts are finally doomed to fail: 'Yet the possibility of a love like
that expressed in Brünnhilde's final act changes everything, in a
way that heroism does not, even in the face of death and the ending
of the world as we know it.'[13]

---

11   Joseph Kerman, *Opera as Drama*. Berkeley: University of California Press,
1988.
12   Kitcher and Schacht, *Finding an Ending*, p. 199.
13   Ibid., p. 201.

Is this ending of the *Ring* not also unique with regard to Wagner's other (six great post-*Rienzi*) operas? They all focus on the dead-lock of a sexual relationship, clearly repeating the Kierkegaardian triad of the aesthetic, the ethical and the religious. In the refusal to compromise desire (even to the point of embracing death), *Tristan* represents the first. *Meistersinger* counters it with the ethical solu-tion: true redemption resides not in following the immortal passion to its self-destructive conclusion; rather, one should learn to over-come it via creative sublimation and to return, in a mood of wise resignation, to the 'daily' life of symbolic obligations. In *Parsifal*, finally, the passion can no longer be overcome via its reintegration into society in which it survives in a gentrified form: one has to deny it thoroughly in the ecstatic assertion of religious *jouissance*. The triad *Tristan–Meistersinger–Parsifal* thus follows a precise logic: *Meistersinger* and *Tristan* render two opposite versions of the Oedipal matrix, within which *Meistersinger* inverts *Tristan* (the son steals the woman from the paternal figure; passion breaks out between the paternal figure and the young woman destined to become the partner of the young man), while *Parsifal* gives the coordinates themselves an anti-Oedipal twist – the lamenting wounded subject is here the paternal figure (Amfortas), not the young transgressor (Tristan). (The closest one comes to lament in *Meistersinger* is Sachs's 'Wahn, wahn!' song from Act III.)

One can argue that this triad repeats the triad *The Flying Dutchman–Tannhäuser–Lohengrin*: *The Flying Dutchman* ends in the deadly apotheosis of the love couple; *Tannhäuser*, like the later *Meistersinger*, focuses on a singing competition, which, following Marx's famous paraphrase of Hegel, occurs first as tragedy and then repeats itself as comedy; Lohengrin is the son of Parsifal. Each time we get the same basic answers to the fate of a love rela-tionship: the obscure sexual death drive, marriage, and asexual compassion. The *Ring*, however, stands out as the exception, with an additional fourth instantiation of fate, as a solution to the dead-lock, in the guise of Brünnhilde's act.

The first thing to point out is that Brünnhilde's final act is precisely that: an act, a gesture of supreme freedom and autonomy, not just resigned acquiescence to some higher power. This fact in itself, this *form* of act, makes it totally foreign to Schopenhauer's thought: 'She acts; and her act is . . . a many-sided embodiment of her many-sided love . . . she does not simply see the world end; she ends it. She also vindicates it, illuminating it anew and offering the possibility of renewal.' [14] How does she achieve this?

What did Brünnhilde know?

To answer this question, one must locate Brünnhilde's act in the totality of the *Ring*, the narrative of which should be read as a series of attempts to find the form of meaningful life. The *Ring*'s philosophy, embodied in the plot and music, is to be taken seriously, for it reaches far beyond Wagner's explicitly formulated philosophy. Therein resides Philip Kitcher and Richard Schacht's thesis: the *Ring* enacts a series of (failures of) what one might call existential projects.

   Wotan's first choice is, to put it in Kierkegaardese, the leap from the aesthetic to the ethical, or, the rule of law imposed on innocent nature. From Valhalla, he will rule the world, bringing peace and justice to it. The attempt fails because of the compromises he must allow, compromises that are more complex than they first appear. They concern not only the well-known topic of illegitimate violence that grounds the rule of law and not only the notion that the rule of law disturbs the innocence of spontaneous natural life. Furthermore, a crucial part of Wotan's tragedy is that 'he has abandoned love in the service of law; another is that along the way to the end of *Die Walküre*, he relinquishes everything that is most precious to him'.[15] The structure here is clearly the one described

---

14   Ibid., pp. 182–4.
15   Ibid., pp. 138–9.

by Lacan as *die Versagung* (denial): after sacrificing everything for the one thing that really matters to him, Wotan discovers that he has thereby lost precisely this thing. This 'everything most precious to him' is embodied in Brünnhilde, his preferred daughter, and his not only political but also ethical breakdown is rendered in the long monologue in front of her in Act II.

In the *Ring*, the source of all evil is not Alberich's fatal choice in the first scene of *Rheingold*: long before this event took place, Wotan broke the natural balance, succumbing to the lure of power, giving preference to power over love. He tore out and destroyed the World-Tree, making out of it his spear, on which he inscribed the runes fixing the laws of his rule, plus he plucked out one of his eyes in order to gain insight into inner truth. Evil thus does not come from the Outside: the insight of Wotan's tragic 'Monologue with Brünnhilde' in Act II of *Die Walküre* is that the power of Alberich and the prospect of the 'end of the world' is ultimately Wotan's own guilt, the result of his ethical fiasco – in Hegelese, external opposition is the effect of inner contradiction. No wonder, then, that Wotan is called the 'White Alb' in contrast to the 'Black Alb' Alberich – if anything, Wotan's choice was ethically worse than Alberich's: Alberich longed for love and only turned towards power after being brutally mocked and turned down by the Rhine Maidens, while Wotan turned to power after fully enjoying the fruits of love and getting tired of them. After his moral fiasco in *Die Walküre*, Wotan turns into 'The Wanderer', a figure of the Wandering Jew already like the first great Wagnerian hero, the Flying Dutchman, that 'Ahasver des Ozeans'.

In order to attain the truth of the story known to us, it often helps to imagine a different direction the story might have taken: it is through such an extraneation effect that we learn to appreciate the contingent and artificial nature of what took place. What about an Antigone who convinces Creon to allow Polynices' burial, thereby (as Creon feared) triggering a new civil war which leads to the destruction of Thebes? What about a Hamlet

who kills Claudius on time, takes over the throne and establishes
a paranoiac dictatorship, involved in a Nero-like pathological
relationship with his mother? Many of Wagner's operas seem
to call for such a mental experiment. What about a *Lohengrin*
in which Elsa succeeds in restraining herself and doesn't ask the
prohibited question, so that the couple lives happily together,
with Lohengrin getting more and more bored by the stifling
marriage? What about a *Tristan* with a *Postman Always Rings
Twice* twist, in which the couple kill Marke in Tristan's Cornwall
castle, then present Marke's death as an accident, marry and rule
together? As for *Parsifal*, we will come back to it later. But the
royal case here would be that of the *Ring*: what if, in Act II of
Die Walküre, Brünnhilde successfully disobeys Wotan, so that
Siegmund kills Hunding? Wotan, who arrives too late, curses her
and arranges that she will have to marry the child of Siegmund
and Sieglinde; furthermore, to make sure that things will end in
a catastrophe, he sleeps with Hagen's mother and breeds Hagen,
the future murderer of Siegfried . . . There is a speculative truth
in this version: the explicitly posited identity between Wotan and
Alberich, the 'white Alb' and the 'black Alb'.

From this point on, Wotan is a broken man and all of his future
solutions will be vain, illusory hopes. The first of these is hinted at
in the very end of *Die Walküre*, where Wotan gets his second idea
– a heroic, innocent act (perhaps replacing mythical violence with
divine violence?). He puts his hopes in an innocent hero outside the
scope of law who can do what is prohibited him as the bearer of the
rule of law. However, he soon sees that his project is condemned
to fail, so he reformulates the problem. Accepting his final failure
and death, Wotan posits himself the task of *finding the right ending*,
of disappearing with honour and dignity. The negative prospect
Wotan tries to avoid is the end of his reign, after which evil plot-
ters like Hagen and Alberich will take over. (The nice touch here
is the underlying solidarity of Fricka and Hagen: the strict rule of
law and brutal, violent manipulation.)

The next existential project is that of Siegmund and Sieglinde, the only truly authentic romantic couple in the entire *Ring*. Although Siegmund is a heroic loner, an outcast helping other people in distress, he fully finds himself in his love for Sieglinde: for the two of them, their incestuous love is all that matters, eclipsing all other considerations. (Compared to their love, Siegfried and Brünnhilde's love is a ridiculous mismatch.) 'If all else perished, and he remained, I should still continue to be; and if all else remained, and he were annihilated, the universe would turn to a mighty stranger: I should not seem a part of it.' This is how, in *Wuthering Heights*, Cathy characterizes her relation to Heathcliff – and provides a succinct ontological definition of the unconditional erotic love which unites Siegmund and Sieglinde. When, on behalf of Wotan, Brünnhilde brings Siegmund the news that he will die in the forthcoming duel with Hunding and paints for him the future bliss of dwelling in Valhalla among the dead heroes and gods, he rejects the company of the gods and prefers to stay a common mortal if his beloved Sieglinde cannot follow him to Valhalla. Devastated, Brünnhilde responds to his refusal: 'So little do you value everlasting bliss? Is she everything to you, this poor woman who, tired and sorrowful, lies limp in your lap? Do you think nothing less glorious?' Ernst Bloch was right to remark that what is lacking in German history are more gestures like Siegmund's. This is the most sacred moment of love. Wagner renders it in music of almost religious solemnity, with a simple, prayer-like rhythm. No wonder Siegmund's determination and vehemence totally shatter Brünnhilde, who decides to break her father's explicit order by helping Siegmund win the duel. One can argue that the failure of Siegmund and Sieglinde is due not only to external circumstances. In other words, such intense, unconditional love can only explode as a miraculous event; it cannot last, it cannot form a new order of things.

It is only at this point, with the birth of Siegfried, Siegmund's and Sieglinde's son, that Wotan's project of the innocent hero who knows no fear and guilt, who is bound by no laws, is unexpectedly (even for Wotan) realized. Here, however, the real trouble

begins: if anything is clear in the last two operas of the *Ring*, it
is that, although he has some sympathetic features (courage,
naïvety), Siegfried is basically a brutal and insensitive thug, one
who is obviously lacking in basic intelligence and wisdom. His
naïve, brutal force makes him an easy victim of schemers who,
one after another, exploit him for their own purposes. Evidence
abounds: his brutality towards Mime, his breathtaking naïvety at
the first sight of Brünnhilde, the ease with which he falls prey to
Hagen's schemes, and the stupidity in his encounter with the Rhine
Maidens just prior to his death. (The love potion served to him by
Gutrune, which makes him forget Brünnhilde, has to be read the
same way as the love potion in *Tristan*. It makes Siegfried drop all
false pretences and act as his naked, true self.)

There is effectively in Wagner's *Siegfried* an unconstrained
'innocent' aggressiveness, an urge to pass directly to the act and
just squash whatever gets on your nerves, as in Siegfried's words
to Mime in Act I of *Siegfried*: 'when I watch you standing, / shuffling and shambling, / servilely stooping, squinting and blinking,
/ I long to seize you by your nodding neck / and make an end
of your obscene blinking!' The sound of the original German is
even more impressive here.[16] The same outburst is repeated twice
in Act II: 'That shuffling and slinking, / those eyelids blinking – /
how long must I / endure the sight? / When shall I be rid of this
fool?', and, just a little bit later: 'Shuffling and slinking, / griz-
zled and gray, / small and crooked, / limping and hunchbacked,
/ with ears that are drooping, eyes that are bleary . . . / Off with
the imp! I hope he's gone for good!' Is this not the most elementary
disgust, repulsion felt by the ego when confronted with the intruding foreign body? One can easily imagine a neo-Nazi skinhead
uttering just the same words in the face of a worn-out Turkish
Gastarbeiter . . .

---

16 'Seh'ich dich stehn, gangeln und gehn, / knicken und nicken, / mit den
Augen zwicken, / beim Genick moecht'ich den Nicker packen, / den Garaus
geben dem garst'gen Zwicker!'

The final scene of Act I of *Götterdämmerung* is an interlude of shocking brutality, possessing a ghost-like, nightmarish quality. When Siegfried approaches Brünnhilde, she extends her arm, trying to use the ring to ward off her assailant. Siegfried tears the ring from her finger. (This gesture has to be read as the repetition of the first extremely violent theft of the ring in scene 4 of *Rheingold*, when Wotan tears the ring off Alberich's hand.) As Brünnhilde collapses, she looks up, momentarily meeting his gaze. He announces his triumph, ordering her into the sleeping cave; before following her in for the bridal night, he pledges that he will keep faith with Gunther by placing his sword, Nothung, between them. The horror of this scene is that it shows Siegfried's brutality naked, in its raw state: it somehow 'de-psychologizes' Siegfried, making him visible as an inhuman monster, the way he 'really is', deprived of his deceiving mask – this is the effect of the potion on him.   There is a mystery here. To put it bluntly, after Siegfried drags Brünnhilde to the cave, does he rape her? Do they make love, or not? Siegfried himself is inconsistent with regard to this point: he claims to have consummated the marriage disguised as Gunther, in 'a complete nuptial night', *and* that he did not dishonour Gunther. When, in Act II, scene 4, Brünnhilde accuses Siegfried in front of the gathered crowd of having done so, he proclaims his willingness to swear an oath. Hagen holds out the point of his spear, on which Siegfried swears that he has been true. Brünnhilde snatches his hand from the spear's point and responds with her own heated avowal that Siegfried has foresworn himself. In the confusion that follows, Siegfried dispels the tension by resorting to male chauvinist wisdom; he urges Gunther to calm his wife.[17] It is only in facing

---

17   What makes this scene additionally interesting is one of the big inconsistencies of the *Ring*: why does Siegfried, after brutally subduing Brünnhilde, put his sword between the two of them (as if to prove that they will not have sex) since he is just doing a service to his friend, the weak king Gunther? To whom does he have to prove this? Is Brünnhilde not supposed to think that he is Gunther?

death that Siegfried matures, gaining elementary insight into what was going on before. In this sense, Siegfried is the true counterpart to Hagen: it is as if the pair, Siegfried and Hagen, mirror their fathers, Wotan and Alberich – the 'white' and 'dark' dwarves. This is why Brünnhilde and Siegfried are a failed couple.

And this is also why the finale of *Siegfried*, the erotic, ecstatic reunion of Brünnhilde and Siegfried, falls strangely flat when one compares it with the ecstatic finale of Act I of *Die Walküre*. In the final scene, Brünnhilde's love for Siegfried is 'transfigured into the new nobility she attains and of which she becomes the apotheosis'.[18] At the beginning of Act III, Brünnhilde refuses Waltraute's plea to return the ring to the Rhine Maidens. The ring stands for the love of Brünnhilde and Siegfried and giving it away would have meant betraying this love. Yet, once Siegfried is dead, she can declare her love anew, offering herself as a token. Sacrifice is thus subjectivized, reflected unto itself. Brünnhilde not only sacrifices the ring, the token of her love, but she sacrifices herself as an object. By sacrificing herself, she provides a kind of resolution to Wotan's problem after all.

Everything from the formal success of the *Ring* as a work of art to its deepest insight as philosophical meditation thus hinges on this point. Is Brünnhilde's final act really an act in the authentic sense, or does it remain an empty, suicidal *passage à l'acte*, bearing witness to an insoluble deadlock? (Or can it be both?) If the *Götterdämmerung* ending fails, it opens up the way for *Parsifal*, with the latter's psychotic rejection of sexual love (instead of its sublimation-transfiguration in *Götterdämmerung*). Everything therefore hinges on this question: does Brünnhilde's act succeed in resolving the tension generated by the impossibility of sexual relationship? (If this is the case, then *Parsifal* is a regression.) Here, one should oppose Wagner's musical work (which varies motifs of the failure of sexual relationship) to his own ideology – the

---

18   Kitcher and Schacht, op. cit., p. 176.

ideology of the sexual relationship, of sexual love as the ultimate reference point that provides meaning in human life. His operas provide new and newer versions of how 'love doesn't work'. The ultimate Wagnerian fantasy, the romantic couple's triumphant self-annihilation in the *Liebestod*, *never* takes place; in *Tristan* and *Götterdämmerung*, the couple does *not* die together. In both cases, the male partner first dies a traumatic, painful death, and the heroine follows him alone in ecstatic self-annihilation.

How are we to discern the underlying libidinal economy of the great self-sacrificial deaths of the Wagnerian heroines? In his perspicuous text 'Why Elsa Asks From Whence He Came: An Epistemological Analysis of Richard Wagner's *Lohengrin*', Steffen Huck[19] provides an original and convincing answer to the enigma announced in the title. (Why does Elsa break down and ask her nameless husband who he is, although she knows the catastrophic consequences of this act?) Dismissing the standard repertoire (feminine possessive curiosity and envy, etc.), Huck mobilizes the distinction between first-order and second-order beliefs: what the subject believes about the world and especially the other subject (can I ever truly know the abyss of another person, can I ever fully trust him or her?), and what the subject believes about other people's beliefs:

> While [Elsa] knows that she is innocent and Lohengrin knows that she is innocent, Elsa cannot – once she entertains the possibility of Lohengrin being a wizard – know that he knows that she is innocent. She knows that he was willing to fight for her but [. . .] there are two possible reasons for why one would: absolute knowledge of her innocence, or doubts about God combined with a superior belief in one's fighting prowess. [. . .] She has no way of telling which of these two possibilities is true. (Except, of

---

19   Unpublished, November 2008. The article may be accessed online at http://else.econ.ucl.ac.uk/papers/uploaded/318.pdf.

course, by listening to Wagner's music that leaves no doubt about Lohengrin's holy nature. This raises the interesting question whether orchestral music in opera is thought to be heard by the opera's characters or only benefits the audience.)

The answer to the question in parentheses is clear: the (psycho)-logical presupposition of opera (Wagner's, at least) is that the orchestral music is supposed *not* to be heard by the opera's charac-ters: it renders the truth they ignore, the blindness which sustains their actions. (A further speculation would have been that there are exceptional moments when the characters *do* hear it – like the 'Grail narrative' from *Lohengrin's* finale which clarifies things to everyone involved.) This, then, is why she cannot resist asking the fatal question – the meta-belief in the question is not just the belief about any belief of the beloved other, but his belief about myself.

One should go an extra step here: doesn't Lohengrin's prohibi-tion on asking the question cast a similar dark shadow on his char-acter? Since, on account of his divine status, he possesses 'absolute knowledge', he certainly also knows what kind of temptation he is exposing Elsa to by his prohibition. What kind of man is he to do such a thing, to consciously propel the woman he marries towards her destruction? Why does the prohibition matter more to him than his love for Elsa?

One might even wonder: is Elsa's predicament not even *more* tragic than it appears? That is to say, isn't it that, whatever answer she gets (Lohengrin is a divine hero who knew about her inno-cence; Lohengrin is just an ordinary guy using some magic), the outcome is catastrophic? Wouldn't it be much more satisfying for Elsa to learn that Lohengrin is an ordinary knight who didn't know the truth, but just trusted Elsa out of love? In this way, his love for her would have been much more authentic.

Read in this way, the question Elsa is prohibited from asking is hysteria at its purest: it is not really 'tell me who are you', but 'tell me who I really am' – which gives rise to another disturbing possibility: what if, even if Elsa is not guilty of the crime she was accused of, her desire *was* involved in the young prince's murder? This brings us to the unexpected conclusion that, of the opera's four main characters, the gullible Telramund is the only atheist and, simultaneously, the only honest man, merely manipulated by Ortrud who, no less than Elsa and Lohengrin, pursues her dark, disavowed goals.

Elsa is, as such, a compromise figure: in contrast to the great 'radical' feminine figures, from Senta through Isolde to Brünnhilde, she lacks the strength to resolve her hysterical tension through the self-sacrificial *passage à l'acte*. Let us explain this apropos *The Flying Dutchman*. The best way to approach Wagner is to start with his 'first' two operas: *The Flying Dutchman* as the first opera where Wagner 'found his own voice' (the highpoint of his earlier work, *Rienzi*, is often referred to – with a fully appropriate irony – as 'Meyerbeer's best opera'), and *Rheingold* as the first music drama, as the first and only work which fully follows the precepts of the music drama (no free melodic improvisations, the music closely follows the drama, and so on).

What we get in *The Flying Dutchman* is something different: the all too direct staging of Wagner's 'fundamental fantasy' (of the woman who sacrifices herself in order to redeem the hero condemned to a painful eternal life and thus enabling him to die in peace) with an embarrassing directness, bordering on obscene kitsch. The operatic equivalent to such an obscene display is, surprisingly, Tchaikovsky's *Eugene Onegin*, whose 'biggest hit', Gremin's aria, is the last of the three *eros energumenos*, cases of a person 'possessed (energized) by *eros*' and exploding in a display of erotic passion. First, there is Tatyana's love-letter scene. At the very beginning of *Onegin*, in the brief orchestral prelude, the short melodic motif ('Tatyana's theme') is not properly developed, but merely repeated in different modes, fully retaining its isolated character of a melodic fragment, not even a full melodic line. There is a genuine melancholic flavour in such a repetition which registers and displays the underlying impotence, the failure of proper development. It is significant that this theme gets properly developed into a kind of organic texture only in the letter scene, in this utopian explosion of Tatyana's desire, a kind of Tchaikovsky equivalent to the Ballad of Senta in *The Flying Dutchman* (another opera which grew out of this central song, and which is also about the heroine immediately recognizing the hero since the Dutchman also 'as yet unseen, [. . .] was already dear to her').

No wonder that Onegin withdraws from Tatyana's embarrassingly open display of erotic passion. There is a dimension of the act in Tatyana's effectively sending her letter to Onegin: she takes the risk and exposes herself in all her vulnerability, which will be injured if Onegin rejects her or if he uses her for a quick affair. This act stands in contrast to the standard melodramatic gesture of a woman who writes a letter to her lover (containing some sensitive and painful message), but then, in the midst of writing it, throws it away and goes to her lover herself, offering herself, the lure of her, to obfuscate the message of the undelivered letter. Tatyana sends the letter instead of offering herself directly, thus avoiding the catastrophe of a scandal – or does she? Gremin's aria shares with the letter scene this dimension of the embarrassing, almost indecent, public display of passion: 'Onegin, I do not know how to disguise the fact: I love Tatyana mindlessly.' One should note here the irony: Tatyana doesn't love Gremin – but does he know this? If yes, is then his love for her a true love? Is not their marriage part of the very superficial/formal society he claims to despise?

Senta's Ballad opens with a weird, darkly obscene vocal rendition of the Dutchman's motif ('Yohohoe! Yohohohoe! Yohohoe! Yohoe!'), and then presents his situation of the undead spectre condemned to wandering on the oceans without aim and rest. What quite logically follows this description is a hint at the possible solution – there is a chance of redemption for the Dutchman. In a typical well-calculated dramaturgy, it is only now, in the third moment, that the Dutchman's curse is explained, that we learn what caused it. A detail to be noticed here is that Wagner's Dutchman is not punished for cursing God or killing his wife, wrongly accusing her of infidelity (as in the traditional Dutchman legend), but for displaying the undead drive, the readiness to pursue his goal for eternity, never compromising it. The punishment thus fits the crime: Satan, who has heard his vow, merely takes him at his word. In the next step, the precise conditions of his redemption are described: every seven years, he can go ashore and search for a faithful wife ready to sacrifice herself for him, but till now he has always been betrayed. Now comes the masterful dramatic climax: the girls around Senta ask the obvious question: who will redeem the poor Dutchman? Senta's answer is an unexpectedly violent subjectivization: changing the entire tonality of her ballad, she throws herself into her own myth and offers herself as the redemptrix. Mary, the old maid who watches the girls, and the girls themselves, of course, react with shock and awe at this obscene blasphemy.

Here already, we encounter a typical Wagnerian procedure often used in his later work: in the midst of the chorus's outcry, Eric, Senta's frustrated lover, enters; the explosive tension of Senta's immersion into a suicidal *éxtasis* is stopped in a kind of musical equivalent to coitus interruptus (which happens, among other places, in Act II of *Tristan*, where the return of King Marke brutally interrupts the lovers' blissful immersion into the deathlust). But even more crucial would have been to link this libidinal tension to the tension between the two modes of collectivity which dominate Act III of *The Flying Dutchman*: The 'normal' popular chorus of the Norwegian sailors is overcome by the obscene chorus of the living-dead Dutchman's sailors; the Norwegians try to resist, gathering strength, but are in the end totally overwhelmed. The structure here is that of the reply of the Real: the feasting Norwegian sailors and girls provoke the silent ship . . . and get more than they were bargaining for. In Wagner's work, choruses are as a rule the element of re-normalization of the excessive outburst of the undead/deadly drive. The only other exception is the chorus of the Gibichung warriors which accompanies Hagen's terrifyingly violent *Maenner-Ruf* in Act II of *Götterdämmerung*.

There is, however, a key difference between *Tristan* (in which we find the ultimate case of the feminine sacrificial death) and *Götterdämmerung*. It can be convincingly demonstrated that Isolde's final appearance and ecstatic death in *Tristan* is the hallucination of the dying Tristan, so that the entirety of Act III, inclusive of the ending, is Tristan's monologue.

The shift from the love duet in Act II to Tristan's monologue in Act III is thus the shift from passion to Passion: from romantic passion to Christian Passion. According to Thomas May:

> A touching moment – one of the opera's most indelible – occurs in Tristan's panic over seeing Isolde still in the clutch of light and day. It marks a transformation. Tristan has evolved from his erotic idea of love to a capacity for disinterested, spiritual love. Like a bodhisattva – a saint who returns to lead the still unenlightened to peace – Tristan's compassion compels him to return from his state of enlightenment and seek out Isolde, who has remained behind.[20]

Is this, however, really the case? Is it not, rather, that far from returning to Isolde like a compassionate bodhisattva, Tristan desperately jumps towards her, *unable to die (and find peace) without her?* When May claims that, in her final song, Isolde herself 'undergoes a remarkable transformation that far more serenely recapitulates what Tristan achieved in his tortured visions',[21] one should discern in that transformation Tristan's own fantasy. In contrast to *Tristan*, in *Götterdämmerung*, Brünnhilde's self-immolation is fully her own act, not the acting-out of another's fantasy.

---

20 Thomas May, *Decoding Wagner*. Milwaukee, WI: Amadeus Press, 2004, p. 77.
21 Ibid., p. 78.

Brünnhilde's final lines are reminiscent of Isolde's death, in that Brünnhilde dies alone (Siegfried, like Tristan, dies first). But there is a key difference here. Her death is not only ecstatic self-annihilation but *also* the purification of sin through fire (involving the destruction of Valhalla and its gods). The only 'fully realized' sexual relationship in the entire *Ring* is the incestuous link between Siegmund and Sieglinde – all other amorous links are fake or go terribly awry. Take Siegfried and his *tante*, Brünnhilde (Wotan, her father, is also his grandfather): the time gap between *Siegfried* and *Götterdämmerung* can be considered a time of sexual bliss, a time when, off-screen, intense lovemaking goes on all night. However, an undeniable hollowness pertains to the triumphant duet which concludes *Siegfried*. Siegfried and Brünnhilde's romantic passion is clearly contrived, a pale shadow of the intensity of Siegmund and Sieglinde's passionate embrace at the end of Act I of *Die Walküre*. And, magnificent as it is, the great awakening of the couple in scene 2 of the prelude to *Götterdämmerung* is the beginning of the road to gradual disintegration. However, this ultimate 'journey with my aunt' enables Brünnhilde to gain the highest knowledge; the outcome of the last events is 'that a woman becomes knowing'. Here, one should not be afraid to ask a simple and direct question: *what*, exactly, does she come to know? The lines in which she is defined as 'knowing' give a very precise explanation: 'the purest had to betray me, so that a woman became knowing!'[22] It is this betrayal that makes her all-knowing: 'All things, all things, all I know now; all to me is revealed.' In what precise way did Siegfried's betrayal make her knowing?

The answer is provided by the so-called motif of renunciation, arguably the most important leitmotif in the entire tetralogy. In interpreting Wagner's motifs, one should always bear in mind

---

22 One should note how the quoted lines refer to the conclusion of *Parsifal*: 'The power of the purest knowledge, given to a feeble fool.' Whatever Brünnhilde is, she is decidedly not a feeble fool like Parsifal; the only true fool in the *Ring*, although not a feeble one, is Siegfried.

their pre-semantic status. Already at the non-musical level, many of them return from one work to another: the hand of the dead man rises up in *Götterdämmerung* (Siegfried's hand) and in *Parsifal* (Titurel's hand); a love potion triggers a deadly passionate attachment in *Götterdämmerung* (Siegfried falls in love with Gudrune) and in *Tristan* (Tristan and Isolde fall in love). Although the parallel reading of such repetitions is crucial for the proper interpretation of Wagner, it should categorically not be done in the Jungian mode; these motifs are not Jungian 'archetypes', they do not always render the same deeper meaning. The different appearances of the same motif should rather be related to each other in the Lévi-Straussian mode, so that meaning (specific in each occurrence) resides in the difference from another occurrence. In other words, one should not look directly for the 'meaning' of a motif, but discern the semantic structure of oppositions which underlies its different appearances. The love triggered by the potion in *Tristan* is the authentic deadly attachment which was already 'in the air' before the potion was drunk (in Hegelese, the potion only changed its status from In-itself to For-itself), while the love triggered by the potion in *Götterdämmerung* is based on the repression of Siegfried's true authentic attachment (to Brünnhilde) – the first potion sets in motion full remembrance; the second potion, repression/forgetting. Similarly, when the dead Siegfried raises his hand, it is a warning against Hagen who wants to tear the ring from it, while Titurel raises his hand to reassert his persistent obscene superego pressure: the first gesture is a warning against a possessive claim, the second, the nightmarish reassertion of such a claim.

The motif of renunciation is first heard in scene 1 of *Rheingold*. In response to Alberich's query, Woglinde discloses that 'only the one who renounces the power of love' can possess the gold. Its next most noticeable appearance occurs towards the end of Act I of *Die Walküre*, at the moment of the most triumphant assertion of love between Sieglinde and Siegmund, just prior to when he pulls the sword from the tree. Siegmund sings it to the words: 'holiest love's highest need'. How are we to read these two occurrences together? What if one treats them as two fragments of the complete sentence that was distorted by 'dreamwork', that is, rendered unreadable by being split into two? The solution is thus to reconstitute the complete proposition: 'Love's highest need is to renounce its own power.' This is what Lacan calls 'symbolic castration': if one is to remain faithful to one's love, one should not elevate it into the direct focus of one's love, one should renounce its centrality.

Perhaps, a detour through the best (or worst) of Hollywood melodrama can help us to clarify this point. The basic lesson of *Rhapsody*, King Vidor's neglected masterpiece, is that, in order to gain the beloved woman's love, the man has to prove that he is able to survive without her, that he prefers his mission or profession to her. There are two immediate choices: (1) my professional career is what matters most to me, the woman is just an amusement, a distracting affair; (2) the woman is everything to me, I am ready to humiliate myself, to forsake all my public and professional dignity for her. They are both false, they both lead to the man being rejected by the woman. The message of true love is thus: even if you are everything to me, I can survive without you, I am ready to forsake you for my mission or profession. The proper way for the woman to test the man's love is thus to 'betray' him at the crucial moment of his career (the first public concert in the film, the key exam, the business negotiation which will decide his career). Only if he can survive the ordeal and accomplish his task successfully, although deeply traumatized by her desertion, will he deserve her and will she return to him. The underlying paradox is that love, precisely as the Absolute, should not be posited as a direct goal; it should retain the status of a by-product, of something we get as an undeserved grace. The point is not that 'there are more important things than love': an authentic amorous encounter remains a kind of absolute point of reference of one's life (to put it in traditional terms, it is 'what makes one's life meaningful'). The hard lesson

Brünnhilde learns is that, precisely as such, love (the amorous relationship) should not be the direct goal of one's life. Rather, if one confronts the choice between love and duty, the latter should prevail.

True love is modest, like that of the couples in Marguerite Duras's novels. While the two lovers hold hands, they do not look into each other's eyes. They look together outwards, to some third point, towards their common Cause. Perhaps there is no greater love than that of a revolutionary couple, where each of the two lovers is ready to abandon the other at any moment if revolution demands it. They do not love each other less than the amorous couple bent on suspending all their terrestrial attachments and obligations in order to burn out in the Night of unconditional passion; if anything, they love each other more. The finale of *Götterdämmerung* is thus Wagner's critical rejection of the three options staged in his three non-*Ring* late operas: the suicidal abyss of *Tristan*, the resigned acceptance of marriage of *Meistersinger*, the psychotic rejection of love in *Parsifal*. True love arises only when one accepts the failure of the intense sexual relationship posited as the direct focus of the lovers' lives, when we return from this abyss to the hard work of our daily lives. It is only against the background of this failure that a love appears which says yes to all passing, but no less sublime, human achievements.

Christ with Wagner

What, then, does Wagner do with Christianity? A reference to his draft of the play *Jesus of Nazareth*, written somewhere between late 1848 and early 1849, will help us to answer this question. Together with the libretto *The Saracen Woman (Die Sarazenin*, written in 1843 between *The Flying Dutchman* and *Tannhäuser*), these two drafts are key elements in Wagner's development: each of them indicates a path which might have been taken but was abandoned; that is, it points towards a what-if scenario of an alternative

Wagner, and thus reminds us of the open character of history. The *Saracen Woman* is, after Wagner found his voice in *The Flying Dutchman*, the last counter-attack of the Grand Opera, a repetition of *Rienzi*. If Wagner had set it to music and if the opera had turned out to be a triumph like *Rienzi*, it is possible that Wagner would have succumbed to this last Meyerbeerian temptation, and would have developed into a thoroughly different composer. Similarly, a couple of years later, after Wagner exhausted his potential for Romantic operas with *Lohengrin* and was searching for a new way, *Jesus* again stands for a path which differs thoroughly from that of the music-dramas and their 'pagan' universe: *Jesus* is something like *Parsifal* written directly, without the long detour through the *Ring*. What Wagner attributes to Jesus in his draft of the play is a series of alternate supplementations of the Commandments:

> The commandment saith: Thou shalt not commit adultery! But I say unto you: Ye shall not marry without love. A marriage without love is broken as soon as entered into, and who so hath wooed without love, already hath broken the wedding. If ye follow my commandment, how can ye ever break it, since it bids you to do what your own heart and soul desire? – But where ye marry without love, ye bind yourselves at variance with God's love, and in your wedding ye sin against God; and this sin avengeth itself by your striving next against the law of man, in that ye break the marriage-vow.[23]

The shift from Jesus's actual words is crucial here: Jesus 'internalizes' the prohibition, rendering it much more severe (the Law says no actual adultery, while I say that if you only covet the other's wife in your mind, it is the same as if you already committed adultery, etc.). Wagner also internalizes it, but in a different

---

23   Richard Wagner, *Jesus of Nazareth and Other Writings*. Lincoln and London: University of Nebraska Press, 1995, p. 303.

way: the inner dimension he evokes is not that of the intention to do it, but that of love that should accompany the Law (marriage). True adultery is not copulating outside marriage, but copulating in a loveless marriage: simple adultery just violates the Law from outside, while loveless marriage destroys it from within, turning the letter of the Law against its spirit. So, to paraphrase Brecht yet again: What is simple adultery compared to (the adultery that is a loveless) marriage? It is not by chance that Wagner's underlying formula 'marriage is adultery' recalls Proudhon's 'property is theft': during the stormy events of 1848, Wagner was not only a Feuerbachian celebrating sexual love, but also a Proudhonian revolutionary demanding the abolition of private property; so no wonder that, later on the same page, Wagner attributes to Jesus a Proudhonian supplement to 'Thou shalt not steal!':

> This also is a good law: Thou shalt not steal, nor covet another man's goods. Who goeth against it, sinneth: but I preserve you from that sin, inasmuch as I teach you: Love thy neighbour as thyself; which also meaneth: Lay not up for thyself treasures, whereby thou stealest from thy neighbour and makest him to starve: for when thou hast thy goods safeguarded by the law of man, thou provokest thy neighbour to sin against the law.[24]

This is how the Christian 'supplement' to the Book should be conceived: as a properly Hegelian 'negation of negation', which resides in the decisive shift from the distortion of a notion to a distortion *constitutive* of this notion, that is, to this notion as a distortion-in-itself. Recall again Proudhon's old dialectical motto 'property is theft': the 'negation of negation' is here the shift from theft as a distortion ('negation', violation) of property to the dimension of theft inscribed into the very notion of property (nobody has the right to fully own the means of production, their nature is

---

24 Ibid., pp. 303–4.

inherently collective, so every claim 'this is mine' is illegitimate). The same goes for crime and the Law, for the passage from crime as the distortion ('negation') of the law to crime as sustaining law itself, that is, to the idea of the Law itself as universalized crime. One should note that, in this notion of the 'negation of negation', the encompassing unity of the two opposed terms is the 'lowest', 'transgressive' one: it is not crime which is a moment of law's self-mediation (or theft which is a moment of property's self-mediation); the opposition between crime and law is inherent to crime, law is a subspecies of crime, crime's self-relating negation (in the same way that property is theft's self-relating negation). And ultimately does the same not go for nature itself? Here, 'negation of negation' is the shift from the idea that we are violating some natural balanced order to the idea that imposing on the Real such a notion of balanced order is in itself the greatest violation . . . which is why the premise, the first axiom even, of every radical ecology is 'there is no Nature'.

These lines cannot but evoke the famous passages from *The Communist Manifesto* which answer the bourgeois reproach that Communists want to abolish freedom, property and family: it is capitalist freedom itself which is effectively the freedom to buy and sell on the market and thus the very form of un-freedom for those who have nothing but their labour to sell; it is capitalist property itself which means the 'abolition' of property for those who own no means of production; it is bourgeois marriage itself which is universalized prostitution. In all these cases, the external opposition is internalized, so that one opposite becomes the form of appearance of the other (bourgeois freedom is the form of appearance of the un-freedom of the majority, etc.). However, for Marx, at least in the case of freedom, this means that Communism will not abolish freedom but, by way of abolishing capitalist servitude, bring about *actual* freedom, the freedom which will no longer be the form of appearance of its opposite. It is thus not freedom itself which is the form of appearance of its opposite, but only false freedom, the freedom distorted by the relations of domination. Is it not, then, that, underlying the dialectic of the 'negation of negation', a Habermasian 'normative' approach imposes itself here immediately: how can we talk about crime if we do not have a preceding notion of legal order violated by criminal transgression? In other words, is the notion of law as universalized/self-negated crime not self-destructive? This, precisely, is what a properly dialectical approach rejects: what exists before transgression is just a neutral state of things, neither good nor bad (neither property nor theft, neither law nor crime); the balance of this state of things is then violated, and the positive norm (Law, property) arises as a secondary move, an attempt to counter-act and contain the transgression. With regard to the dialectic of freedom, this means that it is the very 'alienated, bourgeois' freedom which creates the conditions and opens up the space for 'actual' freedom.

This Hegelian logic is at work in Wagner's universe all the way through to *Parsifal*, whose final message is a profoundly Hegelian one: 'The wound can be healed only by the spear that smote it.' Hegel says the same thing, although with the accent shifted in the opposite direction: the Spirit is itself the wound it tries to heal, that is, the wound is self-inflicted.[25] That is to say, what is 'Spirit' at its most elementary? The 'wound' of nature: the subject is the immense – absolute – power of negativity, of introducing a gap/cut into the given-immediate substantial unity, the power of differentiating, of 'abstracting', of tearing apart and treating as self-standing what in reality is part of an organic unity. This is why the notion of the 'self-alienation' of Spirit (of Spirit losing itself in its otherness, in its objectivization, in its result) is more paradoxical than it may appear: it should be read together with Hegel's assertion of the thoroughly non-substantial character of Spirit: there is no *res cogitans*, no thing which (as its property) also thinks; spirit

---

25   See G. W. F. Hegel, *Aesthetics, Volume 1*. Oxford: Oxford University Press, 1998, p. 98.

is nothing but the process of overcoming natural immediacy, of the cultivation of this immediacy, of withdrawing-into-itself or 'taking off' from it, of – why not? – alienating itself from it. The paradox is thus that there is no Self that precedes the Spirit's 'self-alienation': the very process of alienation creates/generates the 'Self' from which Spirit is alienated and to which it then returns. Hegel here turns around the standard notion that a failed version of X presupposes this X as its norm (measure): X is created, its space is outlined, only through repetitive failures to reach it. The self-alienation of Spirit is the same as, fully coincides with, its aliena-tion from its Other (nature), because it constitutes itself through its 'return-to-itself' from its immersion into natural Otherness. In other words, Spirit's return-to-itself creates the very dimension to which it returns. (This holds for all 'return to origins': when, from the nineteenth century onwards, new nation-states were consti-tuting themselves in Central and Eastern Europe, their discovery and return to 'old ethnic roots' generated these roots.) What this means is that the 'negation of negation', the 'return-to-oneself' from alienation, does not occur where it seems to: in the 'negation of negation', Spirit's negativity is not relativized, subsumed under an encompassing positivity. It is, on the contrary, the 'simple negation' which remains attached to the presupposed positivity it negated, the presupposed Otherness from which it alienates itself, and the 'negation of negation' is nothing but the negation of the substantial character of this Otherness itself, the full acceptance of the abyss of Spirit's self-relating which retroactively posits all its presuppositions. In other words, once we are in negativity, we never quit it and regain the lost innocence of Origins; it is, on the contrary, only in 'negation of negation' that the Origins are truly lost, that their very loss is lost, that they are deprived of the substantial status of that which was lost. The Spirit heals its wound not by directly healing it, but by getting rid of the very full and healthy Body into which the wound was cut. It is a little bit like the (rather tasteless) medical joke: 'The bad news is that we've discovered you have severe Alzheimer's disease. The good news is the same: you have Alzheimer's, so you will have already forgotten the bad news by the time you get back home.'

In Christian theology, Christ's supplement (the repeated 'But I tell you . . .') is often designated as the 'antithesis' to the thesis of the Law: the irony here is that, in the proper Hegelian approach, this antithesis is synthesis itself at its purest. In other words, is what Christ does in his 'fulfilment' of the Law not the Law's *Aufhebung* in the strict Hegelian sense of the term? In its supplement, the Commandment is both negated and maintained by way of being elevated/transposed onto another (higher) level.

One should thus be very careful about attributing pagan ideological motifs to Wagner. Owen Lee observed about the end of *Tannhäuser* that 'just as the papal staff has sprouted leaves, so Wagner's Christian hymn, the "Pilgrims' Chorus," is surrounded at the close by the pulsing music of paganism (the frenzied broken triplets from the Venusberg)'.[26] Is, however, such a 'synthesis' of Christian spirituality and pagan joy not an all too easy solution? Should we not, rather, oppose the two cases conflated by Lee? The sprouting of leaves on the papal staff relates to 'innocent' natural fertility, while the Venusberg music with its 'frenzied broken triplets' stands for a dark and disturbing 'unnatural' passion. The fact that it forms the background of the final chorus hints at an unresolved tension, not at an easy reconciliation. In short, Badiou is right: there is no final reconciliation in *Tannhäuser*. One should take note here of a fact so obvious that it often passes unnoticed. The goddess Venus celebrated by Tannhäuser is a reappearing star – the morning star and the evening star. When Wolfram, elevating pure spiritual love, celebrates the latter, like Tannhäuser, he also celebrates one of the aspects of Venus.

Tannhäuser and Wolfram thus celebrate one and the same object which, viewed from a respectful distance, is the noble

---

26   May, op.cit., p. 48.

'evening star', but when approached too closely appears as the 'morning star' of unconstrained sensuous pleasure. The difference is not substantial but purely parallactic – one more reason to remain sceptical towards the claim that Wagner broke out of the Jewish–Christian horizon and returned to the logic that underlies ancient Greek mythology. For example, in his elaborations on *Lohengrin*, May reiterates the point that

> [the] tale's origin predates 'the Christian bent toward supernaturalism,' instead arising 'from the truest depths of universal human nature.' Wagner hearkens back to Greek mythology to draw parallels. Just as the Flying Dutchman and Tannhäuser are variants on the Hellenic prototype of Odysseus (as wanderer and as an adventurer waylaid by the seduction of Circe), the encounter between Lohengrin and Elsa has its counterpart in the myth of Zeus and Semele.[27]

The 'innermost essence' of 'universal human nature' is for (this Feuerbachian) Wagner the necessity of love:

> The essence of this love, in its truest utterance, is *the longing for utmost physical reality*, for fruition in an object that can be grasped by all the senses, held fast with all the force of actual being. In this finite, physically sure embrace, must not the god dissolve and disappear?[28]

Why this foregrounding of the Hellenic prototype for the Dutchman where the Jewish one of the Wandering Jew is much more pertinent? Is this not Wagner's fundamental Jewish identification which haunted him to his very death in Venice, far from home: 'Exile, in a sense, was a state from which Wagner never

---

27   Ibid., pp. 52–3.
28   Ibid., p. 53.

managed to escape, for all the contradictory blustering of his later nationalism.'[29] To risk going even a step further, is not the '*longing for utmost physical reality*' which forms the essence of true love what propels Christ towards Incarnation? God became man out of love for humanity, where he effectively 'dissolved and disappeared' on the Cross. It is little wonder that, in the last seconds of *Götterdämmerung*, we get a Christian Wagner, along the Pauline lines of 1 Corinthians 13:1–2, 12–13:

> 1. If I speak with the tongues of men and of angels, but have not love, I am become sounding brass, or a clanging cymbal. 2. And if I have the gift of prophecy, and know all mysteries and all knowledge; and if I have all faith, so as to remove mountains, but have not love, I am nothing . . . 12. For now we see in a mirror, darkly; but then face to face: now I know in part; but then shall I know fully even as also I was fully known. 13. But now abideth faith, hope, love, these three; and the greatest of these is love.

Or, as Brunhilde's version might read: 'If I am the most natural innocent living being, but do not have love, I am nothing; if I am the greatest law-giver, but do not have love, I am nothing; if I am the greatest hero, but do not have love, I am nothing. Now abide natural innocence, law, and heroism; but greater than these three is love.'

Paradoxical as it may sound, one should finally reverse the standard claim that the *Ring* is an epic of heroic paganism (since its gods are Nordic-pagan) and that *Parsifal* stands for the Christianization of Wagner (for his kneeling down in front of the Cross, as Nietzsche put it). It is in the *Ring* that Wagner comes closest to Christianity, and *Parsifal*, far from being a Christian work, stages an obscene retranslation of Christianity as a pagan ritual, the

---

29   Kitcher and Schacht, op. cit., p. 198.

circular renewal of fertility through the King's recuperation.[30] A century ago, G. K. Chesterton reversed the standard (mis)perception according to which the ancient pagan attitude is that of the joyful assertion of life, while Christianity imposes a sombre order of guilt and renunciation. It is, on the contrary, the pagan stance which is deeply melancholic: even if it preaches a pleasurable life, it is in the mode of 'enjoy it while it lasts, because, at the end, there is always death and decay'. The message of Christianity is, on the contrary, that of infinite joy beneath the deceptive surface of guilt and renunciation: 'The outer ring of Christianity is a rigid guard of ethical abnegations and professional priests; but inside that inhuman guard you will find the old human life dancing like children, and drinking wine like men; for Christianity is the only frame for pagan freedom.'[31]

Is not Tolkien's *Lord of the Rings* the ultimate proof of this paradox? Only a devout Christian could have imagined such a magnificent pagan universe, thereby confirming that paganism is the ultimate Christian dream. Which is why the conservative Christian critics who recently expressed their concern at how *The Lord of the Rings* undermines Christianity through its message of pagan magic miss the point, the perverse conclusion which is unavoidable here: You want to enjoy the pagan dream of pleasurable life without paying the price of melancholic sadness for it? Choose Christianity. This is why C. S. Lewis's *Narnia* cycle of novels is ultimately a failure: it doesn't work because it tries to infuse the pagan mythic universe with Christian motifs (the Christ-like sacrifice of the lion in the first

---

30   In private conversations, Wagner was quite explicit about the underlying pagan obscenity of *Parsifal*. At a private reception on the eve of *Parsifal*'s first performance, he 'described as a black Mass a work that depicts Holy Communion [. . .] "all of you who are involved in the performance must see to it that you have the devil in you, and you who are present as listeners must ensure that you welcome the devil into your hearts!" '(Joachim Kohler, *Richard Wagner: The Last of the Titans*. New Haven: Yale University Press, 2004, p. 591).

31   Chesterton, *Orthodoxy*. San Francisco: Ignatius Press, 1955, p. 164.

novel, and so on). Instead of Christianizing paganism, such a move paganizes Christianity, re-inscribing it back into the pagan universe where it simply doesn't belong, so the result is a false pagan myth. The paradox here is exactly the same as that of the relationship between Wagner's *Ring* and his *Parsifal*.

This is why one can easily imagine an alternate version of *Parsifal* with a plot that veers off in the middle, and which, in a way, would also be faithful to Wagner – a kind of 'Feuerbachianized' *Parsifal*, in which, in Act II, Kundry does succeed in seducing Parsifal. Far from delivering Parsifal into the clutches of Klingsor, this act delivers Kundry from Klingsor's domination. So when, at the act's end, Klingsor approaches the couple, Parsifal does exactly what we expect him to do (he dissolves Klingsor's castle), but he then leaves for Montsalvat with Kundry. In the finale, Parsifal arrives with Kundry in the last seconds to save Amfortas, proclaiming that the old, sterile, masculine rule of the Grail is over and that, to restore fertility to the land, femininity should be readmitted. One should return to the (pagan) balance of the Masculine and the Feminine. Parsifal takes over as the new king, with Kundry as queen, and one year later Lohengrin is born.

One often fails to take note of the fact, elusive in its very blatancy, that Wagner's *Ring* is the ultimate Paulinian work of art. Its central concern is the failure of the rule of Law, and the shift that best encompasses the inner span of the *Ring* is the shift from Law to love. What happens towards the end of *Götterdämmerung* is that Wagner overcomes his own (pagan, Feuerbachian) ideology (the love of a [hetero]sexual couple is paradigmatic). Brünnhilde's last transformation is the transformation from *eros* to *agape*, from erotic love to political love. *Eros* cannot truly overcome Law; it can only explode in punctual intensity as the Law's momentary transgression, like the flame of Siegmund and Sieglinde that instantly consumes itself. *Agape* is what remains after we take on the consequences of *eros*'s failure.

One should note here that love occurs twice in the quadruple scheme of existential projects that underlies the finale of *Götterdämmerung* (the Rhine Maidens' natural innocence; Wotan's rule of law; Siegmund's and Sieglinde's passionate love; Siegfried's heroic act): first as *eros*, the suicidal-fatal immersion which obliterates all social links (exemplified, or, rather, instantiated by the pair of Sieglinde and Siegmund); then as *agape*, the all-encompassing 'political love'. The first love is a species, and the second one the genus encompassing itself as its own species: in Hegelese, love encounters itself here in its own 'oppositional determination' (*gegensaetzliche Bestimmung*), as its own species.

And Wagner's genius was to propose a woman as the agent of this political love, of the love binding the emancipatory collective, in clear contrast to the standard ideology (to which he usually submits) which reserves the collective domain of political activity to men and constrains women to intimate privacy. Brünnhilde from the end of the *Ring* belongs to the same series as Joan of Arc: a woman leading the emancipatory non-patriarchal collective.

This brings us back to the problem of 'finding an ending': we can conceive the finales of the three preceding parts of the *Ring* as failed attempts at endings: *Rheingold* ends with the contrast between the Rhine Maidens' bemoaning of lost innocence and the majestic assertion of the rule of Law; *Die Walküre* ends with the hope that a heroic act will set things straight; *Siegfried* ends with ecstatic love. They are all false, fake; not only the finale of *Rheingold*, but even more the rather hollow spectacle of the announcement of the hero to come in *Die Walküre* and – the lowest point of them all – the empty-sounding duet of Brünnhilde and Siegfried which concludes *Siegfried*. The much-vilified 'falsity' of these endings is thus part of Wagner's artistic integrity: it registers the falsity of the solution they enact. It is as if all these false endings are denounced in the disturbingly brutal music of Siegfried's death

which brings no solace: it is only Brünnhilde's final act which truly
functions as an ending.[32]

There is, effectively, a Christ-like dimension in Brünnhilde's
death, but only in the precise sense that Christ's death marks the
birth of the Holy Spirit, the community of believers linked by *agape*.
It is little wonder that one of Brünnhilde's last lines is, 'Ruhe, ruhe,
du Gott!' ('Die in peace, God!'). Her act fulfils Wotan's wish to
assume freely his inevitable death. What remains after the destruction of Valhalla is the human crowd silently observing the cata-
clysmic event, a crowd which, in the groundbreaking staging of
Chéreau–Boulez, is left staring out at the spectators when the music
ends, a crowd which is the Holy Spirit embodied. Everything now
rests on them, without any guarantee of God or any other figure of
the big Other. It is up to this crowd to act like the Holy Spirit, prac-
tising *agape*:

> The Redemption motif is a message delivered to the entire world,
> but like all pythonesses, the orchestra is unclear and there are
> several ways of interpreting its message . . . Doesn't one hear it,
> shouldn't one hear it, with mistrust and anxiety, a mistrust which
> would match the boundless hope which this humanity nurses and
> which has always been at stake, silently and invisibly, in the atro-
> cious battles which have torn human beings apart throughout
> the *Ring*? The gods have lived, the values of their world must be
> reconstructed and reinvented. Men are there as if on the edge of
> a cliff – they listen, tensely, to the oracle which rumbles from the
> depths of the earth.[33]

---

32 Karl Boehm effectively acted as a barbarian when, in his Bayreuth
version of the *Ring*, he shortened the passage from Siegfried's *Trauermarsch* to
Brünnhilde's great self-immolation scene, leaving out the short but wonderful anguished appearance of Gudrune worrying about Siegfried's fate: if we
shorten this passage and basically reduce the opera's last hour to two great hits
(Siegfried's death, Brünnhilde's immolation), the entire fragile but very precise
balance of the scene gets lost.

33 Patrice Chéreau, quoted in Carnegy, op. cit., p. 363.

There is no guarantee of redemption-through-love: redemption is merely possible. We are thereby in the very core of Christianity: it is God himself who made a Pascalean wager. By virtue of dying on the cross, he made a risky gesture with no guaranteed final outcome; that is, he provided us – humanity – with the empty S1, Master-Signifier, and it is up to humanity to supplement it with the chain of S2. Far from providing the conclusive dot on the *i*, the divine act rather stands for the openness of a New Beginning, and it is up to humanity to live up to it, to decide its meaning, to make something of it. It is as in Predestination which condemns us to frantic activity: the Event is a *pure empty sign*, and we have to work to generate its meaning. Therein resides the terrible *risk of Revelation*: what 'Revelation' means is that God took upon himself the risk of putting everything at stake, of fully 'existentially engaging himself' by way of, as it were, stepping into his own picture, becoming part of creation, exposing himself to the utter contingency of existence. True Openness is not that of undecidability, but that of living in the aftermath of the Event, of drawing out the consequences – of what? Precisely of the new space opened up by the Event. The anxiety of which Chéreau speaks is the anxiety of act.

Index